EMMY
and the
Rats in
the Belfry

EMMY
and the
Rats in
the Belfry

Lynne Jonell
Art by Jonathan Bean

SQUARE
FISH

HENRY HOLT AND COMPANY
NEW YORK

Special thanks go, in Schenectady, to Bill Buell, historian; David Kennison, warden of St. George's Episcopal Church; and most of all, historian Laurie Wilson, who opened up her home and her heart, lent me her canoe, fed me scones, and filled me to the brim with useful information.

And in Minnesota, to Roy Heinrich of Mt. Olivet Lutheran Church in Plymouth and Jerry Mayers of St. Joseph's Catholic Church in Freeport, for generously giving me belfry tours.

Lastly, thanks as always to my husband and first reader, Bill, who told me everything I ever wanted to know about gel-based polymers; my editor, Reka Simonsen, who keeps asking for revisions until it's right; and my agent, Stephen Barbara, whose support is rocklike in its constancy. I owe them all more than I can say.

SQUARE
FISH

An imprint of Macmillan Publishing Group, LLC
175 Fifth Avenue
New York, NY 10010
mackids.com

EMMY AND THE RATS IN THE BELFRY. Text copyright © 2011 by Lynne Jonelle. Illustrations copyright © 2011 by Jonathan Bean. All rights reserved. Printed in the United States of America by R. R. Donnelley & Sons Company, Harrisonburg, Virginia.

Square Fish and the Square Fish logo are trademarks of Macmillan and are used by Henry Holt and Company under license from Macmillan.

Our books may be purchased in bulk for promotional, educational, or business use. Please contact your local bookseller or the Macmillan Corporate and Premium Sales Department at (800) 221-7945 ext. 5442 or by e-mail at MacmillanSpecialMarkets@macmillan.com.

Library of Congress Cataloging-in-Publication Data
Jonell, Lynne.
Emmy and the rats in the Belfry / Lynne Jonell ;
[illustrations by Jonathan Bean]
p.   cm.
Summary: Ten-year-old Emmy and her rodent friends must fend off the evil former nanny, Miss Barmy, as they search for Ratty's missing mother.
ISBN 978-0-312-64160-3 (paperback)   ISBN 978-1-4668-0381-7 (ebook)
[1. Rodents—Fiction. 2. Humorous stories.] I. Bean, Jonathan, ill. II. Title.
PZ7.J675Emr 2011   [Fic]—dc22   2010047507

Originally published in the United States by Henry Holt and Company
First Square Fish Edition: 2016
Square Fish logo designed by Filomena Tuosto

1 3 5 7 9 10 8 6 4 2

AR: 4.8 / LEXILE: 740L

To my dear son Rob,
in the fond hope that someday, somehow,
he will forgive me for the Spray Pam incident
(though I doubt he will ever forget)
—L. J.

EMMY
and the
Rats in
the Belfry

1

THE PIEBALD RAT laid back her ears, crouched on the third-story windowsill, and looked in the bedroom. The girl on the bed was motionless except for the quiet rise and fall of breath beneath the blanket, and her eyes were closed.

The rat smiled, her sharp teeth showing, and glanced over her shoulder. "She's still sleeping, Cheswick. Get a move on."

A glossy black rodent heaved himself up a last few inches of grapevine and wriggled through the corner tear in the window screen. "Just let me—catch my breath—Jane, dear," he panted, flopping on the blue painted sill.

"Don't be such a weenie, Cheswick. You don't see *me* breathing hard, do you?"

"That's because—I carried you—most of the way," wheezed the black rat. "On my back, my precious— little cupcake."

The piebald rat narrowed her eyes. "Are you

suggesting that I'm *heavy*, Cheswick? Are you saying I need to lose *weight*?"

"No! Not at all!" the black rat cried.

"Then get busy," snapped the piebald rat, grabbing the cord that dangled from the window blind. "You can find me on the bathroom counter when you're done. I do love a nice big mirror."

"As well you should!" gasped Cheswick, but his beloved Jane had already slid down the cord and was halfway across the carpet.

Cheswick sighed. The room, in the early morning light, looked remarkably tidy for a ten-year-old girl's. Books were shelved, the floor was clear of toys, and in the half-open closet he could see clothes hung neatly on their hangers. It was really a pity to mess it up.

Still, if it would make Jane happy . . .

The girl was still sleeping when Cheswick Vole finished his work, but he hardly glanced at the pajama-clad arm outside the blanket or the straight dark hair that fell across one cheek. Through a half-open door he could see blue Italian tile and the straight, smooth side of a Jacuzzi.

The black rat leaped from the floor to the stool lid

to the tank. His hind feet scrabbled on the roll of toilet paper and sent it spinning as he clawed his way up onto the bathroom countertop, narrowly missing an open bottle of mouthwash. He pattered across polished marble to the side of the piebald rat, who stood gazing at the mirror, idly fluffing her patches of brown, tan, and white.

"All done, my little rosebud—"

"Do you think I should dye my fur?" Jane Barmy interrupted. "These patches are all too recognizable."

"But my precious pudding cup, you're beautiful just as you are! I don't want you to change one itsy-bitsy, teeny-weeny—"

"Oh, shut *up*, Cheswick. Don't you *ever* get tired of fawning?"

"Not if it's fawning on you, my little Janie-Wanie . . ." The black rat lifted his upper lip in an uncertain smile and twisted his paws together.

"And enough with the 'Janie-Wanie.'" The piebald rat sniffed twice and curled her tail elegantly around one perfectly manicured paw. "I may not be the beauty queen I once was—"

"You're prettier than ever!" Cheswick said loyally.

"And I may be just a little more furry—"

"Just a trifle! Hardly noticeable!"

"But I am still Miss Jane Barmy, and I'll thank you to remember it. The Barmy name was a proud one, once—and will be again, just as soon as I get my revenge on that nasty little Emmaline Addison!"

The last words were hissed through her long front teeth, and Cheswick Vole shivered in spite of himself, glancing through the doorway to the bed beyond. "Dearest Jane, why do you insist upon revenge? She's only a little girl."

"A little girl who turned me into a *rat!*" snarled Miss Barmy.

"But it wasn't Emmy who did that—it was Raston, that ratty friend of hers, remember? He bit you, and you shrank. He bit you again, and you turned into a rat. It wasn't the little girl at all."

"Close enough." Miss Barmy lifted her lip in a sneer. "And besides, I *hate* rich little girls. I should have been the rich one! Why didn't old William Addison leave it all to *me?*"

"Don't torture yourself, Jane! Forget the past!" Cheswick Vole clasped his paws over his heart. "We could be happy together, you and I. We could raise a family—"

Miss Barmy's whiskers stiffened. "Raise a family? Of what, Cheswick? *Rats?*"

"Well, we're rodents now, after all. It's only logical." The black rat warmed to his subject, a happy smile bunching his furry cheeks until his eyes were squeezed almost shut. "We could find a little place in the country, a nice, sandy riverbank burrow with a view. We could get married . . ." He blushed beneath his fur. "You could have a litter. Six is a nice number, don't you think? Three boys and three girls?"

He opened his eyes, saw Miss Barmy's face, and took a sudden step backward. "Sugarplum! Don't look like that!" The black rat's nose quivered. "I didn't mean anything—of course, it's completely up to you—"

"A litter? A *litter*? Do you think I plan on remaining a rat forever?"

"Well, you don't seem able to change back into a human," said Cheswick hurriedly. "Not in the usual way, you know. Professor Capybara said it was because you needed to learn to love, but that's ridiculous. You're so dear and loving already, aren't you, my little cuddle-bunny-umpkins—"

"Stop blabbering, you old fool," snarled the piebald rat. "Professor Capybara knows how to turn us into humans again, I'm sure. We just need to make him talk."

"Well, I don't know . . ." Cheswick Vole sneaked

a glance in the mirror. He wasn't so sure he wanted to change back. When he had been a human, he'd possessed a narrow chest, beaky nose, thinning hair, and a reedy voice. But as a rat he was big, dark, and handsome, with a fine set of whiskers and a bold, bright eye. Just looking at his reflection in the mirror—such perky ears!—gave him confidence.

"Being a rat has its advantages," he pointed out. "A rat can forage for food. He can live almost anywhere, for free. And no one expects him to pay taxes."

"Yes, yes," said Miss Barmy, "but he's still a *rat*." She clicked her claws together one by one. "Even if I get my revenge on Emmaline, even if I get her parents' money and this mansion and the boats and everything, what am I going to do with it if I'm still a *rodent*?"

"You could create an indoor water park," suggested Cheswick eagerly. "Just the right size for rats! You could wear one of Barbie's bikinis!"

Miss Barmy gave him a withering glare. "Listen, Cheswick. I am not putting on a Barbie-doll bikini, and I am not having any litters, and I am most certainly not marrying you. Not as long as I stay a rat."

Cheswick's eyes widened. "But as a human, Jane? Would you marry me if you were a human again?"

The piebald rat smiled a long, slow smile. Then she edged closer and nuzzled the black rat under his jowls. "Chessie?"

Cheswick closed his eyes with a look of ecstasy and pressed Miss Barmy's paw. "Yes, my little pumpkin?"

"Do you *want* to marry me, my darling?"

"Oh! Oh, Jane! It would be my dream come true!"

"Then you'd better figure out how to turn me into a human again," Miss Barmy said sharply, pushing him away.

Cheswick Vole was panting heavily. "Whatever you say, precious. And is there anything else? Anything at all?"

The piebald smiled, showing all her teeth. "Well, I do have a few more ideas for making Emmy's life perfectly miserable—" She stopped, her ears alert. "What's that noise?"

A soft chittering came from the far windowsill. Cheswick sniffed deeply and froze. "It's rodents from Rodent City! A bunch of them!"

Miss Barmy stared in alarm. "Do something, Chessie! Hide me!"

Cheswick's chest swelled, and his furry shoulders squared with manly determination. He leaped for the bottle of mouthwash and tipped it over, hanging grimly on to the neck as the green liquid, smelling powerfully of mint, poured over Miss Barmy's head.

"*Eeeeheeee—urp!*" choked the piebald rat. "What do you think you're doing, you—you idiot, you *moron*—"

"Must disguise our scent," Cheswick hissed, splashing mouthwash up onto his own fur, "or they'll know we're here. Now hurry! Follow me!"

2

EMMY ADDISON came slowly out of sleep to an odd feeling of heaviness on her rib cage, and the sound of little voices whispering very near her ears.

"Maybe we should let her sleep."

"But this is important!"

"Stop shoving me, Chippy! You almost pushed me right off!"

"You shoved me first, Ratty, old boy—"

"Quiet, everyone! She's coming around!"

Emmy opened her eyes and swallowed a scream. Three chipmunks and two rats were gathered on her chest, staring earnestly into her face.

"I wish you'd knock like everyone else," Emmy said, grumpy at being startled.

"But, dear, we came in the window," said a motherly-looking chipmunk. "You would never have heard us knocking on the sill, not in your sleep."

Emmy had to admit that Mrs. Bunjee had a point. She struggled to her elbows, the rodents pitching on

9

the blanket like small, furry boats in an ocean swell. "What's so important you had to wake me up?"

There was an unintelligible babble of rodent voices, all trying to outsqueak the rest. Emmy rubbed the sleep out of her eyes and looked at them all—Mrs. Bunjee and her two sons, and Raston Rat who was Emmy's first rodent friend, and his twin sister—and tried to feel happy that she had so many rodents in her life. She partly succeeded.

"It's about Miss Barmy—"

"No, it's about the sticky-patches!"

"—there's a warrant out for her arrest—"

"But the professor needs Emmy right *away*—"

"What's that awful, *minty* smell?"

"One at a time!" Mrs. Bunjee's voice was commanding. "Buck, you and Chippy go first."

"Chippy *always* goes first," muttered the Rat.

The wiry chipmunk ignored him, opening a small satchel to pull out a rolled-up piece of paper. Buck grabbed the other side to keep it flat.

Emmy leaned in to get a better view. "Wanted," she read slowly. "For crimes of robbery and fraud. Miss Jane Barmy and Cheswick Vole. Last seen running in the direction of Main Street."

She looked at the drawing of two rats, side by side. One had piebald fur—mixed patches of brown, tan, and white—and was wearing a formal gown in a striking diagonal pattern. The other had black fur and was wearing a tuxedo. Underneath the picture it said, "Cheswick Vole, one-time assistant to Professor Maxwell Capybara, shrank his employer and kidnapped over a hundred rodents before joining forces with Jane Barmy, nanny and kidnapper . . ." Emmy stopped reading when the print got too small.

"We're going to bring those rats to justice," said Buck. "Will you let us put up a poster by the mousehole in your playroom?"

"The one by the electric train," added Chippy with a longing look back at the playroom door.

Emmy grinned. "Sure, put up as many as you want. That drawing really looked like them!"

"*Sissy* did the drawing," said Raston, flinging a furry arm over Cecilia's shoulders as Buck and Chippy scampered off to the playroom.

"Seriously?" Emmy looked in surprise at the shy little rat. "You're good! Where did you learn to draw?"

Cecilia blushed beneath her fur. "When I lived in

a cage, I used to practice drawing in the sawdust all the time."

"Cecilia, you're an artist!" Mrs. Bunjee clapped her paws. "Your mother would be so proud!"

Sissy's whiskers drooped.

"Mommy . . ." Raston began, his voice failing. He swallowed hard. "I'm sure Ratmommy *would* be proud, if only—"

He stopped, cleared his throat, and tried again. "If only she was a . . . a . . ."

Cecilia patted his cheek.

"If only she was *alive!*" the Rat wailed, and broke down entirely, sobbing on his sister's shoulder.

"Now, now," said Mrs. Bunjee, dabbing at his eyes with her handkerchief. "Your dear mother is probably alive and well and living in the same old neighborhood. How well I remember it . . . lovely big tree roots, right at the river's edge . . ."

The Rat snuffled a little. "Really? You think she's still there?"

"I don't see why not. Just because you two were snatched from the nest as little ratlings, doesn't mean that *she* left. Someday you may even see her again. And in the meantime, I'll say it again—she would be proud."

"She would be proud of Rasty," said Cecilia, trying to smile. "He's the educated one."

Emmy reached out a gentle finger to stroke Sissy's paw. Raston had been a classroom pet for years and had gotten a good elementary education. But Cecilia had been locked in the back room of a shop ever since she'd been taken from the nest and had never learned to read, a fact which embarrassed her terribly.

"She'd be proud of us both," said the Rat loyally. "Oh, Ratmom, noblest of rodents, we never appreciated you *enough* . . ."

"Now, Raston," said Mrs. Bunjee, patting him briskly, "stop brooding. Didn't you want to tell Emmy about the sticky-patches?"

The Rat wiped his nose with his paw. "They're *Sissy* sticky-patches. You tell her, Sissy."

Cecilia hesitated. "I can't explain the scientific terms," she said. "Maybe we should just show her." She unbuckled a cotton satchel on her back and pulled out a square the size of a small postage stamp, only thicker. "Go ahead, Rasty—shrink her."

Emmy glanced worriedly at her door. What if her parents or the maid came to wake her up? They wouldn't know what to do if they came in and she was the size of an action figure. "Wait!"

But it was too late. Raston had already given her finger a nip with his front teeth. And just as quickly as that, the old telescoping feeling came over her—as if she were being shut up into a very small suitcase—and Emmy shrank. She dwindled down to rat size right on top of the bed, pajamas and all. The blanket loomed above her like a fluffy blue mountain.

Emmy sighed, looking down at her legs the size of chalk sticks. Sometimes she wished she didn't know so many rodents of power. It was interesting, of course, but often inconvenient. Like now, for example.

"Listen, Sissy," she said, looking up into Cecilia's gray, furry face. "Whatever you wanted to show me has got to wait. Just kiss me on the cheek so I can grow again. Somebody is going to come to wake me any minute now."

"But that's just it! Now I don't *have* to kiss you to make you grow!" Cecilia held up the tiny square patch.

"What's that—" Emmy began, but she was interrupted by a crackle of static and then her mother's voice on the intercom.

"Emmy? Are you up yet?"

Emmy stared up at the intercom, high on the wall. To answer, she had to flick a switch on the speaker panel. But the size she was right now, the button might as well be on the ceiling.

"Hurry!" she whispered to Sissy.

Sissy nodded. "Here, pull off the backing. Now we slap it on your arm—no, roll up your pajama sleeve, it has to touch your skin. That's right. And—see?"

The rodents tumbled off the bed as, all at once, Emmy expanded. Like a dried-up sponge exposed to water, she lengthened and thickened and popped back to her full size in three seconds flat.

Emmy shut her eyes and leaned back on her pillow, feeling dizzy.

"Packs a wallop, doesn't it?" Raston helped Sissy buckle on her satchel again. "But that was the last one, and the professor wants you to help make the next batch. He's still experimenting."

Emmy opened her eyes. "You put an *experimental* patch on me?"

The rodents exchanged glances.

"Sorry, Emmy—"

"*We're* used to being experimented on—"

"Are you all right, dear?" Mrs. Bunjee's chipmunk fur tickled Emmy's ear. "The professor will wait if you're feeling ill."

"I don't think the patches grow people as gently as my kiss does," said Cecilia, patting Emmy's forehead.

"That's not *your* fault," said Raston quickly.

"Hush!" Mrs. Bunjee lifted a paw. "Listen!"

A thin, droning sound came from the playroom. Emmy relaxed. "It's just the train. Chippy must have talked Buck into going for a ride—"

"Not that," said Mrs. Bunjee, cocking her head.

In the silence, voices could be heard murmuring in the hall.

"Get under the blankets!" Mrs. Bunjee ordered. "Hide!"

Someone knocked, and the doorknob turned. "Sweetheart? Time to get up . . . oh, *Emmy.*"

Emmy sat up in bed, rubbing her eyes for effect, and looked at her mother's disappointed face. "Mom? What's wrong?"

"Just look at your room!" Her father's voice, normally so kind, was stern as he flicked on the light. "You promised us you'd clean it last night!"

"But I *did* . . ." Emmy's voice faltered as she looked properly around her for the first time that morning.

Clothes were everywhere: strewn on the floor,

tossed over chairs, and pulled off hangers. Books were tumbled about, pages bent. And papers from last year's school projects had been pulled out of folders and crumpled in corners.

Emmy whirled to face her parents. She had cleaned her room, she really *had*! But they'd never believe her, not with the way it looked now.

Or had she only dreamed that she had picked everything up?

But no. Even when she let her room get messy, it was never as bad as this. "I did clean it," she said. "I don't know what happened, but it was clean when I went to bed last night."

Her mother turned away. In the silence, the metallic hum from the playroom seemed to grow louder.

The lines in her father's face grew even more forbidding. "Turn off your electric train. You left it running all night long."

Emmy looked at him hopelessly. She could hardly say that two chipmunks were to blame.

At least with the train, she knew *why* it was running. But she had no idea how her room had gotten in such a mess.

"*Meeoow?*" A golden furry head poked in the door,

and the housekeeper's cat slipped around Mr. Addison's legs.

"No, Muffy!" Emmy leaped out of bed, snagged the cat by the hind legs, and imprisoned it in her arms. She wasn't about to let the cat loose in a room full of her rodent friends.

She stumbled to her playroom and flicked the train switch. Chippy and Buck were already out of sight.

"And what smells so strongly of mint?" Her mother's footsteps sounded on the bathroom tile. "Oh, *no*."

She turned, hands on her hips. "Emmy, we may have a housekeeper and maids now, but that doesn't mean you shouldn't clean up after yourself when you make a mess."

"I didn't spill it!" said Emmy. "Really, I didn't!"

"You had better stop saying things you know aren't true," her father said heavily. "You've been doing too much of that lately. Now get dressed and clean up your room, Emmy. Immediately."

3

"THERE!" Mrs. Bunjee dusted her paws and looked at Emmy's bedroom, tidy once more. "That's better!"

"Raston didn't help much," said Chippy, who had been rolling up socks with Buck.

The Rat stopped rummaging in Emmy's desk drawer and poked his head out over the side. "I am too helping. I'm looking for something."

Emmy glanced over. "Sorry, Ratty—there aren't any more peanut-butter cups in there. I ate the last one yesterday."

"Ha!" said Chippy.

Raston's ears grew pink at the tips. "Listen, I skipped breakfast. And I'm *starving*."

"I offered you acorn pancakes back in Rodent City," said Mrs. Bunjee tartly. "You said you weren't hungry."

"Er . . ." said the Rat.

Mrs. Bunjee turned around. "Come along, Buckram and Chipster—we need to get back. Don't

forget to meet the professor at the Antique Rat, Emmy."

Emmy nodded. Professor Capybara lived above an antique store that he had turned into a lab for his experiments in rodentology. It wasn't far, but she would have to have breakfast first.

"I wasn't hungry for pancakes made out of *acorns*," muttered Raston as the chipmunks bounded to the windowsill and out into the morning. "And I wasn't interested in seed toast or nut juice, either."

"Rasty!" Cecilia looked up from the bathroom tile, where she was scrubbing away at the grout with a toothbrush. "Mrs. Bunjee was very kind—"

"There's more to life than whole grains, Sissy!" cried the Rat, flinging out his arms. "There's a whole world beyond seeds and nuts! There's *chocolate*! There's raspberry cake and lemon meringue pie and crème brûlée and—and Nesselrode pudding!"

Emmy tried not to laugh. Long ago, someone had papered the Rat's cage with pages from *Nummi Gourmet*, and he had never forgotten the recipes he had read. "Listen, Ratty. I'm sorry about the peanut-butter cups. There are more in the kitchen—I'll bring some up after breakfast."

"Can we go downstairs for breakfast, too?" Raston clasped his paws before his chest. "Please please please *pleeeeease*? You can hide us in your backpack and drop in pieces of bacon!"

"Bacon does sound good," Cecilia admitted, putting down the toothbrush. "And my paws are getting a little tired."

"Thanks for helping," said Emmy. "I don't know how my room got so messed up." She frowned at the grout, still slightly green. The mouthwash had splashed in droplets all the way across the floor and even into the bedroom. She could see small green spots, almost like a trail, leading all the way to the bed.

"Maybe you were sleepwalking," said Raston. "Come on, Sissy, get in the backpack!"

Emmy zipped the backpack partly shut. From the intercom, she could hear muffled sounds: footsteps, a chair scraping? Her parents must have forgotten to turn it off at their end—or the switch was sticking again. She had her hand on the doorknob when she heard her parents' voices.

"What has gotten *into* her?" Kathy Addison's voice floated through the intercom, sounding near tears.

"She used to be such a trustworthy child, Jim, but lately, I can't count on her at all!"

"I know. She left the boat a mess after her sailing lesson yesterday. I found it when I went out for a sail at dawn. Lines tangled, mud everywhere . . . did she think I wouldn't notice?"

"She's been careless with her clothes, too. Maggie has done more mending in the last two weeks than in the past year. And such odd rips in the fabric, too—as if they had been *clawed*."

"And now these lies," came her father's voice. "I want to trust her, but how can I if she doesn't tell the truth?"

Up in her room, Emmy's throat felt thick with words she couldn't say. She wanted her parents to trust her, too. She wanted it more than anything. And she *was* responsible—they just didn't know it.

She *had* cleaned up the boat. She *hadn't* ripped her clothes. And the more she thought about it, the more certain she was that she hadn't trashed her room while sleepwalking.

"She never used to be like this, back when we were poor." Her father's voice interrupted her thoughts.

"Do you think all this money we have now is spoiling Emmy?"

"Maybe. I almost wish your great-uncle William had left everything to those other shirttail relatives of his."

"Do you mean Jane Barmy and her parents?" Mr. Addison sounded shocked. "You must be kidding."

"No, not them. Remember your aunts? The ones we named Emmy after?"

"Emmaline and Augusta. Fine old girls. I used to stay at their place in Schenectady in the summers. They didn't allow any nonsense! They treated me well, and I had a grand time sailing in the Mohawk River, but I had chores, too, every day of the week. And on Sundays I had to go early to church to ring the bells."

Emmy scowled. She didn't want to hear about some old aunts she couldn't remember meeting, or how many chores they'd once made her father do. What she wanted was to hear her parents say they had some faith in their only daughter.

Of course she knew how bad everything looked— all the evidence was against her. But still, she couldn't help wishing they believed in her a little more.

Ding dong! Dinnnng doonnng!

"Oh, it's that nice Joe Benson at the door," said Kathy Addison. "He's such a responsible boy, don't you think? He's in Scouts, and he babysits his brother, too."

"Yes," said Mr. Addison grimly. "I just hope some of it rubs off on Emmy."

The bedroom door closed behind Emmy with a *click*, and her footsteps faded away down the hall. Beneath the bed, two rodents stirred, shook themselves, and crawled out from under the bedskirt, dripping green onto the carpet.

The piebald rat glared. "Happy, Cheswick? Now that you nearly drowned me in mouthwash?"

"But, Jane, dear," said the black rat, "you smell so minty fresh!"

Jane Barmy snorted and dried her fur briskly on the dangling edge of Emmy's bedspread. "Now, listen. First, we're going to wreck her room—"

"Again?" said Cheswick. "Her parents are going to be furious!"

Miss Barmy gave him a chilly glare. "The concept of revenge seems to be eluding you, Cheswick . . .

but never mind." She clawed up a bit of Emmy's carpet, smiling with her thin rodent lips. "Next, we're going to the Antique Rat. There's a nice little hole in the ceiling, just right for spying."

"Spying?" said Cheswick, his ears alert. "What for?"

"I want to find out more about those Sissy-patches. I have"—she rubbed her paws together—"an absolutely *brilliant* idea!"

Emmy stood at the kitchen counter watching Mrs. Brecksniff flip an egg. "But can't I just eat in the kitchen?" She glanced at the door to the dining room, from which her father's voice came faintly. She would rather avoid her parents.

"Of course not!" The housekeeper lifted bacon from a frying pan and set it to drain on a paper towel. "You've got company in there waiting for you."

"But I shouldn't eat in front of company, should I?"

"Mrraow?"

Something furry brushed past Emmy's leg, and she looked down to see Muffy batting at the backpack with a paw. Emmy snatched it up.

"Joe is eating already," said Mrs. Brecksniff, dishing

25

up eggs and bacon. "He's tucking away a second breakfast just as fast as if he hadn't already had a first. Now, give me your backpack—your mother won't want it in the dining room—and go on in and sit down. I'll bring your plate, and then I've got to run upstairs."

The housekeeper plucked the backpack from Emmy's hands and tossed it onto the counter with a thump. A faint squeak came from the interior, immediately silenced.

"Got some squeaky toys in there?" Mrs. Brecksniff picked up Emmy's plate. "No wonder Muffy seems so interested."

Muffy, crouched on the floor, watched the backpack with unblinking yellow eyes. All at once she leaped to the countertop and poked her nose into the half-zippered opening.

"No! Bad Muffy!" Emmy swept the cat off the counter and shoved the backpack, now squeaking uncontrollably, into a tall cabinet. "I'll just put it in here, away from the cat, okay?"

"Fine," grunted Mrs. Brecksniff as she bumped open the dining room door with her hip and disappeared.

Emmy grabbed the cat and put it outside. Then she unzipped the backpack and put her face over the top. "Stop *squeaking*!" she hissed.

Sissy was trembling in the bottom of the pack. Raston patted her on the back and glared at Emmy. "We're going to need *extra* bacon."

"You can have it if you keep quiet!" Emmy reached for the last few slices.

"Crispy, if you don't mind," came the Rat's voice from the cabinet. "Flabby bacon is no good for shock."

In the dining room, Emmy's father was telling Joe a long story about his boyhood. Emmy knew it was long because she had heard it before.

"Yes, every Sunday when I was there I had to ring those bells. That meant I was responsible to get there early, see—"

Emmy kept her head down, ate her eggs as quickly as she could without shoveling them in, and ignored her father's emphasis on the word *responsible*. At least Professor Capybara thought she was responsible. He had asked for her specially, to help him make the Sissy-patches. And Joe could help, too. He knew as much as she did about the rodents of power.

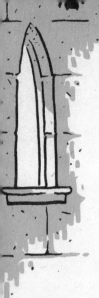

"Then up in the belfry, the bats would fly out, and those bells would ring louder than you can imagine," Jim Addison's voice continued.

"The bell-free?" Joe pronounced the unfamiliar word. "What's a belfry, Mr. Addison?"

"You know the pointy part of a church steeple?" Mr. Addison went on. "High on top of the roof? The belfry is the little room underneath it, where the bells are."

"Does it have those sort of slatted openings?" Joe asked. "Like a big huge air vent or something?"

"That's right. The openings were to let the sound of the bells out so they could be heard from miles away. And then down below, I'd be hanging on to the bell rope for dear life. When it went up, I'd be lifted clear off my feet!"

Emmy stood up and began to clear the table. Maybe her parents would see that she was trying to help out. She was rewarded by a quick smile from her mother and, feeling better, she bumped through the kitchen door.

She opened the cabinet door to check on the rodents, but they weren't in the backpack. They had turned on the interior cabinet light and found the cookbooks that were lined in a row. But they were not lined up neatly anymore. Three cookbooks lay on their sides, and Raston was bent over a fourth, open to a page titled "Delicious and Decadent—Desserts to Die For!" Crisscrossing the page were small, smudged pawprints the color of bacon grease.

Emmy groaned aloud. "Get in the *backpack*, Ratty!"

The Rat looked up, his paw resting on a line of type. "Can I take this cookbook with me?"

"*No!*"

"Just this page, then?" he begged. "Look! 'Whip until frothy'! 'Whisk in vanilla sugar'!"

"Crikey," said Joe, coming up behind and looking over Emmy's shoulder. "Is that rat drool on the page?"

"*Get—in—with—Sissy!*" Emmy pushed the protesting rodent through the backpack opening.

"Lemon zest!" cried the Rat in ecstasy. "Almond paste! Italian *chocolate*, Emmy! Oh, I never knew, I never knew!"

Emmy zipped the pack closed over his head, jammed the cookbooks back on the shelf, and turned just as her mother entered the kitchen.

"Mom? Is it okay if I go with Joe to the Antique

29

Rat? The professor needs us to help him with something. One of his experiments, I guess."

Mrs. Addison nodded slowly. "If it's to help the professor, you may go. But are you sure your room is clean, this time?"

"I'm *positive*," said Emmy.

4

"PROFESSOR CAPYBARA?" Emmy pushed open the door of the Antique Rat, and a bell jingled faintly as she stepped into the dim interior. She looked past the marble-topped tables and carved wooden cabinets to the far side of the store, where two figures hunched over a burning flame.

"Is that Emmy?" The shorter—and fatter—of the two turned, revealing a beaming face above a white beard. "Are Cecila and Raston with you?"

"Right here," Emmy said, unzipping the top of her backpack.

"I came, too, Professor," said Joe, clumping after Emmy to the improvised laboratory, a counter full of beakers and microscopes and stacks of yellowing paper.

The taller, lankier figure straightened, resolving itself into Brian, the professor's teenage assistant. "There are two of them, Professor—do you still need me?"

Professor Capybara flapped his hands at his assistant, waving him away. "You go on, Brian. Emmy and Joe will help me."

Brian ruffled Emmy's hair, gave Joe a thump on the back, grabbed a bag off a chair, and strode out the back door.

"Where's he going?" asked Emmy, as a sudden grinding roar told her Brian had started the ancient old truck he used for deliveries. She laid her backpack carefully on the counter, and Raston poked his nose out of the opening.

"Brian's gone to the Children's Home," said the professor absently, turning down the flame beneath a triangular glass flask, half full of a bubbling golden liquid. "He visits there every week, brings treats and such—all right, Cecilia, are you ready?"

Cecilia followed her brother onto the counter and smoothed her rumpled whiskers. "Ready, sir."

Professor Capybara consulted a piece of paper with a scrawled formula. Then he inserted an eyedropper into a test tube and squeezed the rubber bulb.

"What's in the test tube?" Emmy crowded in close to see.

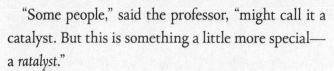

"Some people," said the professor, "might call it a catalyst. But this is something a little more special—a *ratalyst*."

"But what does it do?" asked Joe.

"It helps to store Sissy's kisses." Professor Capybara squeezed the eyedropper over the flask. Three silver drops glistened and fell, swirling into the golden liquid and turning it a deep orange.

"I don't get it," said Emmy.

The professor, red-faced from bending over the hot Bunsen burner, wiped his forehead. "Well, Raston's bites have some unusual effects, right?"

Emmy nodded. The first bite from Ratty allowed you to understand rodent speech. The second bite shrank you to rodent size. And the third bite turned you into an actual rat. But they had discovered all that two months ago.

"And here," said the professor, reaching for a stoppered vial, "is a supply of Saliva Rodentia Rastonia. Rat spit, to be exact."

"Gross," said Joe.

"My spit isn't any grosser than yours!" The Rat poked his nose out of the backpack.

Professor Capybara cleared his throat. "Gross or

not, you must see the benefit of having Raston's spit in a bottle."

Emmy nodded. "It means you don't have to have Ratty around if you want to shrink. You could scratch your skin and rub a little of the spit on the scratch, and it would be the same as a bite."

"Exactly right. Raston's bites are portable, so to speak. But Sissy's kisses, which you need to reverse the bites, are not."

"We found that out the hard way," said Joe. "Remember? That time when we were rescuing those little girls."

Emmy glanced at Sissy, who was smoothing her rumpled whiskers. It was true that it was dangerous to shrink or turn into a rat if Sissy wasn't right there with you. You never knew if you could find her when you wanted to change back. "And you can't put kisses in a bottle," she said, finishing her thought aloud.

"But you *can* capture Sissy's kisses on a sticky-patch and release them when the patch is put directly on your skin! The ratalyst makes it possible!"

"But why do you need us?" asked Joe.

"Creating the sticky-patches is a matter of split-second timing, and it's still in an experimental stage.

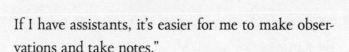

If I have assistants, it's easier for me to make observations and take notes."

"We'll help," said Emmy. "What do you want us to do, Professor?"

"Careful, Emmy," said Professor Capybara. "Hold her steady—that's right. Cecilia, are you quite comfortable?"

"Tell him if you aren't," said the Rat anxiously, watching from the countertop, his furry face lit up by the glow of the Bunsen burner.

Sissy, held upside down in Emmy's hand, twisted her neck to look up at the professor's kindly, worried face. "I'm all right, as long as you hurry. The blood's going to my head."

"Very well," said the professor. "Joe, do you have the paper film ready? The rolling pin?"

"All ready," said Joe.

"Raston, the timer?"

"Check."

The mixture spooled down and spread out like thick honey, glistening and translucent on the shiny backing paper that was marked with grid lines. "Now, Joe!" said the professor.

Joe slapped a sheet of thin, clear film on top of the goop and began to roll it out. The amber goo oozed out the edges and onto the steel plate beneath the backing paper.

"Timer . . . now!" Professor Capybara pulled off the top film, revealing a flat, smooth layer of golden-orange slime, quivering slightly. "Emmy, Cecilia—go!"

Quickly, carefully, Emmy held Sissy upside down over the slime and lowered her until her muzzle was almost touching the surface.

"Whiskers!" said the professor.

"Oh, that's right," said Cecilia, quickly bringing her paws to her face and pressing her whiskers upward. Emmy lowered her a fraction more, and she kissed the orange gel.

"Why does Sissy have to hold back her whiskers?" asked Joe. "Is it just to keep them clean?"

The professor's pen made a scratching sound as he added to his notes. "No. We found that if anything else touched the goo besides Sissy's lips, there were some unusual effects—" He looked up at the ceiling. "What was that?"

All was quiet, except for the slight smacking sound of Cecilia's kisses.

"I didn't hear anything," Joe said.

Raston sneezed. "Me neither. But my ears are all plugged up. I think I have allergies."

Emmy patiently moved Sissy along, square by square. Her arm ached, but she didn't want to let the professor down. *He* thought she was responsible, at least.

"Hey, guys!" Chippy's voice sang out from a hole in the wall, and he scampered across the floor and up onto the countertop. "Need any help?"

"Not really," said Raston, keeping an eye on the timer.

Chippy sniffed the air. "Something smells like—like—"

"Chipmunk?" Raston suggested politely.

"Like toothpaste," said Chippy. "Sort of minty fresh." He tipped his head back to watch. "Hey, why don't you rig up a sling, Professor? Sissy could be suspended at the perfect height."

"It's not a bad idea," said the professor.

"I could design one." Chippy paced back and forth, his paws behind his striped back. "You could do more squares, faster!"

Professor Capybara shook his head. "Cecilia can't

do too many in one day. The goop irritates her lips and makes them sore after a while."

"Time's up!" said the Rat.

"And now to cross-link the polymers with ultraviolet light," said the professor. "Goggles, everyone!"

A bank of tubular lights blazed on as the timer began to tick. And above the ceiling tile, in the space between the floors, a piebald rat stared through a small hole as if mesmerized.

5

"No COOKBOOKS?" said the Rat, pacing the kitchen counter in the professor's upstairs apartment. "No spices?"

"Salt and pepper," said the professor, handing out sodas from the refrigerator.

"He's got ketchup and mustard, too," said Joe, peering in over the professor's shoulder.

Raston snorted.

"And why would I need a cookbook?" Professor Capybara popped open a can for himself. "I just follow the directions on the box."

The Rat mumbled a word that Emmy didn't quite catch.

"Ratty, not everybody likes to cook—" Emmy began, but stopped at the sound of an engine's sputtering cough. The door downstairs banged open, and Brian's voice called out, "I've brought someone you know! Remember Ana?"

Emmy glanced at Joe. Of course they remembered

Ana. She had been the oldest of the girls they had rescued just two weeks before.

The professor started down the staircase at once. "Welcome!" he cried, and Joe followed at a trot.

"Come on, Ratty," said Emmy. "Sissy's downstairs with Chippy. And don't you want to see Ana again?"

"Oh, sure," said the Rat. "Anything to get out of this excuse for a kitchen. Not one single cookbook! And look!" He pointed accusingly at a shelf. "*Imitation* chocolate!"

A lady from the Children's Home had come with Ana, and she was talking. Emmy, walking carefully down the stairs with the Rat on her shoulder, had no trouble hearing her.

"Oh, my, such beautiful antiques, and decorated with such lovely—er, lovely—what *are* these creatures?"

Through the open door, Emmy could see a thin woman with bright red hair pointing to the carved back of a chair.

"Why, rodents, of course," said Professor Capybara. "It's the Antique Rat, you see."

"Oh!" The woman clapped a hand to her mouth and muffled a shriek. "I mean to say, how *special!*"

"Do sit down, my dear Miss—I'm sorry, I didn't quite catch your name?"

"Squipp," she said, clutching her elbows. "Gwenda Squipp. But we can't stay long, Professor . . . Kippy-burpa, was it?"

"Capybara," said the professor, bowing slightly.

"Ana just wanted to say thank you again and good-bye—Ana, dear, come and shake the professor's hand. She's ever so grateful that you rescued her from that terrible situation with the other little girls. Aren't you, Ana?"

Emmy, who had paused on the steps, caught Joe's eye and grinned. They had been the ones to rescue the girls, but of course it had been safer to let Professor Capybara take the credit.

A slender girl with watchful eyes moved into Emmy's field of vision. "Thank you again, Professor," she said in a clear, soft voice.

"She's recovered wonderfully well, considering," said Gwenda Squipp, "and she's had the best counseling the Children's Home has to offer, haven't you, Ana?"

Ana turned slightly away. She pushed her long brown hair back from her eyes and blinked as she caught sight of Emmy on the stairs.

41

"And the other little girls?" asked the Professor. "How are they, Miss Squipp?"

"Oh, call me Squippy—all my friends do!"

"*Squippy?*" said Raston into Emmy's left ear.

"As for the other little girls, they were all snapped up in a matter of days. Lots of loving relatives to take *them* in. We had a little more trouble finding people for Ana," she added, squeezing Ana's shoulder, "but we found some distant cousins at last, and she'll be going to live with them very soon."

Ana ducked out from under the woman's hand.

"Don't go upstairs, dear," called Squippy. "Stay where I can see you. Just sit right there with your friends while I talk to the professor."

"She won't let me out of her sight," muttered Ana, plopping down on the steps between Emmy and Joe. "It's almost like being Miss Barmy's prisoner again."

"No one is as bad as Miss Barmy," said Joe with feeling.

Raston flicked his tail. "Cheswick Vole isn't much better."

"Watch your tail, Ratty, you're tickling my neck," Emmy said. "Listen, Ana, it's going to be okay. You're going to live with your relatives, aren't you?"

"They don't really want me," said Ana, flushing.

Gwenda Squipp had taken the chair the professor had offered her, but she was still speaking in the slightly loud voice some grown-ups use when talking about children. "Yes, Ana and I will be traveling together tomorrow afternoon. A lovely, long trip on the train. And then she'll settle in with a brand-new family—won't that be special, Ana?"

Ana's long brown hair swung forward, hiding half her face. But the half that Emmy could see looked miserable.

Emmy stood up and the Rat gripped a lock of her hair for balance. "Come on, Ana—Joe and I will show you the Sissy-patches. Maybe we can help Brian, too."

"What a *lovely* idea," said Squippy as they passed. "It's so important to be *helpful*, don't you think, Prof— eeeeeeeek! A *rat*!"

"Eeeeeeek, a Squippy!" said Raston. "Seriously, what does everybody have against rats?"

"And now it's *squeaking* at me! Ana, we must leave at once. This is not a safe environment for you!"

"Calm yourself, my dear lady," said Professor Capybara. "It's a trained rat, perfectly safe."

"Really?" Gwenda Squipp gave the Rat a doubtful look.

Raston promptly did a flip on Emmy's shoulder, ending on one knee with paws outstretched.

"Oh! Oh, my!"

"I can sing 'The Star-Spangled Banner,' too," said the Rat, burnishing his claws on his chest fur.

Gwenda Squipp clapped her hands. "Look, it thinks it can talk! It's so cute! Oh, Professor Burpybara, you simply must tell me about your training methods!"

"Cute?" the Rat said in a strangled tone. "Now, listen, lady—"

"So nice to meet you, Miss Squipp!" Emmy said loudly, waving as she backed away.

Raston's voice rose. "I may be exceptionally good-looking, and of course I *do* have remarkably perky ears—"

"Shut up, Ratty!" said Joe under his breath. "Come on, Ana. You can help cut up the Sissy-patches."

"But I'm a manly rodent!" cried the Rat. "Handsome! Not *cute!*"

Emmy sat on a high stool at the far end of the store and kicked her feet against the rungs. She tried to

read the professor's formula for Sissy-patches, but the jumble of numbers and symbols made no sense to her, and she put it back on the counter.

Everyone else was busy. Brian was clinking among blue and green and golden bottles in a tall cabinet and making notes on a chart. Joe and Ana were cutting the Sissy-patches into neat squares. Chippy, gripping a pencil stub between his paws, was drawing a diagram of a sling that would hold Sissy. And Sissy, when she wasn't being measured for the sling, was getting a reading lesson from her brother.

"See? 'S' is for 'Spiny,' and 'Squirrel,' and . . . and 'Schenectady'!" Raston sorted through old cage tags for more words beginning with *s*.

"Schenectady," Joe repeated. "I just heard that name somewhere."

"It's where Ratty and Sissy were born, remember?" Emmy leaned forward. "That's what the tag said— Shrinking Rat of Schenectady. The professor's old lab was there, and Cheswick Vole was the lab assistant. It was Cheswick who went out and found Ratty and Sissy in their nest."

Ana looked up. "I'm going through that town,"

45

she said. "Tomorrow, on the train. It's one of the stops on the way to those people I have to live with."

"Haven't you even met them?" asked Joe.

Ana shook her head, looking miserable. "I wish I could just stay here."

Chippy put his pencil down. "Would you like to come to Rodent City for a visit? Mother invited you, you know. She wants to make you acorn cookies."

Ana glanced over her shoulder at Gwenda Squipp, who was still busily talking with the professor. "I wish I could. But we're leaving tomorrow. And Squippy keeps an eye on me wherever we go."

Emmy swung her legs, thinking hard. *Was* there a chance that Ana could stay in Grayson Lake? Probably not, if there were relatives who would take her. And Emmy knew better than to ask her parents if Ana could live with them—not with the trouble Emmy had been in lately.

But it was exactly that trouble that Emmy could not figure out. How *had* her room gotten so messed up? She certainly didn't think she had been sleepwalking, but as Joe had pointed out on the way to

the Antique Rat, she wouldn't remember it if she had.

Emmy slipped off her stool and stood by Brian. The tall cabinet was full of bottles and vials, each holding a colored liquid or powder and each with its own special rodent power. Would there be something in there that would cure sleepwalking? Who knew, maybe she could even find something that would help Ana.

"Brian," she began, when her eye was caught by a slender bottle half full of a silvery dust.

She lifted it from its shelf and held it close to her face, peering inside. It was almost as fine as powder, and it glittered as if made up of very small, very shiny scales.

"Scaly-Tailed Squirrel Dust," she read from the label. "Suspension of Disbelief." She passed it under her nose and sniffed. "It smells lemony. Like furniture polish."

Brian looked up from his chart. "Better not breathe it in, Emmy."

"But what does it do?"

"I don't know. You'll have to ask the professor." Brian bent over the chart again. "Maybe it

means you stop believing—no, wait. You stop *dis*believing—"

Emmy wasn't paying attention. All at once she was filled with a powerful sense that she *could* do something for Ana. In fact, her idea would not only make Ana happy, it would also impress Emmy's parents! She set the bottle on the counter and ran across the room.

"Professor," she said, "I have a *great* idea! I'd like to have a good-bye party for Ana tomorrow morning. Right here, in the Antique Rat."

The professor beamed. "That *is* a good idea!"

"Why, I don't think—" began Gwenda Squipp.

Emmy held up a hand to interrupt. It was the strangest thing, but she *knew* she could convince Squippy to agree. "I'll plan it all. And I'll buy the food and decorations, too." She could afford it; her parents gave her a generous allowance. She would invite her parents to the party; they would see that she *was* responsible, and be proud of her.

Gwenda Squipp blinked. "You seem very sure of yourself, young lady."

Emmy grinned at her, strangely confident. "But you're going to say yes, aren't you?"

"Well . . . perhaps I should."

"Then it's all settled," said the professor. "We'll hold it right before you and Ana leave on the train. All right, Emmy?"

Emmy nodded. "But Ana has to come early. That's part of the fun," she added quickly. "Two hours early, at least."

"Well," said Gwenda Squipp doubtfully, "I suppose I could arrange my schedule to come with her."

"Oh, you don't need to do that," said Emmy. "Please don't bother."

"But I have to, dear." Miss Squipp shook her head. "Children's Home rules. Ana must always be accompanied, at least until she is delivered to her guardians."

Emmy thought fast. "But do you have to be in the same room as Ana? I mean, couldn't she be upstairs while you were down here?"

Gwenda Squipp frowned.

"There's a good reason," said Emmy recklessly, filled with the happy knowledge that she *would* think of a reason. And then all at once, she did.

Emmy whispered in Squippy's ear.

Gwenda Squipp clasped her hands, sending her

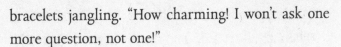

bracelets jangling. "How charming! I won't ask one more question, not one!"

"Wow," said Joe, as the door closed behind Ana and Squippy, and Brian's truck roared into life. "I've never seen you take charge like that before, Emmy."

"I don't know what came over me," Emmy admitted. "But it was like I already believed she was going to say yes! I just sort of told her so."

"What did you whisper to Squippy?" asked Joe.

"I said Ana wanted to make her a very *special* surprise, and I was going to help, and we didn't want her to see it until it was ready."

"Ana wants to give Squippy a surprise?" said Joe. "What?"

"I made that part up," said Emmy. "I mean, we'll come up with some kind of surprise, but that's not why we need the two hours." She grinned. "I'm going to take Ana to visit Rodent City."

Brrriinnnngg! Brrriinnnngg!

The professor stepped to the phone. "Why, yes, Mr. Addison, Emmy is here—just one moment."

Emmy took the receiver. "Dad?"

Her father spoke forcefully. Emmy held the phone

away from her ear, and Joe's eyes widened as he listened.

"*Come back right now to clean your room, young lady. You'll have a few more chores, too!*"

The droning hum of a dial tone filled the air. Emmy stared at the receiver in her hand.

"So you *weren't* sleepwalking," said Joe slowly.

Emmy put the phone back in its cradle as if it had been made of glass. "Somebody," she said, "is out to get me."

6

IT WAS ALMOST MIDNIGHT. All was quiet outside the Antique Rat as two rodents emerged from a hole in the crumbling foundation, sniffed deeply, and scuttled across the street.

One of the rodents was dragging a plastic bag. It glinted briefly in the light from a silver moon, but when the moon slipped behind a cloud, the rats moved across the central patch of grass unseen, the bag bumping behind.

They glanced at a police car that was parked outside a tall, narrow house, and slipped inside the building through a gnawed rathole. They paused at a small poster that had been affixed to the tunnel wall with a thumbtack.

"It doesn't look a bit like us," said the piebald rat, shredding the carefully drawn poster with her claws.

They ran across a wooden floor, scampered up a long flight of stairs, and wiggled around the edge of the heavy door to her parents' spare bedroom.

"Jane, dear," said the black rat, panting, "maybe you shouldn't try this just yet. The police are waiting to catch Miss Barmy—I mean, catch the full-size human that was a nanny to those little girls, and if you grow, you'll be in danger!"

"We'll figure all that out later, Cheswick," said the piebald rat, ripping open the plastic bag with her claws. "I'm not going to wait one more minute to use these patches."

Jane Barmy (the short, furry version) stood on her hind feet, faced the full-length mirror, and took a deep breath. The stolen Sissy-patches were laid out on a terry-cloth towel before her.

"Are you going to use them all at once?" Cheswick asked. "How many are there?"

"I don't know," said Miss Barmy through her teeth. "Not as many as there should be. Didn't you see the professor give two patches to that disgusting Emma-line?"

"Two isn't enough to worry about," said Cheswick. He studied the patches. "Roll fast," he advised. "Pull the towel right around you, and that will keep the patches next to your skin."

The piebald rat nodded, her whiskers quivering.

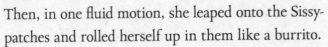

Then, in one fluid motion, she leaped onto the Sissy-patches and rolled herself up in them like a burrito.

"Jane! Oh, Jane, dearest, you're making such terrible noises! Are you in pain, my little sugar-bunny? Speak to me, Jane!"

But Jane Barmy could not speak. Her mouth was twisted in agony, and a high-pitched squeal filled the room. And then she did begin to change—and grow—but not evenly, not first to human and then to full size, but in splotches of human and rat mixed, skin and piebald fur and whiskers and soft dark hair, pink cheeks and lovely eyes and sharp rodent teeth.

Cheswick shuddered as he watched, and he wrung his paws until the fur began to fray, but there was no stopping the transformation that was convulsing his darling. And then, all at once, it was done.

She stood before him, tall and beautiful and entirely human, the woman he adored, fetchingly wrapped in the terry-cloth towel that had grown with her. He had become a rat for love of her, and suddenly he was conscious of the fact that he was *still* a rat. Cheswick bit his claws in sudden despair. Would she think he was too small for her? Too furry, perhaps? Would he have to hide his tail?

Jane Barmy gazed into the mirror as if she could never get enough of her own reflection. She smiled, a slow, lovely smile, her teeth like perfect white chisels—no, like sharp, pointy chisels—no, like ratty chisels in a pointed, whiskered face—no! "No! NOOOOOOOOOOooo!"

The howl that echoed between the walls of the spare room was at first full-voiced, the sound of a grown woman screaming in horror. But it dwindled, it shrank, until it was only a high-pitched squeak, and in front of the mirror was a small, splotchy rodent, brown and tan and white, sobbing bitter tears.

"Oh, my precious fuzzbundle, oh, *Barmsie!*" cried Cheswick, rushing to take her in his furry embrace. And Miss Barmy sank weakly against him, crying on his shoulder, in a way that, so far, had only happened to him in dreams.

"Is everything all right?" Jane Barmy's father, a mild, chubby old man in rumpled pajamas, peered sleepily into the room. "I heard someone scream . . ." He gazed at the piebald rat. Though she had recently turned small and hairy, she was still his daughter, and he noticed with concern the wet tracks of tears along her fuzzy cheeks.

"I'm fine, Father. It was just an experiment. Go to bed."

"But the police might have heard! What will I tell them?"

"Tell them anything. Tell them Mother had a nightmare. Go on, Father! We're busy!"

The white-haired man shuffled obediently out of the room, his down-at-heel slippers scuffing along the hall.

Miss Barmy wiped her eyes and spoke crisply. "Get a pencil and paper, Cheswick, and stop patting me already. We need a plan of action."

Cheswick, who had been mentally diagramming the layout of a nice little burrow in the riverbank—they would need a nursery for the litters to come—came out of his reverie with a start. "A-a plan, Jane?" Surely she understood now that she had to stay a rat. Perhaps she wanted to plan the wedding?

"We have a goal, Cheswick, and therefore we must have a strategy. First, the goal."

Cheswick gripped his pencil and wrote "Marry Jane Barmy." He leaned his whiskered cheek on his paw and gazed at the words, sucking dreamily on the end of his pencil.

"And the goal is," the piebald rat went on, "to turn me back into a full-size human—permanently."

Cheswick gave her a pleading look. "But, Jane! Surely you aren't going to keep trying to grow?"

"Naturally I'm going to keep trying. Write it, Cheswick."

The black rat gripped the pencil stub and wrote "Grow the beautiful Jane" and set aside his dream of a cozy burrow with a long, heartfelt sigh. "I guess we'll need more Sissy-patches."

"Yes, Cheswick, but not just the patches alone. We need that kissy rat herself."

Cheswick shook his head. "She'll never do it."

Miss Barmy gave him a wilting glare. "Do you think I'm planning to ask her permission? We're going to kidnap her, of course. Or—would that be ratnap?"

"Either way," said Cheswick faintly.

"Well, that's the first thing we have to do, then. And next, we have to find a place that isn't watched by the police, where we can keep the kissy rat locked up and keep making the patches until we get it right. Father can mail us the supplies that we need. Ideally, we want a place set up like a lab, where we can—oh! Cheswick!"

"Wha?" Cheswick snapped to attention.

"Are you thinking what I'm thinking?"

"I *want* to be thinking what you're thinking, Jane, dearest," said Cheswick cautiously. "What *are* you thinking?"

"Is that old lab of the professor's still in Schenectady?"

"Why, yes, of course. I had it boarded up, but I still paid the taxes on it every year. I thought maybe someday I would go back and make a name for myself in rodentology, just like the profess—" Cheswick cut himself off and left his mouth hanging open. "Jane! You *want* to go to Schenectady with me?"

"You may be slow, Cheswick, but you always get it eventually. Yes, I'm going to Schenectady with you, and we'll hole up in that old laboratory with the kissy rat until I'm my old self again or we all die, whichever comes first."

Cheswick felt all soft and saggy with love. Alone with Jane . . . in Schenectady! What could possibly be more romantic?

A thought intruded. They wouldn't be *quite* alone. "How are we going to get Sissy Rat there? How are we going to get there ourselves?"

"We'll take the train, of course."

"But even if we tie her up, Sissy will be kicking and squeaking the whole way. And she'll be heavy, too. How are we going to do it without anyone noticing, Jane?"

"You leave that to me, Cheswick. I'm beginning to get an idea . . . a fabulous, brilliant idea . . ." She sat in thought, pink nose twitching. "How is your penmanship, Cheswick?"

Cheswick beamed. "Did you notice those rodent tags on the counter? I wrote all those out by hand, years ago."

"*Very* good." The piebald rat stroked her whiskers. "And how are your claws, these days? Long enough to poke holes in ceiling tile?"

Cheswick guiltily hid his bitten claws behind his back. "If they're not, I can just use a nail, dearest. Or an awl. I'm sure your father will have one in his shoe shop."

"That's true." Miss Barmy got up and began to pace. "By the way, do you know any bats? Postal bats?"

"Well . . ." Cheswick thought for a moment. "I know Stefano. And Guido. Stefano owes me a favor," he added.

"Excellent! You know, this really is a *fabulous*

59

idea—possibly my best yet." Miss Barmy clapped her paws together. "We'd better get started. We've got all night to steal what we need and get into position. Oh, and Cheswick?"

"Yes, my little cuddle dumpling?"

"*We're* not going to bring Sissy to Schenectady. That nasty little Emmaline Addison is going to do it for us. Now, listen. Here's what I want you to do."

7

EMMY COULDN'T SLEEP.

For one thing, she had a cat in her room.

It hadn't been her idea, but everyone else had agreed it was the best thing to do. "Someone is getting in your room when the door is shut," the professor had said. "I wonder if some stray river rats sneaked in to ride on your electric train and vandalized your room. They can be a little wild."

"Could it be Miss Barmy, sir?" Joe had asked. "She hates Emmy. And Cheswick does whatever she tells him to do."

"Surely they know that everyone is looking for them," said Professor Capybara. "I would have thought they'd be far away by now. But I suppose it's possible."

So Emmy had borrowed Muffy for the night. The river rats would hardly go into a room where they smelled a cat. And Emmy had no doubt that even Miss Barmy, as long as she stayed a rat, would think twice before tangling with Muffy.

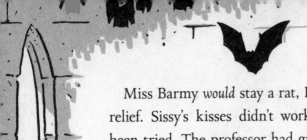

Miss Barmy *would* stay a rat, Emmy thought with relief. Sissy's kisses didn't work on her; they had been tried. The professor had guessed that all Miss Barmy's nastiness clogged up something important inside her and blocked the effect of the kiss. That made perfect sense to Emmy.

She was feeling a little clogged up, herself. She didn't even want to think about the disappointed looks on her parents' faces or the hours of extra chores they had made her do. It wasn't fair, but what could she tell them? Joe thought Miss Barmy was behind it all, but Emmy could hardly expect her parents to believe that her old nanny was now a rat. They already thought she had lied about her room. She didn't want to make things worse.

Her parents had looked happier when she'd told them about Ana's party, though. They had even given permission for her to go back and decorate after her chores were done. And now all was ready for the party in the morning. Emmy and Joe had delivered invitations, hung streamers and blown up balloons, and ordered a cake from the bakery. Emmy had even remembered to ask the professor for two Sissy-patches ahead of time. Tomorrow, when she and Ana shrank to visit Rodent City, they would not have to find Sissy in order to grow to full size again. Which was a good thing, because they would have a party to go to and guests to greet, and they could *not* be late.

Emmy rolled over in bed and pulled the blankets up over her ears. How was she supposed to fall asleep with Muffy making all that noise? It sounded like the cat was banging pots and *pans*—

Emmy sat up abruptly. The clanking sounds were not coming from Muffy, who was curled up on the floor. They were emerging from higher up, on the wall. The intercom switch was still stuck in the on position, and Emmy could hear everything that was going on in the kitchen. Were her parents making a midnight snack, or what? There was a lot of banging around, and even some *squeaking*—

Emmy shot out of bed, grabbed her robe, and ran soft-footed down the stairs to the kitchen. "Ratty! What are you *doing*?"

The Rat, his fur whitened with flour, looked hot, sweaty, and blissful. He was perched on the rim of a blue mixing bowl, and he was gripping a wire whisk with both paws. "Oh, good! You can help me toast the almonds!"

Emmy stared at the open cookbook, gritty with sugar, and an egg that had fallen on the floor and smashed. A thicket of knives lay entangled on the counter—that must have been the clatter she'd heard—and the refrigerator door had swung open.

"I don't *believe* this!" Emmy's whisper was despairing.

"I know!" The Rat flung out his arms and the whisk slid down into the bowl. "Here you have this great kitchen, but nobody ever makes biscotti!"

There was a sound of footsteps in the hall, and Raston ducked behind the toaster as the kitchen door creaked open. Emmy stood perfectly still for one dreadful moment. Then she turned to face her parents.

"Oh, *Emmy*," said Kathy Addison, sinking down on a chair in her nightgown.

"What on earth are you doing now?" Her father's hair was mussed from sleep, but his voice was wide awake and furious.

Emmy cast desperately in her mind for some sort of explanation that would satisfy her parents. "Um— making something for the party?"

Her father lowered his chin and fixed her with

unblinking eyes. "You're making something for the party," he repeated slowly.

"Ana's party," said Emmy. She paused—what would she say if she really had been making something for the party? "Ana doesn't have a family, and she's worried about where she's going . . . I wanted to make her something really special. And I didn't want to bother you," she added in a burst of inspiration.

Jim Addison's gaze traveled over the mess on the counter, the egg on the floor, the wide-open refrigerator. "And what, exactly, were you making?"

Emmy glanced nervously behind the toaster.

"Biscotti!" mouthed the Rat.

"Biscotti," Emmy repeated, hoping her father wouldn't ask her what that was.

The grim set of her father's mouth softened at the corners. He exchanged a glance with his wife.

"Darling," said Emmy's mother, "if you wanted something special for Ana's party, all you had to do was ask. Mrs. Brecksniff or Maggie would have been glad to make those Italian cookies for you."

"Better yet, we'll order some biscotti from the bakery," said her father. "We'll do it in the morning. But right now, clean up this mess!"

"And go straight back to bed when you're done," said her mother, with a hug.

The door shut behind her parents. Emmy reached up to the intercom and jiggled the switch until it clicked off.

The Rat scampered out from behind the toaster. "We can't order biscotti from the bakery!" he said, his eyes wide and alarmed. "It's not the same! It won't be as fresh!"

"Oh, shut *up*, Ratty," said Emmy. "And wipe up that egg. There's no way I'm doing all this alone."

Emmy was groggy the next morning, and she opened her bedroom door before she remembered Muffy. The cat slipped past her legs, clearly annoyed at having been shut in all night.

Then downstairs, when Emmy opened the door to get the paper, she forgot about the cat again. "Drat you, Muffy!"

Muffy, down the steps and five leaps into the lawn, looked back with a smug expression.

"Oh, go on," said Emmy crossly. "You know I can't catch you now. Go ahead and kill a bird or something, you mean thing. But you had better stay away from rodents, if you know what's good for you."

At least Ratty was safely back in Rodent City, she thought as she watched Muffy stalk away. Raston had helped with kitchen cleanup and then he'd left, still complaining about the biscotti.

Emmy couldn't find it in her to care. Her parents would pick up an order of the Italian cookies at the bakery, and that would have to be good enough for Ratty.

Her spirits rose as she skipped up the hill on her way to the Antique Rat. Ahead of her were the school and the playground, and on top of the slide was Joe, waiting for her. His little brother, Thomas, was a short distance away, crouched over something on the ground.

"I have to babysit today," Joe said cheerfully. "But you know Thomas—if grown-ups are around, he's pretty useful."

Emmy grinned. Thomas was only six and a half, but he had large blue eyes, a round, chubby face, and an excellent ability to look innocent at difficult times. "What's he looking at? Worms?"

"Or caterpillars," said Joe, letting go of the slide

railing and flying down on his back. He landed with a thump in the sand and got up, dusting himself off. "So, any more problems with your room getting wrecked?"

Emmy adjusted the shoulder strap on her backpack. "Not since Muffy. But I didn't get much sleep. Hey, Thomas!" she called. "Come on, we're going to the Antique Rat!"

Thomas called back something indistinct.

Emmy looked at Joe. "What did he say?"

"He found something or other. Bring it with you!" Joe called over his shoulder.

They crossed Main Street and turned in to the alley that led to the back streets. Joe was talking about the science badge he was working on for Scouts and how he was going to ask the professor to help him, but Emmy only half listened. She was thinking about her parents.

In a few hours, they would be proud of her again. They would see that she was responsible and trustworthy—at least if all went according to plan. And it *would*. Emmy had a checklist and a timetable; she had all the supplies she needed in her backpack. Right now, Brian was picking up Ana and Squippy, and Ratty would be waiting for them upstairs in the professor's apartment.

They were at the door of the Antique Rat. Joe looked over his shoulder at his brother, who was walking slowly, looking at something in his cupped hands. "Hurry *up*, Thomas!"

Emmy pushed open the door of the Antique Rat and smiled. The party decorations she had put up yesterday looked festive; the balloons and streamers swayed lightly in the draft from the open door. The punch bowl and mints were ready on a little table, and the professor was—

Emmy stopped smiling. Professor Capybara, on the far side of the room, thumped the laboratory counter with his hand, his face reddening.

"My formula!" he cried. "All my Sissy-patches! Gone!"

"Stay calm, Professor!" Emmy cried. "You know what happens—"

Professor Capybara tried to hold his eyelids open, but they closed irresistibly. He swayed, sank to his knees, and toppled over onto the floor with a crash.

"—when you get upset," finished Emmy, as he began to snore.

8

"NOT AGAIN!" Joe stood at her shoulder. "I thought he'd found a cure for the Snoozer virus."

"He was working on a cure." Emmy bent over the professor and straightened the glasses on his nose. "Wake *up*, Professor!"

"It might be a minute, and it might be an hour," said Joe. "You can't hurry him."

Emmy sat back on her heels. "But if Squippy comes and he's out cold, she'll make a big fuss."

"She'll probably call an ambulance," Joe agreed.

Emmy felt in her pocket. At least she had the two Sissy-patches that the professor had given her the day before. They could still make their visit to Rodent City—that is, if Gwenda Squipp would let Ana out of her sight. But with the professor flat on his back, it was doubtful.

"Emmy?" The professor's voice rasped. "I must tell you—"

"Oh, good!" said Emmy. "You're awake already!"

"Listen, please!" Professor Capybara struggled to sit up. "Nothing else was taken or destroyed, just the formula and the Sissy-patches. We must therefore conclude"—he wiped his forehead with his pocket handkerchief, and Emmy saw with concern that his face was growing pink again—"it was *not* the wild river rats, out for some vandalism—"

"Stay calm, Professor!"

"—but Miss Barmy! She's going to use the patches, Emmy!"

"It's okay," Emmy said in her most soothing voice. "They won't do her any good. Sissy's kisses don't work on her, remember?"

The professor shook Emmy's arm. "You're in *danger* . . ." His head lolled to one side as his emotion rose, and his eyes shut like window shades. "Very . . . serious . . . danger . . ."

The handkerchief fluttered to the floor as the professor's body keeled over yet again.

Exasperated, Emmy stood up. Had the formula and patches really been stolen? Or had the professor just forgotten where he had put them?

Joe was opening the street door again, calling to Thomas. Emmy scanned the countertop. She didn't

71

see the missing formula or patches, but the bottle of Scaly-Tailed Squirrel Dust was on the counter where she had set it down. Brian must have forgotten to put it back in the cabinet before he locked it. The bottle had tipped on its side, and some of the glittery silver dust had spilled. There didn't seem to be as much of it as she remembered . . .

Well, she could clean up the spill, at least. Emmy brushed the tiny silver scales off the counter into her hand and got as much of it as she could back into the narrow bottle. She was careful not to breathe it in this time—Brian had warned against that—but she was left with a silvery coating on her palms. She picked up the professor's handkerchief and wiped her hands thoroughly.

There was a scrape of feet at the doorway. "It's about time," said Joe. "What did you find, Thomas?"

Emmy turned, prepared to admire a caterpillar, or a beetle, or a tiny toad. But when she came closer, she saw that the little boy's eyes were round and startled.

"Look." Thomas held out his pudgy hands. Cradled in them was a motionless yellow bird, its beak slightly open, its feet pointing straight up.

"It's dead," said Joe, poking at it.

Thomas's eyes filled with tears.

"Don't feel bad, Thomas," said Emmy hastily. "Maybe it's not *exactly* dead. Maybe it's just stunned."

Joe rolled his eyes.

"Or maybe it has the Snoozer virus," said Emmy, suddenly inspired. "Like the professor!"

"Yeah, or maybe it's *dead*," said Joe.

Thomas sniffled. One fat drop slid off his nose and landed damply on the soft, ruffled feathers. "I don't *want* it to be dead." He sniffled again.

"Here," said Emmy automatically, putting the professor's handkerchief to his nose. "Blow."

Thomas honked loudly into the white square.

"Again."

Thomas took a deep breath and blew his nose a second time. Then he brightened. He looked up at Joe. "Hey! It *is* just sleeping!"

"Look, Thomas, face it. That bird is—"

"Wake up!" cried Thomas, flinging the bird up in the air. "Fly!"

The bird arced up and then dropped like a stone. There was a soft *pluff* as it landed on the floor, its wings splayed out awkwardly.

"See?" said Thomas, picking it up and stroking

73

the limp yellow head. "It's still alive. It just needs time to wake up." He raised the bird to his ear. "I think it's breathing!"

Joe stared at his brother. "Are you mental?"

Emmy looked down at the handkerchief in her hand, still covered with silvery dust. "Maybe it *is* still sleeping," she said slowly.

Joe snorted. "Oh, come on, Emmy, get a grip—"

Emmy caught his eye and shook her head slightly. "Thomas, why don't you take your bird upstairs and put it on the windowsill? Then it can fly out when it wakes up."

Thomas walked happily up the stairs, hunched protectively over his treasure.

Joe turned on Emmy. "What was *that* all about?"

"Remember yesterday?" Emmy whispered. "When I *believed* I could talk Squippy into agreeing to this party and then I did?"

"Yeah, but what does that have to do with a dead bird?"

"Everything! Look!" Emmy dragged him to the lab counter, stepping over the professor's legs, and pointed to the narrow bottle.

"Scaly-Tailed Squirrel Dust," Joe read slowly from

74

the label. "Suspension of Disbelief. What does that mean?"

"If you breathe it in, you can believe things that you usually wouldn't! It worked on me, and it worked on Thomas!" She showed him the handkerchief, still glittering faintly.

Joe lifted his head as the throbbing sound of a truck engine grew louder, then suddenly rattled and died. "Well, let's hope it works on Squippy. Because she's here, and the professor's still snoring."

As it turned out, Gwenda Squipp was easy. The moment she walked in with Ana, Emmy rushed up, holding out the bottle. "Smell this, Miss Squipp! It's Scaly-Tailed Squirrel Dust!"

"But—" said Brian.

"No, Brian." Gwenda Squipp patted the teenager's arm. "I'm not too busy to pay attention to what this very imaginative little girl is trying to show me. Scaly-Tailed Squirrel Dust? How *special*!" She bent her head and took a deep, appreciative sniff. "My, my! It smells so—so—"

"Scaly?" said Emmy.

Gwenda Squipp beamed. "Yes, exactly!"

"I have something else to show you, too." Emmy

took the woman's hand and led her to Professor Capybara, still sleeping.

"Oh, dear! Is he ill?" Gwenda Squipp glanced nervously at Ana. "Perhaps we should go. Is it contagious?"

"Not at all," Emmy said firmly. "It's just that, years ago, a Bushy-Tailed Snoozer Rat sneezed in his face and he came down with the Snoozer virus."

"Really?" Squippy bent over the professor. "How absolutely fascinating! Would you believe I've never heard of it?"

"The scientific name is Ratolepsy," said Brian, pulling out a chair for her. "It's a rodent-induced sleep disorder."

"And whenever he gets too excited, he just falls asleep," Joe added.

"It's funny," said Gwenda Squipp. "I've never heard of it, and it sounds completely impossible—even so, I believe you! Will it help if I fan him?" She began to wave her hands vigorously over his face.

"Good idea! And while you fan him, Ana and I will go upstairs to work on the—you know!" Emmy whispered hoarsely in Ana's ear, loud enough for Gwenda Squipp to hear. "*The surprise for Squippy!*"

Ana's eyes widened thoughtfully as Squippy tried to look as if she hadn't heard.

"And one more thing." Emmy beamed at Squippy. "Ana will be with me, and she'll be perfectly safe. You won't need to check on her at *all*."

"Why, I believe you're right!" Squippy settled contentedly to fanning. "Just call if you need me, dear!"

"That," whispered Joe as they went up the stairs, "is one handy bottle of dust!"

Emmy grinned. "So, Ana—do you want to go to Rodent City?"

Ana looked at Emmy and Joe in dawning realization. It was gloomy in the stairwell, but her face brightened. "*Really?*" she whispered.

"Shh!" said Joe, holding up a warning hand.

"That bird is *not* sleeping." The Rat's voice was exasperated.

They peeked around the corner. Past the kitchen table, Thomas was sitting on a chair by the window, his chin on his hands. Raston Rat was pacing the windowsill.

"Yes, it is," said Thomas placidly.

"It's not! It's dead! It's a dead bird!" Raston grabbed

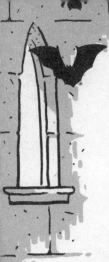

the bird by one stiff foot and lifted. Its head, upside down, rolled limply.

"It's got the Snoozer virus," said Thomas. He smiled a wide, peaceful smile. "It will wake up soon, and fly away."

"It's not going to fly away!" The Rat shook it by the leg, his ears pink with outrage. "The only way this bird would fly is if you shot it out of a cannon!"

"Now you've made it dizzy," said Thomas.

"It's not dizzy!" the Rat shrieked. "This bird is a goner! It's kicked the bucket! It's cashed in its chips! This"—he dropped it on the windowsill with a thump—"is an ex-bird!"

Joe, collapsed against the wall in silent laughter, was no help at all. Emmy handed her backpack to Ana and stepped over to the windowsill. "Come on, Ratty, leave the poor bird alone. We need you to shrink us."

Thomas happily patted the bird's feathers back into place. Brian came up the stairs two steps at a time and set the blue pet carrier down in the middle of the kitchen floor.

"Go ahead, Ana—you shrink first." Emmy rummaged in her backpack and drew out glitter, a large piece of cardboard, construction paper, scissors, and markers. Then she pulled out a can of spray paint and a box of dry macaroni.

There was a muffled cry from Ana as she shrank.

Emmy glanced over her shoulder. "You don't have to bite so hard, Ratty!"

"I'm okay!" called the miniature Ana cheerfully from the door of the pet carrier. "Listen, Ratty, just one more . . ."

Joe, still laughing, came to stand beside Emmy as she spread the contents of her backpack on the kitchen table. "What do you want us to do with that?"

"Make some kind of big card for Squippy. You know—have it say something nice and be from Ana. You can decorate it. Let Thomas help you." Emmy lowered her voice. "And when his back is turned, get rid of that bird. He'll think it flew away."

Joe grinned. "Okay. You've got the Sissy-patches for when you get back?"

"Yup." Emmy unzipped the side pocket of her backpack and pulled out the plastic bag containing the two patches. "I don't know where Sissy is, but we don't need her, as long as you keep these safe—oh, no!"

"What?" said Ana, flicking her tail.

9

IT WAS HOT. The midday sun beat down on the triangular green, wilting its patchy grass. One tree cast a spindly shade over a single park bench and a low planting of yews. Behind them, almost hidden, Emmy sat on the ground with her chin on her knees. The patch of shade was getting smaller, and she was sweating.

She stared moodily at the empty pet carrier and wished again that Ana hadn't gotten Ratty to bite her twice. Sure, Ana was having all kinds of fun visiting Rodent City as a rat, but meanwhile Emmy was stuck waiting around at the back entrance. Because of course she couldn't shrink now. Ana would need both Sissy-patches—one to turn human and one to grow.

Ratty had told Emmy she should shrink anyway. "Sissy just went to get the mail," he had insisted in the professor's apartment. "She'll be back soon."

But Emmy didn't want to take the chance. Enough had gone wrong already; she didn't want to risk missing the party when her parents were coming.

Then, too, if the professor was right and it had been Miss Barmy who had stolen the patches, who knew what she might be planning? No, Emmy had better stay full size—and alert.

But she was getting sick of waiting. Emmy ducked under the spreading branches of the yew and put her mouth to the tunnel opening. "Aaaaannnaaaa!" she called, long and low.

Silence. Emmy glanced at her watch. Should she go get Ratty? He could run down the long passageway to Rodent City and find Ana in Mrs. Bunjee's loft.

"Mraoow?" A furry head butted under the yew beside her and sniffed delicately at the hole in the ground.

"Get lost, Muffy." Emmy glared at the housekeeper's cat, who backed just out of range and curled up under the far branches of the yew, watching Emmy with unblinking eyes.

Well, there was no way she could leave to get Ratty now. Even if she chased Muffy off the green, the cat would come back. Emmy had a brief, unhappy vision of Ana dangling from Muffy's mouth and groaned aloud. She would just have to wait.

She was on her hands and knees, calling into the tunnel for the fifth time, when a voice spoke behind her.

"Emmy! What on earth are you doing out here? Shouldn't you be getting ready for your party?"

Emmy tipped back on her heels to see her father looking down at her and, past him, her mother getting out of the car holding a bakery box. Across the street, Brian was tying balloons to the door of the Antique Rat.

"I'll be there soon, Dad," Emmy said, hoping it was true. "I'm just—I'm just waiting here for somebody."

Her father frowned. "When you're supposed to be hosting a party?"

Emmy gazed up at him, feeling desperate. "It's *about* the party," she said. "It's a surprise."

Her father looked unconvinced, but Kathy Addison called and he turned away. Emmy watched with a flutter of anxiety as her parents walked across the street into the Antique Rat. Would the professor be awake yet? What would Squippy tell them?

"Mrraaow!" There was a sudden soft thump under the yew, and a thin, high squeal from the tunnel's mouth.

"Bad Muffy!" Emmy hauled the cat away by the hind legs and hung on. "Hurry, Ana! Get in the pet carrier!"

A small and fluffy rat scampered into the blue plastic carrier, reached a paw through the barred door, and yanked it shut, breathing hard. "Oh, my gosh, that cat is a monster! But I had such a fun visit—Mrs. Bunjee had three kinds of cookies, and fresh lemonade, and—"

"And you're *late*," said Emmy as she strode across the green, the carrier bumping at her hip. The door of the Antique Rat slammed behind her, and she was halfway to the stairs before Squippy called out, "Did you get the supplies you needed? You know, for"— she lowered her voice with a roguish smile—"the *surprise!*"

Her father turned around. "Emmy told me she was waiting for someone."

"No doubt she was doing both!" Professor Capybara spread his hands, smiling. "There are lots of secrets and surprises with a party!"

Emmy gave him a grateful look, waved at the adults, and disappeared up the stairs.

Thomas and Joe's card for Squippy was beyond

ugly. The minute Emmy let Ana out of the pet carrier, Joe led them to the kitchen table to admire it.

"We had an hour and a half, and a lot of macaroni," said Joe proudly. "Hideous, isn't it?"

"I dumped the glitter on," said Ratty.

Ratty and the boys had pasted colored-paper cutouts on the cardboard Emmy had brought. On top of this, they had arranged dry macaroni to make big, clumsy letters that spelled out THANX SQUIPPY!!! Next they had spray-painted the macaroni gold. Then, more construction paper around the edges to make a border. Then, macaroni on top of that, colored with markers. Lastly they had squiggled what looked to be a massive amount of glue over the whole thing and dumped the entire bottle of silver glitter on top.

Emmy gazed at the monstrosity in awe. "I've never seen anything that comes even close."

Ana, who had scampered up to the tabletop on her own, grinned toothily. "Squippy will love it. She'll probably save it for years."

Thomas leaned his elbows on the table and smiled up at Emmy happily. "My bird flew away," he confided. "I told you it was only sleeping."

Raston coughed behind his paw, but any further

remarks were interrupted by Brian's thumping feet on the stairs.

"Better change back and grow, Ana," the teenager said. "Your guests are here."

Raston pricked his ears, suddenly alert. "It's time for the party already?"

Emmy fished in her pocket for the two Sissy-patches and handed them over. "Careful. They're pretty powerful."

"Maybe not," said Brian, watching Ana peel off the backing with her paws. "Those are from the batch we made yesterday, remember? The professor tweaked the formula so they wouldn't be so strong."

Ana slapped the patch on one short arm, and her squat, fuzzy shape slowly shifted, thinned, and transformed into a tiny figure wearing a red jumper. She looked at them in surprise. "I hardly felt a thing!" She put on the next patch, and grew in slow motion, like a balloon being inflated with gentle puffs of air.

"You're lucky you're not using patches from the old batch, then," said Emmy. "When I grew with one, it was like being kicked by a horse. Ow, Ratty! Pull your claws in when you run up my arm, will you?"

"But Sissy's not here!" Raston's worried face peered at her from her shoulder.

"Where did she go?" asked Brian.

"One of the postal bats said that she had a special delivery waiting, so she went to get the mail." The Rat scrubbed at his muzzle with nervous paws. "She should have been back by now."

"She probably just stopped at Rodent City," said Joe. "Come on, we have to go downstairs."

"But she'd want to show *me* the letter! She can't read, remember?"

Thomas, perched on a high kitchen chair, swung his legs. "Maybe my bird is out looking for her and will come back and tell us where she is!"

Raston put his head in his hands. "Listen, feather-brain, your bird is—"

"At a bird party, probably!" said Emmy brightly. "But we have to go to our own party now, so just wait for her, Ratty, okay?"

"She'd better hurry," muttered the Rat, "or all the biscotti will be gone."

The space between the floors of the Antique Rat was dim. Row upon row of wooden joists supported the apartment above, while squares of ceiling tile rested on a metal grid suspended by wires. Here and there, thin shafts of light pierced upward like bright skewers through gaps in the fiberboard tile.

Two rats lay side by side on a square, their eyes pressed to one of the small, crumbling holes. From the room below came a muffled babble of conversation and the clink of cups and plates.

"We need some more holes, Cheswick," said the piebald rat.

The black rat sighed. He had already made fifteen holes at least. Small enough to avoid detection, yet large enough for a sifting of dust to filter through, they had taken quite a bit of effort on his part. He was happy to do it, of course, but he wouldn't mind a little appreciation. And his right index claw was all ink-stained from writing, too.

He glanced at the plastic bag beside him, full of tiny, silvery scales. "Don't you think we have enough holes?"

Jane Barmy shook her furry head. "The Addisons keep moving around. We need another one by the punch bowl."

Cheswick was reluctant to move. Jane Barmy's

head was very close to his, and he wanted to enjoy the moment. "When is your father coming to deliver the letter?"

"In about ten minutes. So you'd better get busy making those extra holes, Cheswick. I don't want to have done all this work, only to fail because Emmaline's parents weren't standing in the right spot!"

10

Squippy was squealing over the card. "Look, every-one! Ana made me the sweetest thing!" She tapped the macaroni letters for emphasis, and the card shed a fine dusting of silver glitter.

Ana looked embarrassed, as well she might, Emmy thought. The huge and heavy card *looked* as if it had been made by two boys and a rat.

Emmy handed Professor Capybara a cup of punch and was rewarded by a nod of approval from her father and a smile from her mother. Well, good. Maybe this party was helping them think better of her, then.

She caught a movement out of the corner of her eye as she filled another cup and tried to look past the grown-up bodies blocking her way. Was someone going up the stairs? Or was that Thomas's arm, waving in wide arcs from side to side?

"Excuse me," she began, but her voice went un-heard. Gwenda Squipp put an arm around her

shoulder and squeezed. Emmy held on tight to her cup of punch to keep it from spilling.

"And *this* girl," Squippy went on, "arranged it all! The party, and the surprise, and everything! Such a loving, giving child! You must be terribly proud of your daughter, Mr. and Mrs. Addison!"

Emmy smiled in what she hoped was a loving, giving way and tried to bask in the glow of approval that surrounded her, but she was distracted. Thomas was leaping up and down on the stairs now—she could see the round, blond head briefly appearing above the heads of the crowd, the eyes wide and urgent, looking for . . . her?

"Don't worry, dear," said Squippy, pulling in Ana on her other side. "You're sweet children, and now that I've got you both together, I'm going to tell you a story about *my* childhood, when I did something very much the same!"

Emmy, trapped, watched Thomas climb on the stair rail and scan the packed room, his face anxious. Where was Joe?

"Yes, these childhood memories are lovely to recall in years to come . . ."

Emmy looked desperately up at Squippy. She

would probably be talking for another twenty minutes straight, and in the meantime Thomas was
going to kill himself or break a leg at least. What
had happened that was so important? She had to
find out.

Her father was no help—he had mumbled a few
gracious words and melted away into the crowd at
the beginning of Squippy's tale. It was a neat trick,
and one Emmy envied, but it was easier for grown-
ups than for children. She tried to catch her mother's eye, but her mother, too, was carrying on a quiet
conversation with someone at her shoulder and
already edging to one side.

Emmy eyed her cup of punch. She didn't want to
do it, but there was no other way to politely escape.
She waited for Squippy's next squeeze of her shoulder (it didn't take long) and turned her wrist as if
she had been jostled.

"Oh no!" Emmy tried to sound horrified.

Squippy jumped as the punch splashed on the
floor.

"I'll clean it right up!" said Emmy, backing away.
"I'll just go up and get some rags and things."

She threaded her way through the crowd, careful

not to bump any elbows. When she saw Joe, she grabbed him by the sleeve and towed him to the foot of the stairs, where Thomas met them with relief. "Come *on*!" he whispered. "Sissy's got a letter from Schenectady!"

At the kitchen table, Sissy could hardly speak for crying, and Raston wasn't much better. Before them was a white square of paper, unfolded.

Emmy looked closer. There was writing on it, spiky and thin, as if written with a claw dipped in ink. At the bottom was a strange red impression, like a smeared lipstick kiss from two very small, very thin lips, and below that was a signature.

RATMOM

"She's alive! She wants me to come visit her in Schenectady! Oh, Rasty!" sobbed Cecilia. "Just smell her perfume on the letter!"

The two gray rats put their heads down close to the paper, sniffing deeply.

"Watch it, you're going to breathe in all that glitter," Emmy warned. The glitter Ratty had dumped on Squippy's card had gotten everywhere—the floor, the table, and even Sissy's letter were covered with small, silvery scales.

Joe peered at the letter. "Why does she only invite Sissy?"

There was an awkward pause and then everyone spoke at once.

"I'm sure she *meant* to invite you, Ratty."

"Maybe she was in a hurry, and forgot?"

"*Anybody* can make a *mistake*—"

Raston flipped a careless paw. "She probably didn't even know I was here."

"My dear little squoochums," Emmy read aloud. "My precious ratty darling . . ." She looked up. "That sounds like something Cheswick Vole might say."

"It *is* a little weird," Joe agreed.

"It's a mother's love," said Raston, stiffly. "Look!" He pointed to the red smudge beneath the signature.

"What's that?" Joe looked at it with interest. "Blood?"

"No, it's her kiss! What are you, blind?"

"Oh, it *is*!" Cecilia looked more closely. "What a pretty shade of lipstick!"

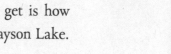

Joe was frowning. "What I still don't get is how your mother knew Sissy was here, in Grayson Lake. Schenectady's pretty far away."

"The postal bats must have told her." The Rat shrugged. "They really get around, you know—flying

back and forth—and I've never met a bat that wasn't nosy. If some of them heard the gossip that Sissy was in Rodent City, and if they went to Schenectady afterward, and if they happened to run into Ratmom, and if they told her . . ."

"That's an awful lot of ifs," said Joe. "And if the bats heard about Sissy, why wouldn't they have heard about you too, Ratty?"

"Who cares?" cried Cecilia. "The point is, she found *one* of us, at least, and—oh, Rasty, we *have* to go to Schenectady! But how, that's the question."

"There's the train . . . but it might be dangerous to ride in the cars. Too many people, not enough hiding places."

"We could ride on the roof of the train—"

"Or ride the rails!"

"We could mail ourselves in a box with air holes . . ."

"But that might feel too cramped."

"Well, you keep working on it," said Emmy. "I've got to find some rags and a bucket."

Emmy wrung out her rag in the bucket of soapy water and mopped the sticky patch of floor by the punch bowl. The party noise had only gotten louder, but Squippy's voice rang out clear and shrill.

". . . then Brian will take us straight to the train station after the party. He's such a dear boy, and so responsible!"

"I used to take that very train when I was a boy," came the voice of Emmy's father, "to visit my aunts. They were spry old girls, and strict, too. They would not let me get away with leaving things in a mess, no sir!"

Emmy scrubbed a little harder. She didn't think it was fair of her father to talk like that, when she was cleaning up at this very minute. She glanced upward and suddenly blinked.

Emmy rubbed at her eye. Ana squatted down. "What's wrong?"

"Got some glitter in it," whispered Emmy. "I wish she'd stop waving that dumb card around!"

"And those relatives of hers!" Squippy cried over their heads. "It's so wonderful that they're taking her in and giving her a home!"

Ana winced, and Emmy suddenly decided she'd had enough. She stood with her bucket. "Ana wants to say good-bye to her friends," she said, and just

95

that easily she and Ana were walking through the crowded room.

They found Joe and Thomas at the lab counter, sitting on stools with a plate of biscotti between them. A steady sound of munching came from the inside of the open pet carrier.

Raston poked his head out. "Where's the professor?" he asked, crumbs spraying from the side of his mouth.

"We've got to show him the letter," said Cecilia from behind him. "And find a way to Schenectady!"

Ana turned her head. "Did I miss something? What letter?"

Emmy and Joe explained, at length.

Ana looked at them thoughtfully. "I'm going through Schenectady. I leave on the train in about an hour."

"But what if the letter isn't really from their mother?" Joe rubbed his forehead. "I have my doubts, actually—"

"Look! It's Mr. B!" Thomas pointed to the window.

The children were suddenly alert. Crossing the green and heading straight for the Antique Rat was a harmless-looking man in a shoemaker's apron.

Joe's eyes narrowed. "What's *he* doing, coming here?"

Ana huddled on her stool, her face pale.

Emmy threw an arm over the girl's shoulders. Mr. B seemed gentle and kind, but he was Miss Barmy's father, and he had helped her keep Ana and four other little girls prisoners for years. Ana probably still had nightmares about him.

The bell tinkled as the street door opened. Joe got off his stool and stood in front of Ana. Near the door, the professor's jovial face turned grave.

The crowd quieted in a wave of silence that began at the door and spread out to fill the whole room. Mr. B smiled hesitantly, then shuffled over to Emmy's parents, pulled an envelope from his pocket, and handed it to Jim Addison. The hum of conversation started up again.

"Thomas!" Emmy hissed. "Go over there and get some punch! They'll talk in front of you if you pretend you're not listening!"

"Use your innocent look," Joe added.

Thomas opened his blue eyes wide.

"Yeah, that one!"

The small, slightly round, blond-haired boy marched

away, looking somehow even younger than his six years.

Ana's mouth turned up a little. "Wow, he's good."

Joe nodded. "I know. It's almost scary."

Emmy, watching intently from her high stool, saw her father open the envelope. As he read, his smile faded. He handed the letter to his wife. There was an animated discussion. Thomas drifted back after a while, holding a punch cup with both hands.

"What? What?" Emmy was too impatient to be polite. "Listen, drink that later, will you?"

Thomas licked the punch-colored stain on his upper lip. "Mr. B said a letter for your parents was sent to his house by mistake."

"And?" demanded Joe.

"It was from Emmy's great-aunts, or something, and they want her to come and visit." Thomas turned to Emmy. "And your mom said they couldn't just send you off without calling first to make sure, but the letter said not to call, the phone was out of order. Your dad thought it all sounded weird, and they don't trust Mr. B, and so they don't want you to go, Emmy, and I want my punch now—spying makes me thirsty."

Emmy stared at her parents from her perch on

the stool. The crowd had shifted, and she could see only the tops of their heads, but as she gazed she suddenly saw a faint shimmer above them, as if the air were full of glitter.

She frowned slightly. Squippy must *really* be waving her card around for the glitter to be flying up over their heads.

Emmy turned to Thomas again. "They said I wouldn't have to go? You're sure?"

Thomas nodded over the rim of his cup.

"It *does* seem weird," said Joe. "Why would a letter to your parents accidentally end up in Mr. B's mailbox? He's not a neighbor. And his last name isn't even close to Addison."

Thomas shrugged. "Your dad asked the same thing, and Mr. B said maybe it was because he used to be the care—the careterk—"

"The caretaker?" Emmy said.

Thomas nodded. "He used to do yard work and stuff for that old guy who was there before you."

"Great-Great-Uncle William," said Emmy.

"Is that true?" asked Ana.

Emmy explained. It had been surprising to her, too, when she had found out. But Mr. and Mrs. B

were distantly related to old William Addison and had lived in a cottage on the estate for many years, taking care of the house and yard. Their daughter, Jane, had grown up with old William's daughter Priscilla, but then Priscilla had died . . .

"It gets complicated," Emmy finished. "And it's boring. I can't keep it all straight."

"So you're related to *Jane Barmy*?" Ana's expression was horrified.

"Barely," said Emmy. "She's, like, a second cousin once removed, or a first cousin twice removed, or something like that."

"But why," Joe asked, "would Mr. B come over *here* to deliver the letter?"

"Maybe he saw Emmy's parents going in," said Thomas. "Can I have another cookie?"

"Shh," murmured Ana. "Look who's coming."

Moving steadily through the crowd like the prow of a ship, Jim Addison bore down on them, with Emmy's mother and Gwenda Squipp in his wake.

"Emmy!" her father boomed, smiling broadly. "We have good news!"

"It's a last-minute invitation, but we knew you'd want to go," said her mother.

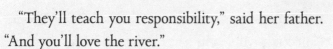

"They'll teach you responsibility," said her father. "And you'll love the river."

"We've got to run home and pack this minute," Kathy Addison said, looking at her watch. "You're leaving in less than an hour!"

"And why!" cried Gwenda Squipp. "Because you're traveling with Ana and me!"

"It all worked out so perfectly," marveled her mother, shaking her head. "Almost as if it had all been *planned*."

The three adults stood beaming at Emmy with the same happy, confident expression. Silver glitter, like tiny scales, dusted their shoulders and hair.

Emmy stared at them blankly. There was something here she didn't understand. "What are you talking about?" she asked with growing apprehension.

Her father chuckled and passed her a letter. Joe and Ana, on either side, looked over her shoulder at the thin, spidery, old-lady writing. Thomas stopped chewing his cookie. Several crumbs fell out of his open mouth.

Jim Addison put a hand on his daughter's shoulder. "You're going to visit your great-aunts

101

Emmaline and Augusta in Schenectady. They're expecting you, and they'll be meeting the next train."

"Schenectady?" shrilled Ratty from the carrier. "We're coming, too, Emmy!"

11

EMMY CLIMBED twenty-seven steps from the train station to the platform and emerged into the bright July afternoon. Cicadas droned in the stubble beyond the railroad tracks, and the concrete slab beneath her feet gave off baking waves of heat.

Joe, behind her, set the blue pet carrier down in the scant shade of the awning. "There's something funny about this whole Schenectady thing."

"You're telling me." Emmy glanced over her shoulder as Ana emerged from the stairwell, followed by the grown-ups and Brian, lugging suitcases. "The professor thinks I'll be in less danger if I go, but I wish you were coming, too."

"No offense, Emmy, but I don't want to visit your great-aunts. Old, and strict too? No thanks." He bent down over the carrier's air vents. "Remember to keep quiet, you guys," he whispered.

"But we're so *hot*," moaned Raston. "Right, Sissy?"

"I'm a little warm," said Sissy faintly.

"You'll be in air-conditioning soon. But don't talk at all—not until Emmy tells you it's okay."

"It'll just sound like squeaking to everyone else," Emmy said in surprise.

"I know," said Joe, "but the less noise they make, the better. I mean, you're not supposed to be taking rats to your great-aunts' house, are you?"

Emmy shook her head. "My parents probably think the pet carrier is Ana's."

"Right. And Squippy probably thinks it's yours. But if the rats start squeaking and the grown-ups notice, you might have to leave them behind."

"I'm not going to say one word!" whispered Raston. "Not even if I'm roasting! Not even if I'm fried! Or—or *grilled*!"

"Shut *up*, Rasty!" said Cecilia sharply, and there was silence.

The others arrived on the platform. Gwenda Squipp grabbed Ana's hand, looking nervously at the tracks. Joe planted himself squarely in front of the pet carrier, and Emmy wandered a few steps away.

She didn't really want to stand near her parents. She knew they still loved her, but then why were they sending her away? Did they really think she needed to learn responsibility that much?

Suddenly Emmy felt a low, rumbling vibration, seemingly in the air and under her feet at the same time. She had been feeling it for a while, she realized, when there came a far-off *hoooo . . . hoooo . . . hoo-hoooo.*

But the track stayed empty even as the rumbling grew louder. The train whistled again beyond the trees, the tones strange and discordant and suddenly louder, and Emmy's heart beat faster as the platform trembled.

Would the train never come? The noise was deafening, but the track was still bare and gleaming in the sun, and then the loudspeaker crackled and a voice announced something—a number, a name— and all at once something tall and silver appeared at the curve, with lights that shone even at midday, coming straight on with a slow roar.

A bell clanged. There was a *whoosh* of air brakes and a screech of metal and then, huge and tall above the platform, the train thundered past, car after car after silver-blue car, slowing, slowing . . . slower still . . . stopped.

Emmy caught a confused glimpse of gigantic wheels and long metal rods beneath, and a row of streamlined windows and a bright yellow number above. A door shaped like a lozenge opened, and a uniformed man jumped out and folded down a set of steps.

"Good-bye, good-bye!" cried everyone, and Emmy was hugged and kissed and set on the steps. The conductor pulled her in, then Ana and Squippy, and bags were swung onto the train after them. Joe handed in the pet carrier last of all and stepped back.

"All aboard!" called a voice. Emmy knelt on a plush window seat, waving through the tinted glass as the train slowly pulled away and her parents and Brian and Joe got smaller and then were gone.

"Well!" said Squippy, from across the aisle. "Isn't this nice? We're on our way at last!"

Emmy leaned against the high back of her seat and looked past Ana to Squippy. The woman had fallen asleep, glasses askew, and she was snoring lightly. A thin line of drool showed at the corner of her open mouth.

Emmy shifted her feet. The pet carrier was an

awkward size and in her way every time she tried to stretch out her legs.

The rats had been very good, though—not a single squeak out of either one.

"It was fun, being a rat," said Ana suddenly. "Do you have a little jar or a plastic bag or something? I want to get some rat spit from Ratty."

Emmy looked at her sideways. "It's no good by it-self, you know. You can't grow back."

"Maybe I won't want to grow back." Ana lifted one shoulder in a half shrug. "Maybe I won't like it at that place where I'm going. They don't want me, anyway."

"How do you know they don't want you?" Emmy picked at the plush seat cushions. "They're your *relatives*. They might love you like crazy."

"Or not." Ana lowered her voice. "Squippy doesn't know it, but I got a look at my file, and I saw the letters they sent. They weren't going to take me until they found out the state would pay them."

Emmy did not know what to say to this. "Maybe," she said at last, "they were really poor and couldn't afford one more mouth to feed. And when they found out they *could* afford it, then they did want you!"

"Maybe. But that would be bad in another way." Ana's thin face suddenly looked fierce and purposeful. "I want to go to medical school someday, and that takes money."

This was interesting. "I didn't know you wanted to be a doctor. Since when?"

"Since I was stuck in that attic for years. There was a stack of old books somebody had picked up from somewhere, and I read them all. One was a medical book, and I couldn't understand it very well, but I read it over and over and it started to make sense. Do you want to hear the twelve cranial nerves?" she asked. "I know them all. Olfactory, optic, oculomotor, trochlear—"

She stopped abruptly as Gwenda Squipp moved in her sleep. The woman's eyes blinked open, then shut again as she changed position. Outside the window, another little town flashed past, and Emmy found herself thinking of her own relatives. Her great-aunts might want *her*, but she wasn't so sure she wanted *them*.

She had their letter in her bag, but she didn't need to read it again to be filled with dread. How long would she have to stay? A week? Two weeks?

Professor Capybara had thought it would be good for Emmy to get out of town for a while—at least as long as Miss Barmy was causing problems—but Emmy felt that even one day was too long to stay with elderly ladies who sounded old-fashioned and strict.

The steady rumble and motion of the train was soothing. Emmy closed her eyes and tried to think of the bright side. Even if her great-aunts were awful, still she could help Ratty and Sissy find their mother. And there was a river, her father had said, and a boat . . .

"Schenectady, next stop," called the conductor from the front of the car.

Ana didn't move. Her face was pale, and she was holding her mouth stiffly, as if trying to keep from being sick.

"Are you okay?" Emmy asked, wondering if she should wake up Squippy.

Ana hunched over her crossed arms. "I'm feeling really strange . . . sort of collapsed inside, like a balloon with no air . . ."

"Can I—" Emmy began, meaning to add "help you to the bathroom," but she never finished her

sentence. For Ana's eyes looked suddenly startled; she put a hand to her stomach and then, with no further warning, she shrank. Hidden from the other passengers by the high seat back, the four-and-a-half-foot-tall girl shriveled to four and a half inches in just under three seconds.

Emmy stared at the doll-size girl on the seat cushion. How could Ana have shrunk? The Rat hadn't bitten her. She had not applied rat saliva to a cut on her skin, either. She had used the Sissy-patches to grow—shouldn't she have stayed big?

The miniature Ana stared up at her, her eyes wide and alarmed—and then, in the space of a blink, the tiny girl shifted and changed shape and grew furry and brown. Ears turned thin and round, a long tail flicked out, and she was a rat.

"Oh no, oh no, oh *no*—" Emmy looked frantically around. Across the aisle, Gwenda Squipp was beginning to wake up.

The conductor made his way down the aisle and stopped at Emmy's row. "Schenectady!" he bellowed as a bell clanged.

Squippy came to with a start and wiped the drool from her mouth.

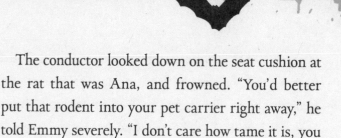

The conductor looked down on the seat cushion at the rat that was Ana, and frowned. "You'd better put that rodent into your pet carrier right away," he told Emmy severely. "I don't care how tame it is, you shouldn't let an animal loose on the train. It's against the rules. Don't you know any better?"

Emmy tried to speak and failed.

"Little missy," said the conductor sternly, "you lock that rat up this instant. Go on, now. I want to see you do it."

"Obey the conductor, dear," said Gwenda Squipp, peering around his uniformed bulk.

Emmy swallowed hard. She scooped up the brown and furry Ana and set her gently inside the carrier.

"That's right," said the conductor, "latch the door. Now, isn't this your stop?"

Emmy nodded wordlessly.

"You're a quiet one, aren't you? Here, follow me. I'll get your suitcase and set it on the platform for you. Somebody meeting you, missy?"

"Yes," croaked Emmy. She staggered in the aisle as the train lurched to a halt and gazed helplessly at Squippy.

Gwenda Squipp pulled Emmy into a firm

embrace. "Don't look so downhearted, dear. You'll have a *wonderful* time with your relatives, just as Ana will with hers." She leaned back to smile into Emmy's face. "Where is Ana, by the way? In the bathroom?"

"Maybe," said Emmy, fired with a sudden idea. "Want me to check?" In the bathroom, she could take Ana out of the carrier, Sissy could kiss her twice, and Ana could walk out, full sized.

"Certainly, dear." Squippy glanced to the front of the car, where the conductor had opened the door to the outside, letting in a stripe of late-afternoon sun. "You'll just have time. Ana will want to say good-bye to you, I'm sure."

Breathing a little easier, Emmy picked up the pet carrier and followed the conductor to the front of the car where the bathroom was. She hoped it wasn't occupied . . . she set down the carrier to fumble with the lock.

"Here, missy, I'll take that!" The conductor plucked the pet carrier off the floor, yanked her luggage from the rack, and jumped out, setting them on the platform. "Now, then!" He held out a hand to help her down the steps.

"But—" said Emmy.

"No time!" said the conductor. "Should have thought of it before! You can use the restroom in the station!"

"But I don't need—"

"Come on, step right out, that's it! Trains don't wait, not even for little girls who have to go potty!" The man in the dark blue uniform swung Emmy out onto the platform, folded back the steps, and hopped into the train that had already begun to move.

"I'll tell Ana you said good-bye!" cried Squippy, waving from the door, and then it shut with a *clack* and the train picked up speed.

Emmy's knees suddenly felt weak. She dropped to the platform bench by her luggage and watched as the train disappeared in the distance. "I guess that new batch of patches isn't as long-lasting," she murmured over the carrier's air vents.

"Squippy's going to be awfully upset when she checks that bathroom," said Ana.

THE CROWD ON THE PLATFORM thinned, dispersed, and was gone. Emmy sat alone. "Now what?" she said aloud.

"Now you get us out of this *prison*," said the Rat, rattling at the lock.

Emmy undid the latch and three rats tumbled out, their fur damp with sweat.

"Maybe your great-aunts are down in the station." Ana jumped onto the bench and shook herself. "They're old, remember? They might not have wanted to climb all those stairs."

Emmy's legs dangled, not quite touching the concrete platform. She felt small and alone and unsure of what to do next. Her aunts *might* be waiting in the station—in fact they probably were. But there was still the question of what to do with Ana.

"Do you want Sissy to make you grow now?" Emmy asked doubtfully. It seemed like a bad idea, somehow, but she couldn't think of a better one.

Ana scampered up the back of the bench, along the top, and down again, her claws skittering merrily on the slatted seat. "Nope! I'm staying a rat."

Emmy stared at her. "Forever?"

Ana shrugged her furry shoulders. "For now, anyway. What else am I going to do? Your aunts invited one girl, not two."

"Well, we could tell someone you got off the train—"

"We'll only get in trouble," said Ana promptly. "I'll get in trouble for leaving. You'll get in trouble for letting me. And your parents and Squippy will never believe what really happened."

Emmy swung her legs. It was true. "I suppose we could prove it to them," she said. "We could show them what happens when Ratty bites and Sissy kisses."

"Excuse me? No way," said the Rat. He leaned against the bench backrest, his short forearms folded. "The minute Squippy found out, she'd want to take *care* of us. She'd put us in a cage—"

"No!" Sissy gasped.

"Oh, it would be a very nice cage. And she'd make sure we got our daily vitamins, and she'd tell us how *special* we were—"

"I won't go back in a cage for anyone!" Sissy said passionately.

"—and she'd tell all kinds of scientists about us, because she'd want to help them, too, and then they'd start to study us and experiment on us."

Sissy whirled on the bench. Her tail nearly hit Ana in the face. "I'm very sorry, but Ratty's right. And I'm not going to kiss you if you're planning to tell Squippy about us."

Emmy twisted her fingers together. What was she supposed to do? She couldn't force them. And Ana was right about one thing for sure. They would both get into trouble.

Emmy gazed at her three furry friends, standing shoulder to shoulder with their chins stubbornly in the air.

"You can't make us," said Ratty, simply stating the obvious.

"It is true, that!" squeaked a thin voice above Emmy's head.

Emmy whipped around, looked up, and nearly screamed. Hanging from the struts of the awning, wings neatly folded, was something brown, furry, and *fanged*.

"It is I, Manlio," said the creature, showing its sharp teeth in an oddly wide smile. "I am—how you say?—a postal bat!"

Emmy made a stern effort to suppress a shudder. Then, getting a grip on herself, she stood on the bench and craned her neck. The bat was hanging wrong side up, its large ears pointed down. Its wings, like shut-up umbrellas, were knobby at the tips, and its body looked like a mouse with no tail.

"How come I can understand you?" Emmy asked. "A bat isn't a rodent." No matter how much you might look like one, she added to herself.

"If you are already to understanding rodent speech," said the bat, "then you are of course also comprehending *Myotis myotis*."

"My—what?"

"*Myotis myotis*," said Ana suddenly, scampering up the back of the bench. "It's the scientific name." She looked at the upside-down bat, her whiskers quivering. "What does it mean?"

"It is for meaning I am a Mouse-Eared Bat. See?" Manlio wiggled his long, pointed ears. "Even better, a *Large* Mouse-Eared Bat. And though some are to saying we don't live in America, what *I* say is maybe

they didn't check the shipping crate from Italy *quite* so good like they thought, see?"

"You came all the way from Italy in a crate?" Sissy, on the bench, stood on her hind feet as she looked up. "My name is Cecilia."

Manlio fluttered down, bumping blindly into the seat back before landing with a thump on the bench slats. He shaded his eyes with one wing. "Cecilia? Ah! Bellissima, such a beautiful name!"

Sissy was too taken aback to do more than giggle.

"I fear I cannot see you so well in the bright of sun as I wish, but already I can tell I stand before the most beautiful, the most elegante of rodents—"

"You're not standing at all," interrupted the Rat. "You're flat on your rear, Bat Boy. And that's my sister you're drooling over."

"Ah, the brother!" Manlio struggled to his feet, his wings unfolding like stretched leather on a frame. "So protective! This is good! Someone so beautiful needs such a brother!"

Raston's frown relaxed. He smoothed his whiskers.

"So big, you are! So strong! So—so—"

The Rat shifted his weight. "So handsome?" he suggested.

"So *magnifico!*" cried the bat. He reached out his long-fingered wing with its claw at the first joint like a tiny thumb and shook Raston's paw. "An honor, sir! I shall to look forward to the better acquaintance! If you have letters or packages to be delivered, sir, you must to call on Manlio!" The bat blinked rapidly. "Not in the day, though. Night is for the flying; day is for the sleeping."

"Why are you here when the sun is still up, then?" asked Ana curiously. She crouched on the bench's backrest, looking down at the furry winged creature with the pug nose.

"Of course, it is for to meet the train," Manlio explained, waving his wings for emphasis. "Who knows who might come and need a letter delivered? Or even a package? I am very strong bat, I." He looked through half-open eyelids at Sissy and smiled dreamily. "Very strong, very hairy. I take the parcel, I wait until evening, and then I fly, fly, to the place of delivery." He unfolded his wings, suddenly businesslike. "And you? These great-aunts you speak of, where is the address?"

Emmy unzipped a side pocket of her suitcase and pulled out the letter from Emmaline and Augusta

Addison. She showed the return address to Manlio, who squinted and peered at it closely.

"Ah, Cucumber Alley! It is not far at all! I would show you, only I cannot fly in the bright of sun. But no matter. If the great-aunts you do not find in the station, it is no *problemo*, no *problemo* at all. It is only one block! One block only or maybe two! You can walk, so easy you can walk three blocks. Or perhaps four. But certainly no more than five!"

It was closer to ten blocks, but Emmy had stopped counting. She sat on her suitcase in the long shadow of a high church made out of blue-gray stone and wiped her damp forehead. She tipped her head back to see the leaves high above and, even higher, the belfry and soaring, pointed steeple at the top of the church. Was this where her father had rung bells as a boy? She was too tired to care. Her suitcase was on little wheels, which helped a lot, but the pet carrier was heavier by an extra rat, and her arm felt as if it were about to fall off.

The great-aunts had not been waiting in the station. Emmy had sat there long enough that the woman in the ticket booth had begun to look at her

oddly. Then Emmy had looked at the large station map, found Cucumber Alley, and waited until the ticket master was busy with a long line of people before slipping out the door.

The first few blocks had been ordinary city streets. But then she had gone under a railroad trestle and turned a corner, and everything was different.

The houses were narrow and the streets were made of brick. The cars went more slowly. Everything was quieter, and she had passed three churches in as many blocks. The neighborhood had the feel of another time, long ago.

But Emmy was tired and thirsty, and she had forgotten to go to the restroom in the train station. She pulled her rolling suitcase past the churchyard with its tall, slanting gravestones, and walked the last blocks to her great-aunts' house.

It was a pretty house on a quiet lane, and behind it she could see the river. Emmy checked the address on the letter one more time, walked up the front steps, and rang the doorbell.

There was a rustling behind the door. The white curtain at the side window moved, and there was a slow sound of shuffling feet. Emmy put her eye to

the window, but she couldn't see anything. She knew someone was there. Why didn't they answer?

She waited another minute and rang the doorbell again.

There was a long, long silence, and then the door opened a crack. "Whatever you're selling, we don't want any," said a reedy voice, and the door began to close.

13

"WAIT!" CRIED EMMY. "Aunt, er—" She took a wild guess. "Aunt Augusta, don't you know me?"

The door opened a little more. A hand appeared around the edge, thin and knobbly. Next came a mass of untidy white hair surrounding a pale, wrinkled face. "I'm not Augusta. I'm Emmaline. And who, exactly, are you?" The elderly woman craned her neck forward like a weary bird and blinked her watery eyes.

"Don't you remember, Aunt Emmaline? You invited me to visit! You said you would meet the train!" Emmy stood on one leg and then the other, hoping that the old lady would invite her in soon. She really needed to use the bathroom.

"Why do you call me aunt? I don't—oh!" The frail Miss Addison, her back so bent that she wasn't much taller than Emmy, straightened a little in surprise. "Can you be Jimmy's little girl?"

Emmy didn't really think of her father as Jimmy,

but she supposed Aunt Emmaline might. "Yes," she said, relieved. Surely now she would be invited in.

The door opened a little wider. Great-Aunt Emmaline stood in her slippers and robe, the belt trailing in the dust on the floor. Her eyes darted to the stairway behind her and then back to Emmy's face, as if she couldn't think what to do next.

Emmy had tried her best to be polite, but this was getting ridiculous. And what on earth was her aunt doing in her robe and slippers this late in the day? "I'd like to come in, please, Aunt," she said, trying to keep the annoyance out of her voice.

Aunt Emmaline looked more frightened than ever. "My dear," she fluttered, "I'm afraid there's been some mistake. I don't remember inviting you."

"But you sent a letter," Emmy began—then stopped. She didn't have time to argue. "Will you please just let me in? I *really* have to use the bathroom!"

Emmy sat at the kitchen table, the pet carrier in front of her. Across an expanse of dirty tiled floor, Aunt Emmaline stood at the counter, pouring lemonade from a cracked pitcher into two glasses.

It wasn't just the floor that was filthy, thought

Emmy as she looked around. The curtains were dingy and stained. The fruit bowl on the counter was filled with blackened bananas. And the sink was piled high with dirty dishes.

And this was the aunt who was supposed to teach her discipline? Emmy regarded the sticky kitchen table with disgust. Maybe it was the other aunt who was the tidy one. But if so, she hadn't been on the job lately.

Aunt Emmaline set the glass of lemonade in front of Emmy with a faltering smile. "I'm sorry if I didn't seem welcoming, Emmy. I'm afraid it was just so unexpected."

"That's all right, Aunt Emmaline." Emmy lifted her glass of lemonade and took a sip.

"Call me Melly, dear. I never did take to the name Emmaline—too long, I always thought— Why, whatever is the matter?"

Emmy was doing her valiant best to look as if nothing was wrong, but her whole face puckered sharply with the effort. With a heroism she hadn't known she possessed, she swallowed.

Aunt Melly took an experimental sip from her own glass. "Oh!" She set it down abruptly, and her

face crumpled. "I forgot the sugar! Oh, dear, I can't remember *anything* anymore!" She buried her face in her veined, trembling hands.

"It's okay!" Emmy said. "Seriously, Aunt Melly, it's not a big deal—"

The old lady started to cry.

Emmy moved back a little in her chair. What was she supposed to do now? She hesitated, then patted the old lady on the shoulder. "Where is Aunt Augusta?" Emmy asked. Maybe the other aunt would be less emotional.

But at the mention of her sister, Aunt Melly wailed aloud. "It's all too much—just too much! Oh, Gussie, I don't know if I can do it!" She put her head down on the sticky table and sobbed.

Emmy cleared her throat. "Is something . . . wrong with Aunt Augusta? Is she—is she—"

"Dead?" Aunt Melly blew her nose with a honk. "No, but she will be soon! And all I can do is make her comfortable, and I'm even failing at that!"

Emmy stared at her.

"I'm an old lady," Aunt Melly went on, mopping her eyes. "I may not look it—I'm only eighty-five—but I *feel* ninety!"

Emmy thought Aunt Melly looked to be at least a hundred, but she kept that opinion to herself.

"Emmy," said Aunt Melly with sudden firmness, "you're family, and I can hardly turn you out on the street. But can you keep a secret?"

Emmy nodded, glancing at the pet carrier. "I keep secrets all the time."

"Well, then. Come upstairs and soon you'll understand everything."

Aunt Melly shuffled toward the stairs. Emmy, about to follow, heard a sudden squeak. "Take us with you!"

Lugging the blue pet carrier, Emmy followed the thin, bent form of her great-aunt past the bookshelves in the hall, around an antique dollhouse on a stand, and up the long, creaking stairs. She trailed one hand along the side of the curved wooden banister, shaving off a layer of dust with her palm. At the top of the staircase, all was dim. In the shadowed landing was an old cedar chest, three burned-out lightbulbs, and a dead potted palm.

"In here," said Aunt Melly, opening a door.

Emmy walked into the room and stopped in surprise. There was no dust in this room, no lightbulbs

that had not been replaced, no accumulation of dirt. Starched white curtains swung at the window, open to let in a soft evening breeze. Light from the setting sun touched upon fresh flowers in a crystal vase. A needlepointed cushion sat plumply on a polished wooden rocker.

In the middle of the room was a bed piled high with pillows. And lying back against the pillows was a tiny old woman with a face almost as white as her neatly arranged hair. Thin blue veins stood out on her neck and on the skeletal hands that rested atop the comforter. Her eyes were closed; she looked so pale and she lay so still that Emmy wondered if she were dead already.

"Gussie, dear," said Aunt Melly, "I've brought a visitor."

The papery eyelids fluttered open to reveal eyes of a surprisingly vivid blue.

Aunt Melly steered Emmy gently to the bedside. "Gussie, this is Jimmy's girl. Emmy, this is your great-aunt Augusta."

"Oh my!" The voice that issued from the woman on the bed was just a thin thread of sound, but the mouth quirked sweetly. "That Jimmy . . . was a rascal . . . but you . . . look perfectly . . . lovely!"

"Don't talk, dear; you get so out of breath." Aunt Melly plumped up her sister's pillows, put a hand on the pale forehead, and looked worried. "Is there much pain?"

"Not . . . so much," whispered Aunt Augusta.

Now that she looked, Emmy could see the signs of suffering everywhere on the wasted face. The mouth smiled, but the lines on either side were deep. The blue eyes were bright, but the space between them was tensely knit.

"We'll let you rest now, dear. But before I go, is there anything you need? Could you eat a little something? A poached egg, perhaps?"

Aunt Augusta closed her eyes. Her head turned slightly to one side.

"A nice cup of tea, then, and maybe a cookie? I have Russian tea cakes, Gussie—your favorite kind." Aunt Melly tightened the belt of her robe and spoke more firmly. "You must eat something to keep up your strength, or I shall have to call the doctor."

The eyes flew open, and the blue-veined hands lifted in sudden protest. "No!" Aunt Augusta's whisper was like the cry of a frightened bird. "You promised, Melly!"

"Then you *must* eat something."

Aunt Augusta shut her eyes again. "All right," she said faintly, and was still.

The bedroom door shut behind them with a *click*. Aunt Melly sank down on the cedar chest and looked up at Emmy. "You see," she said.

Emmy knelt beside her. "Why doesn't she want you to call the doctor?"

"Because she knows the doctor would put her in the hospital or a nursing home. But she wants to stay here—where she's lived all her life—in her own home, in her own room, with me to take care of her."

Emmy fiddled with the handle of the pet carrier. Ana and the rats were being unusually quiet, but that probably meant they were listening all the more. "Isn't it hard for you to take care of her all by yourself?" She tried not to look at the mess all around her.

"Hard?" Aunt Melly flared. "I bathe her and make her favorite foods and do her laundry and wash her hair and turn her over in bed, and I run up and down the stairs fifty times a day. It's terribly hard, but I'd do it all ten times over just to keep

130

her with me, if I had the strength." Aunt Melly stared at her gnarled hands. "At least she doesn't suspect how I've let things go in the rest of the house. She only sees her room, and I keep that looking nice . . ."

Emmy was silent a moment, thinking. The aunts were supposed to be rich, just like Great-Great-Uncle William had been. "Why don't you hire someone to come in and help you?"

Aunt Melly lifted a ravaged face. "You don't suppose I haven't thought of that? I did hire someone, last winter. But this is such a small neighborhood, the cleaning lady started talking to the neighbors and telling them how ill Gussie was and that she should really be in the hospital, and it was all I could do to convince people that she only had a bad cold. Sometimes people just won't mind their own business!" she finished fiercely. "Gussie doesn't want to die in a hospital, all hooked up to tubes and things, and I don't blame her one bit. And now—" She stood, bracing herself against the wall.

"And now what?" Emmy asked.

"And now you know everything," she said, giving Emmy an appealing look. "But don't tell your parents.

Or anyone else. *Please*—" She put a hand to her forehead, swaying slightly. "Oh dear . . ."

She groped blindly and staggered, her hand hitting the wall and sliding off. Emmy grabbed for the old lady's arm, but it was too late. Aunt Melly crumpled at the knees and slid slowly to the floor in a dead faint. Two blackened fronds dropped from the potted palm.

Emmy straightened her aunt's robe, tucked it around her legs, and sat back on her heels. "Now what?" she said for the second time that day. She opened the carrier door. "Any ideas?"

Raston breathed loudly through his nose. Cecilia twisted her paws together, looking anxious.

"I can think of one," said Ana, hopping out with a flick of her tail. "Kiss me, Sissy. Kiss me twice."

Aunt Melly was heavy and awkward to lift, but between them, the two girls carried her to the bedroom next door and tucked her in. Emmy drew the covers up under the old lady's chin, and Ana shut the blinds. Sissy lined up her slippers neatly on the floor. Raston jumped on her pillow to plump it.

"She's all worn out," said Ana in a low voice. "I know how that feels."

Emmy glanced up at the older girl. "You do?" She smoothed the comforter over her great-aunt. "I mean, I know you were a prisoner with the other little girls, but I didn't think you had to do much actual work."

"But I was the oldest," said Ana. "I had to take care of them. I taught them lessons, and told them stories, and tucked them in, and tried to keep them safe. I just—felt alone, you know? Like it was all up to me."

Emmy looked down at Aunt Melly's lined, care-worn face in sudden pity. "Everything's been up to her, too."

"But now," said Ana firmly, "it's up to us."

"We'll help, too," said Sissy. "Right, Rasty?"

"You bet," said Raston. "Got any more pillows to jump on?"

They began with the kitchen.

"It's in the worst shape," said Ana, "and we'll want to make something to eat after a while."

"Do you know how to cook?" asked Emmy. She was at the sink, scraping crusted food off the dishes.

"I watched Mr. B do it for years," Ana answered,

making a clatter in the broom closet. She emerged, triumphant, with a bucket, cleaning rags, and a feather duster. "I can make toast and tea, anyway."

"I can boil an egg," said Emmy. She ran a sink full of sudsy water and began to wash the glassware, grateful that she had not always been rich with servants to clean up after her. Back before her father had inherited the Addison estate, she had learned to do dishes and vacuum and shovel snow and keep her room tidy. "And I can make grilled cheese and heat up soup. And once I baked cookies."

"There are cookbooks on the shelf." Ana scrubbed at the kitchen table with energy. "We can follow directions. How hard can it be?"

"Cookbooks?" said Raston, twisting around to look.

"Hold still, Rasty." Sissy clawed holes in a rag for Raston's forearms and stuck feathers from the duster through the cloth. "Now you can dust the books in the hall. Just run over them and twirl around."

Raston looked down at his feathered skirt with dismay. "What do you think I am, a ballerina?"

"Would you rather clean the grout in the bathroom?" Sissy held up a toothbrush.

"I'd rather bake biscotti! Why don't you let me be the cook? I've always wanted to make *filet de boeuf!*"

"Cleaning first," Ana said firmly. "And you can dust the hall furniture while you're at it."

"But be careful with your claws," Emmy said. "Don't scratch anything."

The Rat glared at them. "How come everybody's giving me orders all of a sudden? If it's because I'm the only boy, then it's not *fair.*"

"Life isn't fair." Ana wrung out her wet cloth. "Get used to it."

"You'd better start working, Rasty," Sissy added, "if you want any dinner."

Raston stomped off, his feathers quivering with indignation. "How come we have to clean, anyway?" he muttered. "This place looks just fine the way it *is.*"

"Poor, pitiful Ratty," said Ana in a singsong, drying off the table. "He works so *hard.*"

"We need another boy around here!" yelled the Rat from the hall. "The professor! Joe! I'd even take Thomas!"

"Actually," said Emmy, "we *could* use Joe. I'm pretty sure he knows how to use a mower."

Ana reached for a broom and began to sweep.

"But how can we get him invited here? We don't want to lie to your aunt—"

"I certainly hope not." Aunt Melly spoke sharply from the kitchen doorway. "And just who, exactly, are you?"

14

EMMY'S HEART BUMPED twice, hard. The broom fell from Ana's hands with a clatter.

"Well?" demanded Aunt Melly, gripping the doorknob for support.

Emmy's heart settled into a steadier beat. She rinsed the plate she was washing and set it down. What could she tell Aunt Melly? That Ana had gotten off the train by mistake? But then Aunt Melly would call the Children's Home, and Ana would be sent away to her relatives after all.

"Don't tell," whispered Ana, and her eyes were pleading. "I'll just go away."

Emmy dried her hands on a towel. It was the second time in an hour that someone had begged her not to tell a secret.

Aunt Melly was talking again. "Speak up, Emmy. What is this strange girl doing in my kitchen?" Her tone was stern, but her voice wavered and the doorknob rattled slightly under her fingers.

Emmy pulled out a kitchen chair. "Please, Aunt Melly. Sit down." She glanced around the floor and was relieved to see that Sissy and Ratty had sense enough to stay out of sight.

Aunt Melly sat down stiffly and knotted her trembling fingers together. "Just because I'm an old lady doesn't mean you can take over my home and invite strangers in without my permission!"

Emmy leaned forward across the table. "Listen, Aunt Melly. You have a secret, right?"

Aunt Melly grew rigid. "Telling secrets to family is one thing. Telling them to strangers is something else entirely."

Emmy touched Aunt Melly's gnarled fingers. "I'm Jimmy's daughter, I'm *named* after you, Aunt Emmaline—you can trust me, okay?"

Aunt Melly blinked. Her eyes grew moist.

Emmy smoothed the ropy veins on the back of her aunt's thin hand. "I'll keep your secret. But I need you to keep mine, too."

"And that is?" quavered Aunt Melly.

Emmy glanced at Ana. They had to come up with some explanation for Ana's presence, but the true one—that Ana had shrunk and turned into a rat

and been brought into the house in a pet carrier—
would be a little hard for Aunt Melly to believe.

Ana quietly found a tissue and tucked it in the old
lady's hand. "*I'm* the secret," she said. "I—sort of
ran away."

Aunt Melly blew her nose. "Well, did you or didn't
you?"

"I was on the train with this lady who was taking
me to my new home. And I got off the train when it
stopped, and I didn't get back on in time. I didn't really do it on purpose," said Ana, and then added in a
burst of honesty, "but I'm glad it happened. Because
I didn't want to go live with my relatives, anyway."

"They only took her for the money!" added Emmy
indignantly.

Aunt Melly crumpled the tissue and looked from
one girl to the other, frowning. "That doesn't add up.
No conductor would let a child get off the train by
herself when it wasn't her stop."

"Well, he didn't exactly see me," said Ana.

Aunt Melly narrowed her eyes as if she could
draw the entire story from Ana just by looking.
Watching her, Emmy suddenly saw what her father
had meant when he said the aunts were strict.

"No, my dear," said Aunt Melly with sudden decision, "that won't do. You must tell me the whole truth."

"You won't believe the truth," said Emmy helplessly.

"Well, I'm certainly not believing what you're telling me now." Aunt Melly tapped a finger on the wooden tabletop. "If I'm going to help you, if I'm going to keep your secret, I must have the facts."

Ana and Emmy exchanged glances. "The facts are sort of weird," said Ana, tracing a pattern on the table with her thumb.

"*Very* weird," added Emmy.

Aunt Melly gave an elderly snort. "I used to be a schoolteacher, my dears. I've heard every story in the book."

"You might be surprised," muttered Emmy. "Okay, Ana, you explain. I'll find Ratty and Sissy. Maybe they'll let Aunt Melly see what they can do."

She found Cecilia in the bathroom, working patiently at the grout with a toothbrush, and explained where matters stood.

Sissy tipped back her head. "You're sure your aunt won't tell anyone else about us if we show her our powers?"

"Pretty sure," said Emmy. "She doesn't want us to tell about Aunt Gussie."

"True." Sissy's claws clicked on the bathroom tile as she headed for the hall. "Let's check with Rasty."

They found Raston by the bookshelf. He had abandoned the dusting and was crouched over the pages of an open book, flexing his muscles. The chapter title, featuring a man with an oiled chest that looked remarkably bumpy, read "Are You Weak, Run-Down, Tired of Being Pushed Around? Ditch Your Flab and Get Flabulous!"

Emmy cocked an eyebrow. It didn't exactly seem like Aunt Melly's sort of book.

"Look, Sissy!" Raston unsheathed a claw to point. "Ten Easy Steps to a Flab-Free Life!"

"I can't *read*, Rasty," said Cecilia patiently. "You know I can't."

"Huh? Oh, right." Raston stared intently at the paragraph beneath him. "Hey, wow! Brussels sprouts have a fat-burning ratio of seventeen to one!"

Emmy put her hand over the page. "Listen, Ratty. Would you mind showing Aunt Melly how you shrink people, if she promised not to tell anyone?"

The Rat crouched over a paragraph of small print, his nose almost touching the paper. "Yeah, sure." He raised his head and gazed at her earnestly. "But listen to this—there's no 'fat' in 'fitness'!"

Aunt Melly shook her head severely. "You cannot seriously expect me to believe all this nonsense. You must think I'm senile."

"We could show you how the shrinking works," Emmy said. "You could shrink yourself, if you didn't mind a little rat bite."

Ratty and Sissy poked their heads out of the carrier door and looked at Aunt Melly.

"Absolutely not!" Aunt Melly pulled her hands off the table. "And furthermore"—she looked sternly at Ana—"it's one thing for me to keep Gussie out of the hospital when she wants to stay home. It's another thing entirely for you to run away from people who want you."

"They *don't* want me," said Ana, flushing. "And I'd stay home, too, if I had one!"

"But your social worker must be worried sick!" Aunt Melly's hands began a nervous patting on the table. "I know I asked you to keep my secret, but what am I going to say if someone calls here for you? I simply can't lie about something like this—"

Brrriiinng! Brrrriiinng!

Aunt Melly looked at the phone on the counter as if it were a poisonous lizard. She picked it up with two fingers. "Hello?"

Ana and Emmy watched her with concentrated attention.

"How lovely to hear from you, Jim!" said Aunt Melly, straightening. "And Kathy, too!"

The rodents climbed out of the pet carrier. "Emmy!" Sissy whispered. "Is your aunt going to make you go back home?"

"Even if Emmy goes, we still have to *stay*," Raston whispered urgently. "We've got to find Ratmom!"

Cecilia nodded, clasping and unclasping her paws.

"Yes, Emmy's here, safe and sound. She's been"— Aunt Melly glanced at the sink full of suds—"doing the dishes for me. Among other things."

There was a pause. "Teaching her to be responsible?" Aunt Melly's thin lips quirked in a half smile as she looked around the kitchen, now much cleaner than before. "I'd say she's very responsible already. But she does seem to have quite an imagination . . ."

Ana bit a fingernail, never taking her eyes off the white-haired woman.

"What did you say? I must have fixed the phone? I don't understand."

Emmy snatched the letter from her pocket and unfolded it on the kitchen table, pointing to the spidery letters that spelled out

DON'T CALL! THE PHONE IS OUT OF ORDER.

Aunt Melly gazed at the letter. Her brows drew together, and her lips tightened. "I see. Well, it's working now."

There was another pause. "Gwenda Squipp? Who's that? Yes, yes . . . I see . . ."

The squawking sound of a voice came through the earpiece, loud and clear. ". . . so we were just wondering if she might have gotten off the train with Emmy."

Aunt Melly looked almost desperate as the voice of Emmy's father went on.

"And of course you'd think Emmy would call, but she's been acting a little odd lately, and you know how children can be—they love keeping secrets and don't always realize . . ."

Aunt Melly's hand gripped the phone until the

knuckles showed white. "I'm afraid I must tell you, Jim . . ." She looked at Ana with pleading eyes.

"Bite my finger, Ratty," said Ana. "Hurry!"

Raston obliged at once with a small nip. Ana promptly shrank to rat size.

Aunt Melly made a strangled sound in the back of her throat.

"Again!" said Ana, and in three seconds she was a small brown rat.

Aunt Melly stared at the rat that was Ana with a strange mixture of relief and terror. The phone, forgotten, sank down.

It squawked in her hand. "You're afraid you must tell me . . . what?"

The elderly woman raised the receiver again. "I'm sorry," she said faintly, "but the only girl here is Emmy." And she slid to the floor like a limp noodle.

Emmy grabbed the phone. "Hi, Dad! Hi, Mom!" She motioned frantically, and the three rats leaped off the table. Sissy and Ana began to fan Aunt Melly with a napkin. Ratty hopped up on the old lady's shoulder and slapped her cheek briskly with his paw.

"Yes, I'm fine—what? Aunt Augusta?" Emmy wished she had time to think. Everything was moving

too fast. She glanced at the stairway to the second floor and found herself saying, "Aunt Augusta is taking a nap right now."

"Really?" Her father's voice came through the receiver, sounding tinny. "That's not like her. She was always the most energetic and zippy of us all."

"They're getting older, Dad. They need a little more help now." Emmy stopped, afraid to go on. She couldn't tell her father the true state of affairs. But her aunts *did* need help, and lots of it.

"Actually," she said slowly, "the aunts could use someone to do yard work. And I was thinking, maybe Joe?" She glanced at Aunt Melly, still on the floor. Her eyes were fluttering open, and the rats scampered off her chest and up onto the tabletop before she could scream.

Emmy squatted down, facing her aunt, and spoke more loudly. "I think Aunt Melly would love to have Joe here. She could teach *him* responsibility, too."

There was silence at the other end. Emmy began to think she had overdone it, but then her mother's voice came on. "That's a sensible idea, but we'll have to check with your aunt. Put her on, please."

Emmy covered the mouthpiece with her hand.

"My parents want to know if you would like to invite my friend Joe here." She gave her aunt a look full of meaning. "I think it would be a very good idea. He could *help* us. With the *yard* work. And *other* things." She put the phone into Aunt Melly's unsteady hand.

"Yes? Melly here . . . yes, of course . . ."

Aunt Melly still looked a little dazed. But something in her seemed to rise to a challenge. She was holding up well, Emmy thought, considering everything. Better than most grown-ups would have, probably. There was a bit of steel inside the old lady that Emmy admired.

"Er," said Aunt Melly, "of course Joe could help with the mowing if he likes. And it might be safer for Emmy to have a friend with her, if she went boating." She glanced up at Emmy, who nodded encouragingly.

"Yes . . . I'll make up the extra guest room. Perhaps you could ask his parents for me," Aunt Melly went on. "And do let me know . . . yes, the sooner the better. He could come on tomorrow's train."

She hung up and struggled to a sitting position. "Now, Emmy," she said, "I don't understand any of this, and I'm not entirely sure that I haven't been

working too hard." She looked at the rats and passed a hand over her eyes.

"You *have* been working too hard," said Emmy, "but it's all true. Ana, show her again."

The brown rat that was Ana pattered across the tabletop, got a kiss from Sissy, and transformed into a girl without any fuss. Three seconds and another kiss later, she was back to full size and climbing down onto the floor.

Aunt Melly looked at Ana with the wide eyes of shock. "This can't be *happening*."

"It's happening, all right." Emmy picked up the letter that Aunt Melly had written to her parents and fanned her with it. "You've seen it with your own eyes."

Aunt Melly fastened her gaze on the waving letter. "I suppose I could be dreaming. But in any case, I must tell you something about that lett—eeeek!" She looked up at the open window, suddenly filled with a brown and furry fluttering.

"No need for to tell anything! No need for the explaining so tedious!" A large brown bat alighted on the windowsill, folded his umbrella wings, and smiled a wide, fanged grin. "For the evening, she is here, so

148

beautiful—but Cecilia, she is more beautifuller still! And I, Manlio, have come for to take her away!"

"Oh, no you don't," snapped Raston.

"Am I losing my mind?" cried Aunt Melly. "Why are all these *bats* here?" She covered her untidy white hair with her hands.

Manlio waved an expansive wing at the bats who were swooping out of the evening sky to hang from the window sash, the blinds, the curtains, the branches just outside the sill. "Have no fear, postal bats have no interest in the hair of old lady persons! We are arrived on the business official—but," he added, leering at Cecilia, "in this case the business, it coincides with the pleasure, no?"

"And why do these creatures keep *squeaking* at me as if they're *talking*?" Aunt Melly's voice rose to the level of hysteria. Her hair, loosened from its bobby pins, fell halfway to her shoulders.

"Calm down, Aunt Melly, please!" Emmy glanced at Cecilia, still safe on the tabletop. "If you let Ratty bite your finger, you'll understand everything they're saying. It's just a little nip, Aunt," she added earnestly.

"Oh, what does it matter?" said Aunt Melly wildly,

holding out her finger. "I'm probably going insane, anyway—OW!"

"I didn't bite *that* hard," said Raston. "Sheesh."

"Hard enough," Aunt Melly said with spirit and then, shocked—"That rat. He *talks*."

"Really?" said the Rat, peering down at her. "Are you sure?"

"Don't be sarcastic, Ratty," said Emmy. "Sissy! Get off the windowsill!"

"Hey, you greasy bat!" cried Raston, leaping from the table to his sister's side. "Get your claws off my sister!"

"Raston! How rude!" Cecilia ducked out from beneath the bat's sheltering wing and straightened to her full height. "Manny was just showing me something."

"Manny? *Manny*?" The Rat sneered. "What was he showing you, his *bat toys*?"

The bats outside the window stirred restlessly.

"Of course not, don't be silly. Here, look." Cecilia stepped back to reveal a complicated arrangement of straps and buckles, connected to a multitude of long filaments that looked like fishing line.

"It is—how you say?—a harness!" said Manlio,

sweeping his wings wide. "It is for the flying of the rodents through the sky!"

"And why," said Raston through his teeth, "would we want to fly with *you*?"

Manlio reached into a small satchel and pulled out a folded piece of paper the size of a large postage stamp. "For to see the Rat Mamma, of course! Here is for the letter from her to the most beloved ratlings!"

"Oh!" cried Cecilia. She clutched the paper in her paws and stared at it with longing. "If only I could read it! Oh, Rasty!"

Raston snatched the paper and bent over it. "I need a better light," he muttered, and scrambled from the windowsill to the counter where a lamp burned brightly.

Emmy and Ana leaned in from either side and peered at the letter, trying to read the tiny printing.

Behind them, on the windowsill, Manlio moved closer to Cecilia. "Would you like for to try it on?" he murmured. "It is the very latest style, Italian leather of course, and the strap color it is so beautiful with the soft gray fur . . . there, you see? One little strap to fit over the beautiful shoulder . . . then another . . . now we buckle under the sweet fuzzy arms."

"Are you sure it will hold me?" Cecilia whispered.

"*Tesora mia,* my treasured Cecilia! It is to offend, this!" Manlio clasped his wings together at the thumb joint and raised his eyes heavenward. "Would I trust my oh-so *preziosa* Cecilia to the straps if they were not one hundred *per cento*?" He twisted his head to look at the hanging bats behind him and gave a brief nod. A hundred bats roused, unfolded their wings, and began to flutter upward, each trailing a nylon filament attached to Sissy's harness.

The agitation of bat wings sent a slight waft of air against Emmy's cheek. She turned to see Sissy still on the windowsill, now strapped tightly into the harness and beginning to sway as the nylon filaments grew taut.

"Hey!" cried the Rat. "Not so fast!" He launched himself at the windowsill but fell short, smacking hard against the wall. He scrabbled at the sill and hung by his claws, gasping as he tried to pull himself up over the edge.

"Ratty, are you all right?" Emmy cried. "Manlio, don't take her yet. Ratty doesn't want her to go—"

"All together we *lift* the most beautiful rodent, we *fly* her through the air . . ." Manlio's teeth showed

white and sharp, and his beaded eyes were bright in his furry face as the filaments pulled at the harness and Sissy was dragged off the sill. The gray rat dropped briefly out of sight and then rose again, swinging in space as the bats beat steadily upward in a flurry of wings.

Raston grunted with supreme effort and dragged himself onto the windowsill at last, panting.

"Ladies first!" said Manlio. "Handsome-but-weighty gentleman rats next time!" He fanned his wings and launched himself from the sill, just escaping Raston's sudden frantic leap.

"There's only one harness, Rasty!" cried Sissy, swinging in space outside the window. "I'll send the bats back for you, I promise! And I'll tell Ratmommy you're coming!"

Emmy rushed to the window, but by the time she got there, all she could see of Sissy were the bottoms of her feet and a curved tail hanging down.

In a moment the rodent was just a dark blot high above—and then Emmy could see nothing at all but the darkening sky and a pale coin of moon just rising.

A STREETLIGHT SHONE DOWN on a narrow building in the old part of Schenectady, turning boarded windows pale and edging the crumbling front steps with a rough glow. Beside the steps, in deep shadow, sat a square box wrapped in brown paper. The paper had been chewed—the box, gnawed open at one corner.

No one watched as a sleek rat backed out of the hole in the box, slung a bag over his shoulder, and hurried up a slender board that led from the ground to a gap in the siding above the foundation.

Cheswick Vole pushed his way past a hanging flap of tar paper and tossed the bag down three inches to a scarred wooden floor. He paused to catch his breath, looking around.

The laboratory's long counters and high stools were thick with dust, but no vandals had broken in during the years Professor Capybara had been away. Everything was as he had left it—the laboratory equipment, the roll-top desk with its manual

typewriter, the old-fashioned projector with an educational video still in it from the library, never returned. Professor Capybara used to play videos so the rodents wouldn't be bored, and even the sheet he had used for a screen was still hanging on a wire.

A wall of cages, stacked one on the other, showed where the rodents of power had once been kept. Cheswick remembered having to clean the cages, back in the days when he had been the professor's assistant. It had not been his favorite activity.

But now that he was a rat, he viewed these things differently. And the cages—extra large, with every convenience: water bottles, scratching posts, exercise wheels, play tubes—looked surprisingly attractive.

But most attractive of all was his beloved Miss Barmy. Cheswick lifted his muzzle and sniffed. She was here, but he couldn't see her. He scanned the large room, dimly lit by a single Bunsen burner. Perhaps she was up on the high counter, unpacking the bags of supplies?

He brightened at the thought. Jane wasn't usually the sort to pitch in and help. But here in Schenectady, maybe things would be different!

The black rat hauled the bag over to a leg of the counter where a long string hung looped, its two ends dangling over a hook high above. He tied the bag to one of the ends and yanked hard on the loose end of the string. The bag rose, swaying in the air, and when it bumped against the lip of the counter, Cheswick wound the bottom string on a protruding nail and stepped back, wiping his forehead with a weary paw.

It had been a long and exhausting couple of days. It hadn't been easy, messing up Emmy's room twice, and stealing the formula and supplies from the Antique Rat had been dangerous as well as exhausting. Then he'd had to drag a whole bag of Squirrel Dust up to the rafters, and after *that*, he'd had to poke holes in the ceiling tile!

But it had all been worth it. Miss Barmy, his dearest Jane, had been with him the whole time. He blushed hotly as he recalled how she had lain next to him between the rafters, cheek to fuzzy cheek, as they watched the party going on below. And when he had lifted the bag of Scaly-Tailed Squirrel Dust, and sifted it through the hole precisely above the Addisons—when the dust had swirled, sparkling,

landing on their hair, their shoulders, floating lightly in the very air they breathed—oh, at that magical, never-to-be-forgotten moment, Miss Barmy had actually kissed him! Only on his ear, of course, and in her excitement she had unfortunately bitten it a little, but still—it had been *wonderful*.

She hadn't been quite so friendly inside the box, though.

Mr. B had tucked the two rats in the packing box together with their supplies and given them plenty of air holes, a doll's bottle of water, and some sesame seed snacks. He had sent the box express delivery, clearly marked FRAGILE and THIS SIDE UP, and they *had* stayed right side up, mostly.

But even though it had been cozy in the box, and dark, Miss Barmy had stayed well away from him. She said she had a headache.

Well, she had to be feeling better now. The express driver had left them at the doorstep of Professor Capybara's old laboratory, as directed. And the postal bats should be arriving soon, if Guido and Stefano had passed on the message properly.

Yes, everything was going according to plan, Cheswick thought as he clawed his way up a tall wooden

stool and scrambled onto the countertop. And such a plan! Carefully thought out in every detail, even down to the final revenge on Emmaline Addison . . .

Cheswick hunched his furry shoulders and looked down over the edge of the counter, feeling oddly ashamed. Of course Jane knew best. Still, he didn't quite understand why she needed to harm a little girl. Wasn't it enough for her that she was going to grow and become human again? The police couldn't watch her house forever. Soon enough, she would be able to find a new place—maybe out of the country—where she could start over. Perhaps a nice place on the Riviera, in the south of France? Cheswick had never been to France, and he had always wanted to go.

The black rat hauled the last bag of supplies over the rim of the counter and fell back on his rump, hard. Where *was* Jane? He looked past the microscopes, past the test tubes and the Bunsen burner's steady flame, and saw at last the piebald rat. She was up on a windowsill, leaning on the sash with her back to him.

Cheswick watched Miss Barmy as she gazed out through the glass, apparently lost in thought. Her

fuzzy cheeks bunched, and he could tell she was smiling.

Was she gazing at the moon? Or the stars? She looked positively *enchanted* . . .

Ah! Cheswick pressed his paws to his chest, almost bursting with emotion. He understood it now! The sight of such far, high beauty had called up Jane's better self, the nobility that he had always known was there. And now she had no need for revenge, or even to grow human again . . . She would be content to be his ratty love, with a litter of ratlings in a sandy riverbank somewhere. France would be perfect! They could raise the children to be bilingual!

He leaped to the windowsill in a single bound. He would look out with Jane, side by side. Together, they would look up at the stars, and dream, and hope, and plan . . .

But no. The window was boarded up. There was no view outside; there was nothing to be seen but darkness.

No, wait—there *was* something. The flame from the Bunsen burner gave a little light, casting a reflection on the surface of the glass. Cheswick could

even see his own face! His whiskered muzzle, his pointed ears, and next to him—

Oh.

Cheswick slumped a little. Now he could see what Jane had been looking at all this time.

Miss Barmy fluffed her patches of white and tan and arranged the fur between her ears with a skillful paw. Then she curled her tail gracefully over her shoulder and smiled again at her own reflection.

"Chessie?"

The black rat straightened with an effort. "Yes, Jane?"

"I like this lighting. It's very—"

"Romantic?" said Cheswick, with a flicker of hope.

"Flattering," Miss Barmy finished.

Cheswick gazed at her softly lit reflection, and sighed. He supposed he couldn't blame her. After all, it was a very pretty reflection . . . if a bit fuzzy.

"There's a nice little breeze coming in," he said. He put his ear to the gap in the window frame and listened with pleasure to the night sounds of crickets, the peep of frogs from some nearby reeds, and a light fluttering of leaves that sounded like the beating of a hundred thin wings—a hundred *bat* wings—

There was a sharp knock at the siding near the floor, and a flat, fuzzy face poked beneath the hanging tar paper. "We've got her," said a raspy voice. "And now you must to pay Manlio and the bats, no?"

"Twenty-five mealworms," said Cheswick, counting them out. He folded back the tar paper and looked up into the sky, where a cloud of bats descended in a series of erratic drops. Below them, swaying, was a dark blot the size of a pear, and against the faint light of the moon a slender tail could be seen hanging down.

"Fifty," said Manlio, watching the squirming white worms drop one by one into his bag. "You forget— there is the brother for to bring, too."

"The brother?" Cheswick said sharply. "*He's* here?"

"*Certamente,* there is the brother. He is a heavy one—I think maybe we charge *thirty* mealworms for him. But we must to make the special trip for him, see? When the sweet fuzzy one, she is inside with the Mamma, yes?"

"We don't want the brother," said Cheswick, glancing nervously over his shoulder back inside.

Manlio Bat drew back, staring at the large black rat. "The Rat Mamma, she no want her *son?*"

161

"Er . . . not yet," said Cheswick. "She wants to have time alone with her daughter, first."

"She want the daughter, but not the son?" Manlio repeated, his thin voice rising. "Is none of my business, maybe, but what kind of Mamma *is* this?"

Cheswick ignored the question, watching instead as the colony of bats settled ever lower, squeaking like a hundred tiny rusty gates. The swaying rat in the harness touched the ground, lifted, then dropped again, stumbling as she tried to land on her feet.

"*Attenzione!* Be careful!" cried Manlio.

"I want the harness," said Cheswick as Manlio agitated his wings and fluttered to where Sissy lay on the ground, entangled in limp strings.

"Then you will to pay," snapped Manlio, busily snipping through knots with his sharp small teeth. "A harness, she costs. There, my so beautiful Cecilia, you have had the great adventure in the sky! But now you are back to the earth, and soon you will see the Rat Mamma, no?"

Sissy staggered, clutching Manlio for balance.

"Hey, Giovanni!" Manlio patted Sissy on the shoulder with his wing as a large, hairy bat sidled forward. "Giovanni, he will help you stand until you recover the balance, no? I must to go make the arrangements . . ."

Sissy glanced up, looking dazed. "And then you'll get Rasty?"

Manlio hopped to the gap in the siding, where Cheswick waited in the shadows. "For the harness, fifteen worms more," the bat said briskly. "And listen—the little Cecilia, she think her brother is to coming soon. They have much the love for each other, much the—how you say, the feeling *famiglia*?"

"Family feeling," said Cheswick. "I understand it's considered important."

"Considered important? *Considered?* Guido, my cousin, he almost to break his wingtips flying for to deliver the message to us, all the way from the Grayson Lake . . . this, because he my cousin, my *famiglia*! And I, I do all I can—for the honor of the Bats *Postale*! The postal bats, *comprendo*?"

"I comprehend," said Cheswick sharply. "But what you don't seem to comprehend is that it's none of your business! You have been hired to transport one rat—*one*, got it? And not to give advice when you haven't been asked!"

Manlio sighed. "Is right. Is not none of my business. But the beautiful Cecilia, she will be oh so sad—"

Cheswick glared at him, and the bat fell silent. "Now bring her in, but blindfold her, first."

"Blindfold?" Manlio's voice rose again.

"Her mother wants to surprise her, see?" snapped Cheswick. "And you give me any more objections, I'll take my business elsewhere! I hear you've got a lot of mouths to feed up there in your belfry, Mister Bat!"

Manlio swirled his wings about him like a cape, and bowed. "*Comprendo,* Signor Ratto—I understand. The sweet fuzzy one, she will break her heart, and the brother will wait and wait, and no one will come for him."

Cheswick frowned. "Maybe I'd better give you a note to drop in his paws, or he might come looking for her. Wait just a minute."

16

EMMY WOKE and lifted her head off the table. Sun was streaming through dirty curtains, and she looked around, confused. Where was she? Why wasn't she in her own bed, and who was that girl sleeping on the floor?

Then she remembered. She was at Great-Aunt Melly's house with a runaway orphan and a broken-hearted rat.

They had stayed up late. Aunt Melly, still half stunned—rats could *talk*? and *shrink*?—had gone up in a daze to settle Aunt Gussie for the night, and called down faintly that the guest room at the top of the stairs had two beds. But Emmy and Ana had kept on cleaning long into the night, waiting with Raston for the return of the bats.

They hadn't come and they hadn't come. Finally, Emmy had put her head down on the table just to rest for a minute—and not woken up till morning. Ana must have collapsed on the floor in exhaustion.

But the Rat was sitting on the windowsill, a tiny piece of paper clutched in his paw.

Emmy sat up and combed back her hair with her fingers. "Ratty," she said.

No answer.

Emmy moved closer. "Maybe the bats got tired, Ratty. Maybe they can only do one heavy delivery a night."

The Rat, a dejected-looking lump of fur, threw one paw over his eyes. With the other he extended the tiny note. "It's all a mistake," he said in a hollow voice. "Ratmom doesn't want me. She only wants Sissy."

"What? I don't believe it." Emmy snatched the note and held it close to her eyes, scanning the miniature writing.

But it was true. There, in black and white, were the cruel words "I don't want to see you right now."

"Who brought this?" Emmy demanded. "Manlio?"

Raston nodded.

"But didn't he say anything else? Did he at least tell you where your mother lives?"

Raston shook his head. "He just swooped by, dropped the note on the windowsill, and flew off. I tried to grab one of his wings, but I wasn't fast enough." He sniffled, wiping his eyes with his paw. "And I wasn't fast enough to stop him when he took Sissy away in the first place. If I'd been eating my Brussels sprouts, I could have stopped him, I bet. And now I don't even know where my sister *is*, and it's all because I'm—I'm just—"

"Just what, Ratty?" said Ana, sitting up.

"*Flabby!*" Raston said, sobbing bitterly. "I'm a soft, floppy, weak excuse for a rodent, is what I am!"

"But, Ratty—"

"Don't deny it!" cried the Rat. "I haven't been eating right! I haven't been exercising! I've been scarfing down peanut-butter cups and biscotti, and lounging about, and now see what it's got me? No sister, no mother, and . . ." He bent his arm, trying to make his biceps pop up, without success. "No *muscles!*" he wailed.

"Listen, Ratty," said Emmy. "It's not your fault."

"You can't be expected to catch a bat," added Ana, but the Rat just shook his head and trudged off to the bookshelf in the hall. And soon after, the girls could hear his rhythmic grunts as he began to go through the exercises shown on the brightly colored pages of *Get Flabulous!*

It was a busy morning for everyone. Raston built up his muscles. Aunt Melly got dressed and tended to Aunt Gussie. And the girls finished the kitchen and started work on the entryway and front rooms. Ana was dusting the antique dollhouse and Emmy was vacuuming the hall when the doorbell rang.

Emmy jumped. She caught sight of a dark blue sleeve through the front curtains, and the glint of metal on an official-looking belt, and backed away, leaving the vacuum running noisily.

Aunt Melly peered down from the top of the stairs, looking frightened. "Who's at the door?"

"The police!"

Aunt Melly clutched at her chest. "Some nosy neighbor told them about Gussie! They've come to take her away!"

Emmy grabbed Ana and shoved her into the hall closet. The Rat, alarmed, jumped off his book and scurried after.

"Don't make a sound!" Emmy hissed. Then she ran around the newel post and up the stairs. "Quick, Aunt Melly, straighten your collar—comb your hair—that's right. Now come on down; you have to answer the door."

The old woman leaned heavily on the banister. "Can't they let her die in peace? It won't be long, now. She was even worse this morning . . ."

"Aunt Melly! Stop looking so scared!" Emmy gripped her great-aunt's arm and helped her down the final step. "Nobody's going to take Aunt Gussie away. You're dressed instead of in your robe, and the house is clean—at least the part they'll see—and you look like you're taking care of things. The police are probably here because of—" She shot a look at the hall closet door, still open an inch.

"Psst!" Ana's finger beckoned frantically through the crack.

Emmy spoke sideways, not turning her head. "What?"

The doorbell rang again and was accompanied by a loud knock. Aunt Melly glanced nervously over her shoulder. "I'd better answer that, or they'll wonder what's wrong."

"*Please* don't tell the police I'm here," Ana begged. But Aunt Melly was shutting off the vacuum, her back turned, and did not respond.

Emmy risked a quick look back. "I won't tell."

"But what if *she* does? I'd rather be a rat forever than live with people who don't want me!"

"Now, then," said Officer Crumlett, consulting his notebook, "we know that Ana Stephans did not get off the train at Schenectady, because we have reviewed the video from the train station platform." He crossed his legs, leaned back, and took a glass of iced tea from the tray Emmy held out.

Emmy brought the tray back to the kitchen, thinking it was a good thing Ana hadn't changed from a rat to a girl in front of the video camera, or the police would have had a big surprise. She arranged her face in what she hoped was an innocent expression and returned to the front room. It was a perfectly clean and tidy front room, too—they had even dusted the keys of the upright piano in the corner—and Emmy was confident that everything looked good.

Unfortunately, Aunt Melly looked distinctly uneasy. She sat rigidly on a chair, her hands knotted in her lap, and glanced at the hall closet door more times than Emmy thought wise.

"Now, little girl, I need to ask you. Was Ana

talking to anyone else on the train? Anyone she might have gone off with?" Officer Crumlett clicked his pen against his teeth.

Emmy shook her head.

"Did Ana say anything to you about running away?"

"It is a terrible thing," Aunt Melly interrupted in a wavering voice, "when a child goes missing."

"Yes, but I was asking—"

"Even if the child is perfectly safe somewhere"—her eyes strayed once again toward the closet door—"*other* people don't know that, and of *course* they are worried."

"Naturally, but—"

"And if anyone *knew* where the child was," Aunt Melly went on, "they might think they had a duty to inform the authorities, even if—even if—" She faltered and buried her face in her knotted hands. "Oh, dear!"

Officer Crumlett looked both confused and suddenly alert. Emmy patted the elderly woman on the back, thinking fast, and looked up at the police officer. "Aunt Melly used to be a schoolteacher, and she gets very emotional when kids are in trouble."

Aunt Melly groped for a handkerchief and

dabbed at her eyes. "Really, I simply *cannot* go on with this."

"I'm sorry to upset you, ma'am," said Officer Crumlett, shifting uncomfortably in his seat. "Just a few more questions—"

Aunt Melly wailed aloud.

Emmy glanced past the policeman to the closet door—she couldn't help herself—and saw to her horror that it had swung open. If Officer Crumlett turned around, he would see Ana for sure.

But it seemed likely that he would find out about Ana in any case. Aunt Melly was just feeling too guilty to keep the secret. And really, Emmy could see her point. Everyone was worried about Ana now—her relatives, the police, the people at the orphanage, the social worker. Squippy was probably in a lot of trouble for losing track of Ana, and she might even lose her job.

Officer Crumlett leaned forward, solid and stern, his hands on his knees. "Emmy, you must tell me. Did Ana say anything, anywhere, at any time, about running away?"

"Well . . ." Emmy looked past him to the hall closet. Ana's head was poking around the doorjamb, and the desperation in her face was like a shout. Ana lifted her left hand—the Rat was perched on her palm—and then she placed her right forefinger very close to the Rat's sharp front teeth.

Emmy knew at once what Ana was trying to say.

Aunt Melly, though, was still mopping her eyes. She blew her nose with an elderly honk, sniffled twice, and looked up at Officer Crumlett's broad blue shirtfront.

"Officer," she quavered, "I'm afraid I must tell—"

"Aunt Melly!" Emmy gripped her aunt by the shoulder and shook it slightly. "Please don't torture yourself! Officer Crumlett *knows* you can't tell him anything. He doesn't blame you."

"No, indeed," began the policeman, but Emmy was not finished. If Aunt Melly wanted to tell the truth, then Emmy would tell the truth. "Ana didn't exactly talk about running away. But she *did* say she wished she could turn into a rodent."

"A . . . rodent?" Officer Crumlett rubbed his red-veined nose.

Emmy nodded. "She said that if she could turn into a rat, then she wouldn't have to live with people who didn't want her." She fixed Aunt Melly with an earnest gaze. "She said *she might never change back.*"

Aunt Melly took in a little breath. She glanced

quickly past the policeman to the hall closet, and her eyes widened.

Officer Crumlett clicked his pen and put it in his pocket. "I trust you realize this is a serious matter. I am not asking if Ana Stephans liked to pretend, or wished she could change into a little furry animal, or believed in fairies. The police force is interested in facts. And the fact is, we want to find that little girl and keep her safe."

Aunt Melly's spine stiffened, and she spoke with sudden decision. "That is exactly what we hope for as well—that you will find her safe and *unchanged*."

The policeman looked slightly confused, but he pulled out a small card from his pocket. "If you remember anything else, here's my number. We're checking all the towns on the railroad line from the last time Ana was seen. And believe me, we are questioning Miss Gwenda Squipp *very* closely."

"Now, Ana," said Aunt Melly after the door shut behind Officer Crumlett, "I can't say I like the way you forced me to choose between doing the right thing and keeping you safe, er, human."

Ana emerged from the closet with the Rat on her

shoulder. "I'm sorry, really I am. But I don't think it's the right thing to send me away to people who don't even *want* me."

"Nevertheless," said Aunt Melly with surprising firmness, "we simply cannot keep up this deception." She pushed down on the arms of her chair and rose slowly to her feet. "You must try to understand—"

"I'm *tired* of trying to understand!" Ana cried. "It's horrible to live with someone who doesn't care about me! I've done it already, for *years!*"

The Rat patted her earlobe with his paw. "Say it, don't spray it," he suggested.

"But, my child," said Aunt Melly gently, "the judge ordered it. You still need someone to take care of you."

"I can take care of myself!" Ana wiped at her cheek with the back of her hand. "If I was a rat, I wouldn't need anyone. I could scavenge for crumbs and sleep in culverts and attics and things, and I wouldn't even go to *school!*" She turned away suddenly, burying her face in the crook of her elbow.

"She really *wants* to go to school," Emmy explained to Aunt Melly. "She wants to be a doctor someday."

"I won't be one if I'm a rat," came Ana's muffled voice from beneath her arm.

"You could lead exercise classes, though," Raston said brightly. "I'd come!"

Aunt Melly's face took on an austere expression. She lifted the Rat from Ana's shoulder and set him on the bookshelf. "You may choose a book, Raston," she said, sounding more like a teacher than ever, "and read it—quietly. Ana, dear, here's a tissue. Blow your nose and sit down on the sofa. It's time we had a talk. Oh, and Emmy?" She put a hand on Emmy's shoulder and propelled her toward the front door. "You'd better hurry to the train station. Your friend Joe should be arriving any minute now."

17

"Okay, so let me get this straight," said Joe. "You asked your aunt to invite me here so I could *work*?"

Emmy sighed. She had tried to explain things on their walk from the train station back to Cucumber Alley, but apparently she had not made this point clear. Then as soon as they got to the house, Aunt Melly and Ana had divided up the chores, and from that moment on, they'd been busy. Even Raston had been put to work, dusting hard-to-reach surfaces on light fixtures and the tops of shelves.

And now it was evening. The three children were sprawled on patio furniture on the second-floor porch, exhausted. Raston, still wearing his feather duster, was perched on the flat top of the railing, gazing pensively into the distance at the river and the sun that was slipping behind the treetops.

Emmy glanced at Joe. "I told my parents that Aunt Melly needed you to help with the yard work. Didn't they tell yours?"

Joe lifted his head off the lounge chair. "Sure, but I thought that was just an excuse! I figured you wanted me here to help Ratty and Sissy find their mother!"

"Shh!" said Ana, with a nod toward the Rat, but he had already heard. A low, broken murmur came from the rodent on the railing.

"Ratmommy . . . only wanted her . . . *favorite* child . . ." There was the sound of a sniffle.

Joe pushed his sweaty, straw-colored hair out of his eyes and lowered his voice. "Not to complain or anything, but I've been mowing all afternoon. With a *push mower*. You know, the kind they had in the Dark Ages? And when I wasn't mowing, I was pulling weeds. And when I wasn't pulling weeds, I was clipping the hedge. And when I wasn't doing *that*—"

"We get the picture," said Ana. "We were working, too. And we made supper and everything."

"Tea! And toast! And boiled eggs! You call that *supper?*"

"You think you can do better?" Ana demanded.

"I can nuke a hot dog in the microwave. I can put in a frozen pizza. That would have been way better."

178

"Sure," said Ana, "*if* they had a microwave, which they *don't*—and *if* they had any pizzas in the freezer, which they *didn't.*"

"Quiet, you guys!" Emmy motioned toward the porch door that opened into the house. Aunt Melly could be seen at the far end of the hallway, bringing a tray out of Gussie's room. "Listen, Joe, I'm sorry. But can't you see? They really need us."

Joe glanced into the dim interior as Aunt Melly's shadow disappeared down the staircase. "They need somebody, that's for sure, but why does it have to be us? I was working on my scouting badge for science with the professor, and on another badge with my Scout leader, and I quit everything to come here. I thought there was some kind of big huge mystery and you wanted me to help find Ratty's mom—"

A whimper came from the direction of the railing.

Joe rolled his eyes. "But *now* all I'm doing is slaving for two old ladies I don't even know. And if you ask me, your aunt Gussie *should* be in a hospital! She looks like she won't even last the week!"

Ana glared at him.

"Well, it's true," said Joe sulkily. "That is one *old* lady."

179

"Don't keep calling her that!" said Emmy. "You say it like it's something bad."

"Well, it's not exactly good." Joe shrugged. "She can't take care of herself, she feels terrible all the time, she can hardly breathe—that sounds pretty bad to me."

Emmy didn't say anything. Joe was right.

"It won't last," said Ana quietly. "Aunt Melly—I mean, Miss Emmaline—told me that if I promised not to turn into a rat, she would speak to the judge and make sure they found me a better place to live. But she said we could wait a few days . . . because you're right, Joe. I don't think Aunt Gussie *will* last the week."

"And how weird is that?" Joe sat up, looking exasperated. "We're just hanging around, waiting for an old lady to die?"

"We're *not* just hanging around." Raston sat on the railing, his tail dangling, and looked at them gloomily. "We're working."

Joe groaned and flopped back down on the lounge chair. "Don't remind me. I must have thirty-seven blisters."

"At least you don't have to wear a bunch of feathers when you mow the lawn," said the Rat. "At least *your* mom wants you."

180

"Most of the time," said Joe. "Listen, though, Ratty—what makes you so sure your mom doesn't want you? Just that note? Let's see it."

Raston pulled two small and crumpled pieces of paper from his waistband and held them out, turning his head away. "You find the one you want. I can't stand to read them again."

Joe pored over the postage-stamp-sized notes, squinting. "Hmm. I guess she makes it pretty clear who she's inviting."

Raston hid his face in his paws.

"But it still seems fishy to me." Joe looked up. "I just don't believe that a mother would only want to see one of her kids."

"Maybe I was a bad ratling," said the Rat, his voice muffled.

"Or maybe she's a bad mother," said Joe, looking down at the notes again.

Raston's head whipped up. "You take that back! You hear me?"

"Shh, Ratty," said Emmy, looking over her shoulder at the sound of footsteps in the hall. "He was just kidding; right, Joe?"

"Oh, sure," said Joe. "Ratty's mother was perfect, and he was a baby delinquent. I totally buy that.

181

Listen, Emmy, do you still have that letter your aunt sent you? I want to check something out."

Emmy dug in her pocket for the letter, as the sound of footsteps grew louder. Aunt Melly was standing in the doorway.

Joe stood to offer her the lounge chair, but she sank down on a straight-backed chair instead, smiling. "After how hard you worked today, I think I'll let you have the lounge. I can't possibly thank you all enough."

The children said polite variations of "we were glad to help" (partly true), and "oh, it was nothing" (completely false).

"You just don't know what this means to Gussie and to me," Aunt Melly went on. "I should have told you to take some time out to play. I can't believe you worked straight through!"

Joe looked proud of himself. Emmy tried not to laugh.

Aunt Melly gazed out over the lawn and down to the boathouse at the water's edge. "It's too late to rig the sailboat, but you still have over an hour of sunlight left. You could put the little canoe in the water and try it out, if you like. It's meant to hold just one adult, but I don't see why it couldn't hold two children. Your father told me you are comfortable with boats, Emmy?" Aunt Melly looked down at her great-niece, then stiffened as she caught sight of the letter in Emmy's hand. "Dear me. I started to tell you this yesterday, but then—well, I'm afraid what with Ana shrinking and growing, and rats talking, and bats coming to the window, it just went right out of my head."

She unfolded the letter and looked at it with such a worried frown that Emmy hastened to reassure her. "It's okay that you forgot you invited me, Aunt Melly. I understand."

"I'm afraid you don't understand," said Aunt Melly. "That is not my handwriting. I did *not* send this letter." She set it down on a small table.

The sound of crickets was suddenly loud in the stillness.

"I thought there was something funny about it!" said Joe. "And look here." He laid Ratmom's two tiny notes next to the letter that had been sent to Emmy's parents.

Emmy squinted at the spidery writing, and then went rigid. "I can't believe I didn't notice that."

183

"You probably never compared them side by side before," said Joe, smoothing the letters flat.

"What's wrong?" cried Raston from the railing.

"It's exactly the same handwriting," said Emmy, "only different sizes. And look—there's some more of that glitter you guys used on Squippy's card." She pointed to a small sparkle, caught in a crease. "I wish you hadn't dumped the whole bottle on, Ratty. That stuff got into everything."

Joe bent over the letter again, frowning.

Raston reared back on his hind legs. "Are you saying that Ratmom wrote the big letter, too? Are you trying to blame *everything* on my mother?"

"Calm down, Ratty," said Emmy, looking down again at the letters. "We don't know that. We're just saying that the *same* person—or rodent—wrote all three."

"But who?" asked Aunt Melly. "Who would want to bring Emmy to Schenectady, just to leave her at the station with no one to meet her? What would be the point?"

"Maybe Manlio Bat heard how beautiful Sissy was and set it all up so he could meet her," Raston said darkly. "Oooh, if I ever get my paws on him—"

184

Ana shook her head. "If some bat wanted to see Sissy, why wouldn't he just fly to Grayson Lake? And why would he write to Emmy's parents?"

"They're postal bats," said Emmy. "They're paid to deliver messages and things. Maybe we should be asking who hired the bats. And why."

"Good question," Ana said. "Why *would* anybody want you to leave home and go to Schenectady?"

"Maybe Miss Barmy wanted to get you out of the way," suggested Raston, "so she could mess up your room again and get you in even more trouble."

"But that doesn't even make sense." Emmy's head was beginning to hurt. "My parents couldn't possibly blame me for anything if I was out of town."

"Excuse me," said Aunt Melly, "I don't understand everything you're talking about, but it seems to me that the whole point wasn't to get Emmy to Schenectady, but Sissy Rat. After all, *she's* the one the bats came to pick up."

"That's true." Emmy twisted a lock of her hair around her finger. "But why would someone want Sissy?"

"Well," Aunt Melly said, looking like a teacher again, "let's think. What's special about her?"

"I know! I know!" The Rat leaped up. "She won the Rodent City beauty contest last month!"

"Er . . . that wasn't exactly what I meant."

"And I bet Ratmom heard about it," Raston went on, speaking over Aunt Melly's objection, "and is going to enter her in the Miss Schenectady contest!"

"Really, Raston, I hardly think—"

"And *that's* why I wasn't invited," said Raston. "They'll be doing girly stuff now, makeovers and dresses and things, and I'd just be in the way. But when they're done, they'll send the bats back for me, too! Oooh, Ratmommy was clever to write all those letters and get you to bring us here!"

Full of enthusiasm, Raston leaped from the railing, his feather duster fluttering, and scampered to the doorway. "While I'm waiting for them to come back, I might as well get flabulous!" He dropped to all fours, did a few leg lifts to warm up, and began a series of wind sprints down the length of the hall.

"That is one weird rodent," said Joe at last.

Emmy watched the little scampering form. "Raston might be deluded—"

"No kidding!"

"But *somebody* went to a lot of trouble to get Sissy here and then get her away from us."

"But who—"

Emmy put up a hand. "Aunt Melly asked what was special about Sissy, but we all know that. She reverses Ratty's bites."

"Yeah, but—"

"Listen." Emmy leaned forward and lowered her voice. "Anybody who gets shrunk, or turned into a rat, just asks Sissy to kiss them, right? It's easy. But there's somebody who had *trouble* growing, remember? Somebody we hope *doesn't* grow . . ."

There was an appalled silence.

"Miss Barmy," breathed Ana. Her fingers curled. "But why would she want Sissy in Schenectady— Oh! You think she's here!"

"I just bet she is," said Joe. "And look here." He pointed to the letter. "This isn't glitter. I think it's a bit of Scaly-Tailed Squirrel Dust."

"You can tell the difference?" Emmy looked closely at the tiny scales.

"I spent half a morning dumping glitter all over that stupid card," Joe said. "Glitter has a different shine and a regular edge. This isn't glitter."

Emmy tipped her head back, her eyes half closed, remembering how the sparkling glitter had swirled over her parents' heads at the party, landing on their shoulders, their hair, as they read the letter Mr. B had given to them. But of course it hadn't been glitter at all. It had been Scaly-Tailed Squirrel Dust, and it had made them want to believe everything in the letter, no matter how improbable.

Joe and Ana were busy working out how all the pieces fit together—the fake letters, Mr. B, the robbery at the Antique Rat—but Emmy shut her eyes and put her fingers in her ears. She had to think. If Miss Barmy really had used the bats to kidnap Sissy—if Miss Barmy had Sissy right *now*—they had to find her, and fast. But how? They couldn't very well fly into the air after the bats . . .

Emmy stood abruptly and walked to the railing, leaving Ana and Joe's conversation behind. She stared out at the river.

Manlio Bat had waited for them at the train station. She doubted he would be waiting around there anymore, but it was at least one place they could check. But there must be other places . . . Where *did* bats hang out? An unformed thought nagged at the corner of her mind, as if she had forgotten something important, but she couldn't quite remember what it was.

What they really needed to do was to find the rodents of power in Schenectady, if there were any left. They might be willing to tell Raston if there were new rats in town and where they were hiding. And at the very least, they would know where to look for Manlio and his bats.

"Aunt Melly," said Emmy, "can we still use your little canoe? I have an idea."

"EASY—KEEP IT STEADY with the paddle while I get in," said Joe, shoving the small canoe holding Emmy and Raston a little way out from shore.

Emmy jammed the double-bladed kayak paddle into the rocky bottom of the river and held the floating canoe in place. "Step in the *middle*," Emmy reminded him. "Ratty, get out of Joe's way—*yeeouch!*"

"You said to get out of the way," said the Rat, who had run up her bare arm to her shoulder as Joe stepped into the canoe. "I can't help it if my claws are sharp."

"You didn't have to draw blood," said Emmy, examining her arm tenderly. The boat rocked suddenly as Joe sat down, and Emmy pushed off with the long, double-bladed paddle.

She looked back at the house, its west side bright in the late sun. Ana had stayed indoors, naturally. With the police looking for her, it seemed wise. But Aunt Melly had shown her the piano, the bookshelf, and the antique dollhouse, and had even dug out her father's old medical kit so Ana wouldn't be bored.

No one had told Ratty their suspicions about what had happened to Sissy, because no one could bear to break it to him that his sister might have been kidnapped. But Emmy had suggested that they try to find his old neighborhood, just for fun.

"Okay, Ratty," Emmy said as they glided smoothly past the boathouse. "Mrs. Bunjee said your old nest was by the river, right? What else do you remember about it?"

The sun reflected off the water in pockets of liquid gold, sliding over the dimpled surface of the moving river, and Ratty shifted restlessly on her shoulder. "I think I remember . . . tree roots."

"Hey, great clue." Joe pointed down the main channel of the Mohawk River, lined with stately trees as far as the eye could see. "We ought to find your old nest in—what do you think, Emmy, ten years or so?"

Raston hung on to Emmy's ear for balance. "And I suppose you remember everything about your nest when you were a baby?"

"Well, I didn't have a *nest*, exactly . . ."

Emmy dug in her paddle, up and down in a rhythmic motion, and the drops flew off the ends in glistening arcs. "Keep a lookout, Ratty, and yell if you see anything that looks familiar."

The stately houses on the shore gave way to a long green park with swings and a teeter-totter and a cannon, which looked as if it came from the Revolutionary War. Looming ahead was a high bridge, and Emmy, needing a rest, pulled in next to the stone abutment.

The canoe was large enough to hold two children and a rat, but small enough to slide in beneath some overhanging branches near the surface of the water. Joe grabbed an outer branch, then an inner, and hung on. In a moment the canoe was almost completely hidden, floating quietly under a tent of dense green leaves.

It felt like another world, dappled with slanting light and shifting green, and the suck and slap of the river against the sides of the little canoe was oddly peaceful. Raston climbed down from Emmy's shoulder and perched on the bow of the canoe, gazing down at the water. No one spoke for a long minute—and then the silence was broken by a snicker.

"Get a load of the rat in the feather skirt. What's he going to do, dance *Swan Lake?*"

Emmy glanced up through the leaves to see two large brown rats lounging on the stone walk that ran under the bridge, with their feet dangling over the edge.

"Nah, he's just a pet. Humans like to play dress-up with 'em."

The first rat scratched an armpit. "Some rodents have no dignity."

"Well, the wild ones don't even know what dignity is. And if they're pets, they're already degraded, man."

Raston, who had forgotten to take off his feather duster, reared back, his ears pink. "You—you—I'm *not*—"

"Aw, isn't that cute?" The first rat peered at Raston through the leaves. "He's trying to talk."

"You can tell he's not one of us. Too stupid-looking. No vocabulary to speak of, no appreciation for the finer things in life."

"Speaking of the finer things, dude, it's sundown— let's go to The Surly! I'll buy the first ginger beer!"

The Rat, crimson to the tip of his tail, jumped into the bottom of the canoe where he ripped off the feather duster and stomped on it. Then he scrambled back up to the bow, only to see the two rats swimming strongly away from shore.

"Come back and fight like a rat!" Raston shook his paw in the air.

"You should have said that while they were still here," said Joe, grinning.

"What, you think I didn't want to fight them? I've been doing exercises!"

"Yeah, for how long, one day?"

Emmy parted the leaves with her hand and watched as the rats grew smaller the farther they swam, their sleek backs showing clearly amid the brilliant orange-and-gold ripples. Then suddenly the last bright edge of sun was gone. The river turned the color of lead, and the rats were small, dark blotches in dark water, and then Emmy couldn't see them at all.

But they hadn't changed direction. They were swimming straight for the long island in the middle of the Mohawk, and as Emmy turned to Joe, she could see that he had been watching, too.

"That's not far," Joe said. "Not even a quarter of a mile. We could paddle there, easy."

They had to go home first, of course. The sun was setting, and Aunt Melly would be worried.

But after the elderly aunts had gone to bed, the

children had a conference in the girls' bedroom with Ratty. Joe, seated on the floor with the Rat on his knee, tried delicately to explain the situation.

"We think we should try to find Sissy," he said.

Raston's ears popped up. "But she's with Ratmom! And they're going to send the bats for me tomorrow night . . . or maybe the next. Sissy promised!"

"Er . . . right." Joe glanced at the others. "But we'd feel better if we knew where Sissy was. And when we ran into those two rats by the river—"

"Big meanies," said Raston, picking at his toes.

"Yeah, well, they didn't understand about the feather duster. But they were going to that island—"

"To some place called The Surly," Emmy added.

"And it sounded like there would be a bunch of other rats there. Don't you see, Ratty? If we paddle over and drop you off, you could ask around, and maybe somebody somewhere would have seen Sissy, or heard of your ratmom, or know where the bats hang out."

"But what if they make fun of me again?" The Rat tapped his claws together in a nervous tattoo. "Or what if we find Sissy but she's too busy for me?"

Joe scoffed. "When has Sissy *ever* been too busy for

you? She's the most adoring sister in the world. And no one will make fun of you as long as you don't show up in a feather skirt."

The Rat kneaded his paws together, one over the other. "But what if—" He swallowed and tried again. "What if Ratmom really *doesn't* want me?" He stopped, and looked away. He sniffled.

Emmy took a tissue from the bedside table and dabbed at the Rat's eyes. "If we find her, she'll want you. Of *course* she'll want you."

Raston climbed slowly off Joe's knee to the faded blue carpet and stood there for a moment, looking small and forlorn. "Are you going now?"

Emmy glanced out into the hall. A thin line of light still showed under Aunt Melly's bedroom door. "We'll have to wait awhile."

The Rat hugged himself, his shoulders slightly hunched. "I'll just . . . go on, then. I have some more exercises to do." He shuffled out of the room and down the hall, his tail dragging.

Ana turned to Emmy and Joe. "I wish you weren't going on the river in the dark. Aunt Melly would be terribly worried. And it's not even safe."

"But if we wait till daytime, the rodents will all be asleep," said Joe.

"We'll be careful," Emmy said. "But Sissy is in trouble. We've *got* to find her."

The water was black as oil, and cold. Emmy shivered, huddled in the small canoe, as Joe paddled strongly away from shore. She had gotten her feet wet shoving off, and the bottoms of her jeans were clammy and chilly against her calves.

The river moved under them, smooth and silent, and a flicker of moonlight dipped in and out among the long ripples. Everything was shadow; the bridges stood like giants with legs of stone.

Joe grunted, digging the paddle deeper into the inky water.

"What's wrong?" Emmy asked. "Are you getting tired?"

"More current—in the middle," he said between his teeth. "Got to—steer upstream—so we don't miss— the island."

Emmy gripped the sides of the canoe with both hands and gazed across the water. The island ahead was darker than the surrounding night, and the trees looked solid as a wall.

The Rat, tucked inside Emmy's life jacket, poked his nose out as the land came ever closer. Emmy

could feel him trembling against her chest, and she stroked him gently between the ears. "Don't worry, Ratty. You'll do fine."

"But where are we *going*?" His voice cracked. "It's all so *dark*."

"Shh!" Joe's paddle stilled, and the canoe drifted into slack water.

On the upstream bridge a single car sped past, its headlights streaking. Somewhere behind them a fish jumped, slapping the water. And from the island there came a steady rasp of crickets, and a stirring of leaves, and a faint sound of wild, squeaking laughter.

Joe picked up the paddle and quietly poled the canoe along the shallows.

"Watch out for the rock," Emmy whispered.

Joe pressed the paddle against a large, square boulder that suddenly loomed out of the darkness, and with a slight grating sound, the canoe went past. As they rounded the far edge, the laughter grew suddenly louder, and flickering light gleamed from within a tangled mass of roots hanging just above the water.

Emmy put out a silent hand, grabbed a dark knob of wood, and hung on. The canoe, rocking slightly, inched beneath the overhanging bank into deep shadow.

The twisted, polished roots looped in and around one another, and inside them were hollow spaces lit by a hundred tiny torches. But the hollow spaces weren't empty. They were crammed with rodents—a mass of heaving, laughing, shouting rodents, sitting at tiny tables, hoisting thimble-sized mugs, swaying with their paws on one another's shoulders as they squeaked with raucous laughter. Over the main arched entrance a painted sign read THE SURLY RAT, and a thin haze of smoke pooled in the room behind it.

Raston crept onto Emmy's shoulder and gazed at the spectacle, his mouth half open. "Let's go back," he whispered urgently. "Ratmom would *never* go to a place like this."

"BUT SOMEBODY HERE might know where she is," Emmy whispered back, falling silent as two burly rats came to the arched entrance, holding a struggling chipmunk between them.

"Out you go," said the largest rat, and with no further comment, the chipmunk was tossed in a high, flying arc. There was a tiny wail, a small splash, and then a sound of thrashing paws.

"Rough crowd tonight, Jacky," said the big rat, picking his teeth. "Even the chipmunks are dancing on tables."

Jacky leaned on a curving root, watching the chipmunk's progress to shore. "I haven't seen the 'munk yet who could hold his ginger beer." He laughed and spat into the water. "Unlike old Della Rat. She can put away five bottlecaps full in one night, Sal—I've seen her."

"Is she here tonight *again*?" Sal yawned and stretched, knocking against the sign that swung from a paper-clip chain. "She does that same old routine with the song and the potted fern every time she comes. I can't believe anybody still buys her drinks."

"It's a pretty good trick with the fern, though." Jacky shrugged his muscular shoulders. "I can't figure out how she does it."

Sal chuckled. "*She* doesn't even know how she does it. I was here the night when she did it the first time, and she was just as surprised as the rest of us."

Emmy watched the bouncer rats move inside, shouldering their way through the crowd. She could feel the Rat stirring uneasily on her shoulder.

"Okay, Ratty, go on in," said Joe quietly. "Here, I'll give you a lift." He picked up the Rat and set him on a thick root, just out of the light.

The Rat struggled free. "We're looking in the wrong place! She would never come near a place like this—not *my* mother, not the sweetest ratmommy *ever*—"

"All the same, you've got to ask around," said Joe.

"If I were hung on the highest hill," Raston quoted, standing on his hind legs, "Ratmom o' mine, O Ratmom o' mine, I know whose love would follow me still—"

"Oh, come *on* already—"

"She was an angel!" The Rat stamped his hind foot on the wood as he paced. "All that I am, or ever hope to be, I owe to her mother love! Are you seriously saying that the noblest and best rodent ever to rock a ratling's cradle could be found here, in this low, trashy, common riverfront *bar*?"

"Hush, Ratty!" Emmy slid the canoe farther into the shadows as Sal stuck his nose out of the front entrance and looked around.

"Hey, you!"

Raston, whose pacing had taken him one step into the lighted part of the root system, froze. "Who, me?"

"If you want to listen to the music, buddy, come in and buy a drink like everyone else—you don't hang around outside, listening for free, at The Surly!"

The Rat cast one panicked, pleading look over his shoulder and moved forward as if he were being dragged.

Sal clapped him on the back. "What'll it be, rat-boy? Ginger beer? Root beer? Pear cider?"

"Root beer," the Rat said faintly, and he was ushered inside.

The tinkling of a toy piano sounded above the

babble of voices. The crowd quieted a little as a sultry, slurred voice began to sing.

> *All by myself in Schenectady,*
> *All by myself in this bar . . .*

"Psst!" Joe hissed. "Emmy, can you see?"

Emmy shook her head. "But everybody's inside now. Maybe we can get closer."

> *I cry all alone for my ratlings dear*
> *So unhappy here*
> *I cry a tear . . .*

Emmy switched her grip on the roots and floated the canoe forward, inch by inch. Just under the entrance to the riverfront bar, Joe grabbed a protruding root and poked his head up slowly, peering inside.

> *All by myself I get lonely*
> *Since my husband was crunched by a cat . . .*

"What's going on?" Emmy whispered. "Can you see Ratty?"

Joe nodded, and sat down. "He's at a little table at the side. Somebody just filled his bottlecap again. And there's this sort of sloppy-looking rodent up on stage, kind of swaying while she sings, with this—I don't know, it looks like a fern or something. In a pot. If that's Della," he finished, "she looks pretty weird to me."

> Since my ratlings were stolen right out of the nest
> I can't get no rest
> I don't care how I'm dressed . . .

Emmy stood up carefully, paying attention to her balance, and got a grip on a knobby root as the canoe rocked beneath her. The crowd had grown quieter with each succeeding line, and as Emmy put her eye to the entrance, all rodent attention was focused on the stage where a large, heavy rat was singing to a potted plant.

Della did look sloppy. One sock was brown and one was black, her shapeless dress had a torn hem, and her soiled cardigan sweater had been buttoned unevenly, so the bottom right corner hung down. In one paw she held a large bottlecap of something foamy, which spilled into her neck fur every time she took a swallow. But in spite of all that, she could *sing*.

Della's low, throaty voice gained in power as she barreled into the final lines, scraping on the high notes with emotion. Even from a distance, Emmy could see the shine of tears on the furry face.

> *Now I guzzle root beer*
> *As I . . . cry . . . a teeeeeeear!*

Every rodent seemed to be holding its breath. Over against the side wall, Raston had frozen with his cup halfway to his lips. Then, as the last, sobbing note died away, Della leaned over the green fern, and one single tear dropped on the topmost frond.

And the fern died. There was no other way to put it, Emmy thought as she watched it shrivel, curling up and dwindling down into nothing at all. It had been green and thriving, and now there was nothing left but dirt in a pot.

The bar erupted in a mixture of applause and heckling. Near Emmy, a couple of gophers snickered.

"*That's* all she does? What's the big deal? *I* can kill a plant."

"I can too," said the second gopher. "All I have to do is lift my leg, like this—"

The gophers fell into fits of giggles and staggered off, holding their stomachs. Emmy looked around for Raston, but the crowd was suddenly moving and restless again, and the table where he had been sitting was empty.

Emmy was suddenly, overwhelmingly tired. It was way past her bedtime, and Ratty didn't seem to be asking anyone any questions. She was just about to sit down in the canoe again—the crowd's attention had shifted, and she might be spotted—when a piercing shriek filled the thick, smoky air.

Every head turned to the stage, where Della was still standing with a pot in her hand. Her attention was not on the plant (or what was left of it), but rather on a young gray rat with a white patch behind his left ear.

It was Raston. And while Emmy watched, Della shrieked again, tossed the pot over her shoulder, and clutched him in her massive arms.

"Rasty!" she cried. "Come to *Mommy*!"

Raston turned his head at the last moment to avoid being smothered and stared desperately with one eye, his other mashed against Della's enormous chest.

"What's going *on*?" Joe whispered loudly from the bottom of the canoe. "Let me see!" He grabbed a protruding root and pulled himself up next to Emmy, while the canoe rocked unsteadily.

"My sweet little Rasty-Roo!" blubbered Della. Her arms clenched even tighter, and Raston's hind feet kicked frantically as his nose and mouth were completely engulfed.

"She's cutting off his air!" Joe shouted. "Hey, lady! Let him go!"

The silence was instant and complete. Every rodent whirled, ears pricked on high alert, to stare in shock at Emmy's and Joe's large and human faces—and in the next moment the bar was a mass of heaving fur swarming for the exits. Dark, sinuous shadows slipped into the night with a scrabbling sound of claws on wood and a rustling in the underbrush above. In thirty seconds there was no sound but the wash of the river against the pebbled shore.

Della's arms slackened and the Rat backed away, his sides heaving, as the bouncers pushed past the empty tables.

"We don't need *your* kind here." Sal gripped Raston's left elbow.

"Your humans chased away the *paying* customers." Jacky gripped Raston's right elbow, and the Rat's toes dragged the floor as they propelled him forward.

The bouncers grinned at Emmy's and Joe's faces in the entrance, baring their long, yellowed teeth. "You humans can back away so we can toss him out, or . . ."

"Or what?" said Joe rashly.

"Or this," said Sal, chuckling as he shifted his grip on the Rat.

"We have our ways," said Jacky, reaching under Raston's hairy arms.

"Oooooh! Nooooo! Hee hee hee heeeeee—help! Mommeeeeee!"

"Stop tickling my boy!" cried Della, charging heavily toward the bouncers. "Hang on, baby. Ratmom will save you!"

Emmy and Joe sat down abruptly, nearly upsetting the canoe. They steadied it just in time to look up and see the Rat soaring overhead, a dark, flailing blot against the starlit sky, and hear his high, faint squeal.

There was a splash. From inside the bar came a

sound like nuts cracking, or perhaps two small skulls being violently smacked together, and then a thunderous series of footsteps.

"Ratmommy is coming!" Della screamed, and she launched her ponderous bulk up and over the rooted railing.

There was another splash, distinctly louder, and a burbling thrashing sound intermixed with squeaks. Emmy grabbed the paddle and pushed off in the direction of the considerable noise being made by the rats.

As it turned out, the noise was solely Ratmom's, because Raston was completely underwater.

"Hang on, baby—Mommy's got you," wheezed Della, swimming vigorously with one arm while the other gripped her submerged son in a headlock. "Don't struggle! I've taken Lifesaving 101!"

Raston's tail—the only part of him above water—whipped frantically from side to side as his mother swam on.

"Holy cats, she's drowning him," said Joe. "Quick, Emmy, the paddle!"

Emmy pushed the paddle underneath the thrashing rodents, lifted, and almost dropped them again. "Help, Joe! They're heavy!"

Joe pushed down on the far end of the paddle, like a counterweight on a seesaw, and together they swung the rats into the canoe and safety.

Raston, wheezing, coughing, hacking up water, sucked in great gulps of air as he sprawled on the bottom of the canoe. Della heaved herself to her knees and leaned over him, pressing his rib cage with her powerful arms. "*Out* goes the bad air, *in* comes the good!"

Raston moaned in feeble protest.

Joe grasped Della firmly around her substantial middle and pulled her off her son. "She *took* Lifesaving 101," he muttered to Emmy, "but did she *pass* it?"

"Doubtful," said Emmy, dipping her paddle in the river and giving a strong push toward the far bank. "Let's just get Ratty back home."

The Rat, wheezing, struggled to sit up. "But we—*heeesp!*—can't go—*heeesp!*—without Sissy!" He looked accusingly at Della. "Where *is* she?"

Tears mingled with river water on Della's tragic, furry face. "Why ask *me*?" she cried. "I haven't seen my little Cecilia since the day she was taken from the nest!"

20

Sissy was crying, too, but silently, so no one could hear her.

It was hard not to cry. The leather straps of the harness had chafed her skin until it was red and inflamed beneath the fur. She had a hammering headache from hanging upside down. And worst of all, the skin around her mouth was peeling off in painful shreds from kissing the Sissy-patch gel hundreds of times a day.

She knew now why the bats had harnessed her up and flown off with her into the night, and it had nothing to do with meeting her mother. Miss Barmy wanted to grow and become human once more, and she was determined to do it, no matter who got hurt in the process.

In fact, Sissy had come to understand that Miss Barmy actually *enjoyed* hurting rodents—or people— or anyone at all. Which is exactly the reason Sissy refused to cry in front of her, or even show that she

was in any kind of distress. She had done so once, and the twisted little smile that had played across Miss Barmy's spotty face had made Sissy determined never again to give her the satisfaction.

A pattering of rodent feet sounded on the lab counter, and Sissy hastily wiped her eyes.

"Ready for another batch?" Cheswick's voice was falsely cheerful. "I've turned on the video for you again!"

Sissy gave him a glance so contemptuous that Cheswick flinched and turned his head, busying himself with the mixing of chemicals. He consulted the formula now and then—the formula stolen from the Antique Rat, written in Professor Capybara's own hand—but he hardly needed it, after so many times. He busied himself stirring it all up in a flask and called out to Miss Barmy.

"Oh, Jaaaaaane! We're almost ready for you!"

"I'm not interested in 'almost,' Cheswick." Miss Barmy's voice floated down from the roll-top desk, slightly testy. "Let me know when you're *really* ready. I'm busy typing a letter about Emmaline."

Cheswick paused, looking troubled. "Really, Jane? You don't think you've punished Emmy enough yet?"

Miss Barmy's sharp-nosed face appeared over the edge of the desk. "You almost sound like you've forgotten what she's done to me, Cheswick."

"Well, no . . ." Cheswick stirred the amber contents of the small flask with sudden energy.

"Besides," said Miss Barmy, smiling a cold rat smile, "it's terribly important that everyone understands what a bad girl Emmy really is. Then they can help her to improve, you see."

"Oh! So you're not just after revenge?"

"Of course not!" Miss Barmy waved her paw in dismissal. "I have always had Emmaline's best interests at heart, Cheswick. The fact that she's a vicious, nasty, *evil* child who never thinks of anyone but *herself* is completely beside the point."

Cheswick blinked up at Miss Barmy. "She doesn't seem that bad. Perhaps she only needs a *little* lesson."

"Cheswick, Cheswick, Cheswick." Miss Barmy looked down on him from the desk. "You always do believe the best about people, even when you're horribly mistaken. It's really very sweet, if a bit fatheaded."

Cheswick blushed from his ears to the tip of his tail. "Jane, darling—"

"Unfortunately," Miss Barmy cut in crisply, "you *are* mistaken about Emmaline. I'll be doing her aunts a favor when I let them know the truth."

Cheswick sighed. He supposed Jane was right. She was almost always right about everything . . .

He picked up a clamp, lifted the flask with a grunt, and poured the heated amber goo onto the backing paper that he had prepared. It was heavy work, and he could have used an extra pair of paws, but Miss Barmy had gone back to the typewriter. He flipped a sheet of thin clear film over the spreading goop, jumped on it, and began to roll. His body wasn't quite as smooth as a rolling pin, but he was getting to be an expert at going around the corners without falling off.

There. He was done. Cheswick peeled off the backing paper, flung it aside, and cranked the winch that raised Sissy up and over the quivering orange slime. "Kiss!" he ordered, moving the lever that flipped her upside down in the leather harness.

Sissy beat back a shudder, gritted her teeth, and held her whiskers out of the way. As Cheswick moved the crank lever, the ratchet gear inched Sissy across the poured and flattened layer. At each click, he paused to allow the slender gray rodent to kiss the surface.

Sissy's lips felt as if they were on fire. The pain seared across her face and up into her ears. But she knew better than to refuse to kiss the gel. She had done that once before, and Miss Barmy had made Cheswick hang her up by her tail until she pleaded, sobbing, to be let down.

But she needed something to take her mind off the pain. Sissy stared hard at the video that Cheswick had put on for her. It was the same one, over and over—there didn't seem to be another one—and she had become used to it as nothing more than background noise. But all at once, something on the screen made sense to her.

She went stiffly alert in the harness. Would it still make sense when she was right side up?

The ratchet made one final click, and Sissy, startled, kissed the last square. Now at last Cheswick would bring her down and she could sit upright. She could hardly bear to wait the few seconds until he did. The blood was pooling in her head, and her ears felt swollen and tender.

But no—she had forgotten the ultraviolet light.

She flung an arm over her eyes just in the nick of time. Cheswick hadn't supplied her with goggles, of course.

The bright light was gone. Miss Barmy leaped from the roll-top desk and snapped off the video projector. "At last you're done! Quick, Cheswick, get the patches together!"

Sissy waited, nose down, the pressure in her eyes growing. She could see Miss Barmy and Cheswick, their small rodent shadows dark against the screen as they moved busily about, lit from behind by the Bunsen burner.

She twisted in her harness, swaying slightly, but the straps were too tight for her to shift position. She felt her eyes bulging, and her vision seemed tinged with pink. Sissy arched her back and then rounded it, pumping her body as if on a swing. Back and forth she swayed, the arc greater each time. She couldn't reach the metal crosspiece from which she hung, but she could perhaps grab the chain—she almost had it—

There! Her claws caught and held. Curling like a caterpillar, Sissy gripped the chain that was clipped to her harness and hauled herself upright, paw by paw. The sudden change of pressure in her head brought first a slicing pain, then relief as her vision cleared and her headache eased.

Cheswick and Miss Barmy were murmuring, their shadows close together behind the screen. Sissy caught a few words: "patches," "roll," "ready." And then Miss Barmy climbed onto a little block of something—a brick? a book?—and stood poised for a breathless moment, lifting her short, furry arms.

"Now!" cried Cheswick, and Miss Barmy leaped, rolling as she hit the floor.

Sissy had seen it before—yesterday, in fact—but she watched again in spite of herself, revolted and fascinated as Jane Barmy shrieked, moaned, and grew large behind the sheet, a shadowy monster with claws changing to hands, rounded ears sliding lower on the head, tail disappearing like spaghetti sucked up from a bowl.

All was still. The silhouette of a graceful woman stood etched against the screen.

Sissy, hanging on to the chain with every muscle tense, waited for the moment Miss Barmy would shrink again. The patches never worked for long.

But Miss Barmy wasn't shrinking. And she was laughing.

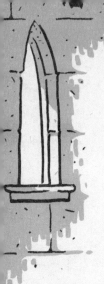

"It's working! It's working!" squeaked Cheswick, leaping about near Miss Barmy's ankles. "Oh, my sweet violet, my precious little—er, my precious *big*—"

"Shut up, Cheswick, and stop dancing on those extra patches! Quick, I need another one!"

Sissy tried to make sense of what she was seeing, but the harness caught her with a painful jerk as she dropped and swayed, turning dizzily in the air. She whimpered before she could stop herself.

"What's that?" Miss Barmy's voice was sharp.

"Oh, it's just that little kissy rat, what's-her-name . . ."

An elegant woman came around the corner of the screen, wearing an outfit of creamy silk that Sissy had last seen on a Barbie doll. On Miss Barmy's shoulder, holding a plastic bag between his paws, was Cheswick Rat.

"Are you feeling any symptoms yet, Jane dear?" he inquired.

"No, not yet—wait. Is my nose twitching?"

Cheswick peered up at her face. "Perhaps just a bit, and growing pinker, too." He dug in the bag, pulled out a Sissy-patch, and slapped it on her neck.

Sissy watched as Miss Barmy's nose (which had been sniffing the air like any normal rodent's) quieted and seemed to grow rounder and less pink at the tip.

Miss Barmy, gazing into a hand mirror, smiled tenderly.

Cheswick put out a hesitant paw and stroked the underside of her jaw. "Oh, my lovely Jane," he whispered. "You're prettier than ever."

A becoming dimple showed in Miss Barmy's cheek. "I *am* pretty, aren't I?" She frowned slightly. "A little older, perhaps."

"More *mature*, Jane!" cried Cheswick at once. "A ripe peach! A fragrant melon! You're a juicy mango of a woman, my dear, and never forget it!"

Miss Barmy ignored this. "Get me another one, and hurry. Look, whiskers." She tapped the side of her nose.

The glossy black rat reached for another patch, peeled off the backing, and pressed it to her skin. Rodent whiskers, which had begun to sprout on either side of her face, shrank back to nubbins and then disappeared altogether. Miss Barmy looked in the mirror and gave a satisfied nod.

"It's a medical condition. I can live with it, Cheswick."

The black rat bobbed his head. "Some people need pills, or shots—"

"And I need patches." Miss Barmy moved closer to Sissy and eyed the dangling rat. "A regular, never-ending supply of patches . . ." She put out a long forefinger and stroked the rodent's back.

Sissy swung back and forth helplessly, twirling on her chain.

Miss Barmy smiled and cupped Sissy in her palm. "Do your lips hurt, my pet? Would you like to get down?"

Sissy couldn't help it—she nodded.

"And are you hungry? Thirsty, perhaps?"

At the mention of food and drink, Sissy became aware of how dry her mouth was, and her stomach rumbled in longing.

"If you're very good, perhaps we can get a new video for you. Something more interesting than this dull educational stuff." Miss Barmy rubbed Sissy between the ears and spoke to Cheswick. "Now that we know it can be done, I'll call Father to send some clothes and everything else I need. As for you—"

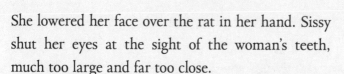

She lowered her face over the rat in her hand. Sissy shut her eyes at the sight of the woman's teeth, much too large and far too close.

"We're going to be very good friends, you and I," whispered Miss Barmy. "From this day on, you will *never* leave my side."

Sissy turned her head away, feeling sick.

Miss Barmy's fingernails grew pointed and claw-like. "Chessie! Another patch!"

Cheswick turned the bag inside out. "That's all there is, Barmsie, dear. I'm afraid we'll just have to make more."

Miss Barmy smiled at Sissy, her teeth suddenly rat-sharp, her cheeks downy with new fur. "Oh, we'll make more patches," she said as her claws length-ened and her tail grew. "*Lots* more."

They let Sissy rest and eat supper at last. Cheswick turned on the projector again, without the sound. Sissy was tethered to a brace on the counter, but she got as comfortable as she could and watched the video one more time. It made even more sense right side up.

She looked at Miss Barmy, pulling her letter out

of the typewriter, and at Cheswick on the desk, swinging his feet. They didn't know, and Sissy was certainly not going to tell them, but they had done her a tremendous favor.

The last slanting rays of the setting sun poked through a crack in the boarded-up window, shooting a straight arrow of light into the gloomy interior. Sissy gazed upward, entranced. She looked forward to this moment every day. It lasted only a minute, but for that brief time she could see that there was still a world outside this prison, and she took heart, and hoped for escape.

The amber light was abruptly blocked as Miss Barmy stood on her haunches, holding the letter up for admiration. Behind her, Cheswick looked over her shoulder.

From the counter, Sissy craned her neck to look up at the letter, too. She could not see it all, but the few lines she could see filled her with so much joy that she almost forgot the pain of her sores and shredded lips. It was really true! She could read at last!

Of course Raston had given her a start by teaching her the alphabet. But it wasn't until this video

that she had learned how to put letter sounds together to make words. And though the lesson had
seemed impossible to understand the first time she
had seen it, somehow the repeated instruction had
seeped into her brain. She could read! She could
read!

Sissy's joy diminished as she squinted at the letter
again, reading not just words, but sentences. Miss
Barmy was cruel. Why was she trying so hard to
make Emmy look bad? Sissy was indignant, but all
at once her heart pattered faster with a new idea.

If she could read—that meant she could *write*, too.
And if she could write, she could send a message for
help and rescue.

The bats. Every night, some bat or other came to
the gap in the siding to drop off or pick up messages.
If she were very smart, and very clever, could she
perhaps find some way to get a written message to
her friends and brother?

On the desk, Cheswick cleared his throat. "There's
only one *s* in *nasty*, my precious little honeybee . . .
and 'sneaks out of your house at night'—did she
really? How do you know?"

"Bats are not just for carrying letters, you know.

Manlio operates a little business on the side. BatSpy, he calls it. I've arranged to have the old aunts' house watched and Emmaline followed."

Sissy felt all her fur rise on end. She had hoped that Manlio didn't really know he had delivered her into captivity. She had tried to believe he was just an innocent postal bat doing a job, but now there seemed to be no doubt. He was on Miss Barmy's side. And if Sissy did manage to get a letter to one of Manlio's postal bats, she doubted that it would ever be delivered.

Sissy sighed deeply.

Miss Barmy poked her nose over the edge of the desk, her ears alert. "Cheswick, that rodent has rested enough. Let's get her back to kissing patches. I want at least a thousand."

21

EMMY SANK DOWN on the second-floor landing, exhausted. She had just made her twenty-third trip upstairs, this time to deliver Aunt Gussie's supper tray. It was three days since they had found Della in The Surly Rat, and it had not been an easy three days.

For one thing, taking care of two elderly ladies, a big house, and a yard was a lot of work for three children—especially when they were searching a whole city for one small rat.

They had canoed back to the island and questioned all the rodents they could find, but no one had heard of any new rats in town. Emmy and Joe had hung around the train station often enough that the stationmaster had suggested they find something else to do, but they hadn't seen a single bat. And though Raston roamed the streets every night in search of clues, so far he hadn't found one.

To make things worse, Ratty and his mother were having trouble getting along. Emmy looked through

the banister posts to the hallway below, where Aunt Melly's antique dollhouse sat atop the bookcase. From its open windows came the sound of squeaking voices raised in argument.

"I'm not your little ratling anymore, Mom! And if I go out at night, I might pick up Sissy's scent. She's the one in danger! *She's* the one you should be worried about!"

"So I'll help you find her," cried Ratmom, hiccuping. "Tonight, as soon as it gets dark."

"No! You're too fat and slow—there are *cats* out there!"

"Too fat? *too fat?*" Della hiccuped again. "I am *not* fat. I'm just . . . well padded. And as for slow—"

The back door slammed. Emmy heard the creak of the refrigerator door, the sudden spurting hiss that meant a can of soda was being opened, and then Joe's footsteps in the hall.

"Is that ginger beer?" Ratmom called.

Emmy watched as Joe stopped at the antique dollhouse. "Root beer."

"Close enough." Ratmom's light gray paw poked a bottlecap out of an upper window. "Fill 'er up!"

"Again?" came Raston's voice. "Don't you think you're overdoing it?"

"So I take a little drink now and then. I've been through a lot of heartache!"

"You'd feel better if you'd stop drinking and start exercising with this book, *Get Flabulous*. You've got to get in shape if you want to find Sissy!"

Emmy leaned her head against the banister as Joe mounted the stairs. She was beginning to wonder if they ever *would* find Sissy. Nothing they were doing was working.

Joe dropped a second can of soda into Emmy's lap. Notes from the piano drifted upward, making a tinkling and hesitant music.

"Is that Ana?" Joe cocked his head, listening. "She's getting better."

"She took lessons for a couple of years, before Miss Barmy. I think it's coming back to her."

"Good," said Joe. "She needs *some* fun while she's stuck inside." He dug in his back pocket and pulled out a small book.

Emmy winced. Although he didn't complain, Joe looked at his Scout handbook every chance he got. He would rather be at home, earning his badges, Emmy knew.

As for herself, she hardly knew where she wanted to be. It was hard labor at the house on Cucumber

Alley. But she didn't want to go home, not as long as the great-aunts needed her. And not until she had found Sissy.

"Kick! Kick! Higher!" Raston urged from below.

Emmy looked down. The rats had moved to the terrace on top of the dollhouse, where there was more room to move around.

Ratmom grunted, her eyes bulging. "I *am* kicking!" she whimpered. "This is as high as my legs go!"

"Feel the power in your spine, press your sacrum to the ground—"

"Press my *what?*"

"—and chant 'I am feeling flabulous! I am feeling flabulous!'"

"I am feeling *pain!*"

"That's not pain, that's the feeling of flab leaving your body," said the Rat earnestly.

Emmy and Joe snorted at the exact same time and got root beer up their noses. By the time they had calmed down and found tissues, Ratmom was crying again, slobbery and loud.

"We're going to have to hide the root beer," Joe murmured. "And the ginger ale, just to be safe. She's always weepy when she's guzzling."

"Who knew it could affect rats like that?" Emmy rubbed at her nose, which still felt fizzy. "Or some rats, anyway. Maybe only rats of power that live on the island."

"Speaking of rat powers . . ." Joe shut his Scout handbook and tucked it away. "I've been wondering about that thing Ratmom does with the plant. It seems pretty useless—"

"No kidding!"

"But I wonder if there's more to it than just making a plant curl up and die."

"What do you mean?" Emmy shrugged. "She dropped a tear on a fern, and it shrank down into the dirt. That's all."

Joe frowned slightly. "Still, it might be a dangerous power, don't you think? I mean, what if her tears could kill something besides a plant?"

Emmy watched as Raston prodded at his mother, who had wiped her eyes and was on her back attempting to do leg lifts. "She doesn't look like a killer."

There was a heavy thump as Ratmom's legs gave out and hit the floor. In the next instant she was wailing. "I'm a failure . . . a total failure . . ."

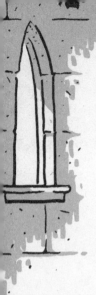

"Well, not *total*," said the Rat.

"It was my fault that I lost you!" she cried. "I left the nest for a minute to visit the next burrow for a new recipe—fried grubs, very tasty—and when I came back, you were gone! Oh, let me hold you—let me pretend you're still my little ratbunny . . ."

"Oh, all *right*," said Raston testily. "But I'm not wearing a baby bonnet." He lay his head in his mother's lap and crossed his arms over his chest.

Ratmom burst into a flood of tears, rocking him back and forth. "Oh, Rasty, my little Rasty-Roo . . ."

"Do you have to blubber all over me?" demanded the Rat. "You're getting my fur wet!"

"Hey!" Joe moved suddenly on the stairs. "Stop crying, it's *dangerous*! Your tears could kill him, just like they killed that fern!"

Raston looked up, his mouth open.

Ratmom shook her head. "My tears never kill the plant. They just make it curl right up again and go back to being—" She blinked.

"A seed?" demanded Joe.

"A spore," whispered Ratmom, moving a moment too late to catch the single tear that rolled off her cheek and straight into Raston's open mouth. And then, as quickly as the fern had gone back to being a spore, Raston curled up, grew small, and—

"Waaah! Waaah! Waaaaaaaah!" cried baby Rasty.

Emmy and Joe dashed down the stairs. Ana left the piano. For one long, speechless moment, they all stared at the squalling, squirming, furry infant in Della's arms.

Joe stuck his hands in his pockets. "No offense, but I'm not changing his diapers."

Ratmom's shocked expression changed to dismay. "Oh, Rasty! I didn't mean to do it!"

"Don't drop any more tears in his mouth, whatever you do!" Emmy snatched baby Raston up and cradled him in her palm, safely away from the blubbering Della.

"Waaaaaaah! Wah wah wah wah waaaaaaaaaah!" howled Ratty, kicking her thumb.

"Put him *down*, Emmy," said Joe. "What if he bites you?"

Hurriedly Emmy searched the dollhouse for a cradle and tucked Ratty in with a bit of blanket. "Keep Ratmom away from him," she ordered. "I'll be right back."

She rummaged in the kitchen cupboards until she

found what she needed: a tiny glass bottle. She rinsed it out and brought it back, drying it on her shirt.

She presented the bottle to Della. "Listen. Your tears are *dangerous*. So anytime you cry, collect them in this bottle. And don't forget to put the cap back on—tight!"

Della, sobbing even harder, dipped her head so the tears slid down her nose. The clear, shining drops fell in the bottle.

Raston was still screaming. It was a piercing sound, shrill and surprisingly loud. Upstairs, Aunt Melly appeared at the landing. "What on earth is that noise? Gussie needs quiet." Her hand fluttered to her throat. "Oh, she's suffering so!"

Ana went quickly up the stairs. "I'll help, Aunt Melly." She whispered over her shoulder, "Keep him *quiet*!"

Emmy and Joe tried. They rocked him in the cradle. Emmy sang to him, and Joe made funny faces, but baby Ratty only screamed harder.

"Food!" said Emmy. "Maybe he's hungry!"

"But what do we feed a baby rat?" Joe shifted his weight uneasily.

"Milk," said Ratmom, sniffling in a corner of the dollhouse terrace. "Two percent."

But a drop of milk, aimed directly into his open mouth, only made him sputter and spit it out. And when Emmy, in desperation, gave him a crumb of a peanut-butter cup, he choked.

"Oh, my baby, my baby!" wept Ratmom, lumbering toward the cradle.

"Hey! Don't touch him while you're crying!" Joe blocked Ratmom's progress with a doll's dresser. "Crikey, I wish they'd all just dry up. Here, Ratty, I'll give you a horsey ride."

Baby Raston was screaming so hard his tail was stiff and his ears were bright red. Joe tipped the cradle and the Rat came out in a tangle of blankets and kicking feet, his tiny mouth wide open like a steam whistle.

"I need some earplugs," said Joe, balancing the Rat on his forefinger and moving it up and down. "Here, Ratty, this is the way the horsey goes, walk, walk, walk!" He moved his finger a little faster, and said, "This is the way the horsey goes, trot, trot, trot!" Then faster still: "This is the way the horsey goes, gallop, gallop, gallop!"

Joe tipped up his finger, tumbling the ratling into his waiting palm. Baby Raston gave one last sob, hiccuped, and lifted his tiny head. "Mo!"

Joe looked down at him. "What?"

"MO!"

"I think he means 'more,'" said Emmy, grinning. "Looks like you have the magic touch."

"Yeah, but I don't want to keep bouncing him all day *long*—"

"MO MO MO MO MO!" demanded the baby rat, scrunching up his furry face.

"Okay, okay!" Joe hastily put the Rat back on his fingertip and began to bounce. "This is the way the horsey goes . . . Listen, Della, how long until he goes back to normal? This is going to wear off, right?"

"Don't ask me," said Ratmom, capturing a final tear in the bottle. "Maybe it doesn't wear off."

"Oh, great," said Joe. "*Just* what I wanted to hear."

"Twot!" shouted baby Raston.

Joe gave Emmy a haggard look.

"I think he means 'trot,'" said Emmy. "And weren't you the one who said I shouldn't hold him in my hand? You'd better get Aunt Melly to lend you a glove."

"Oh, yeah, right!" Joe hurriedly set Ratty in the cradle. The ratling, after one incredulous look, squeezed his eyes shut, opened his mouth, and began to wail—heartbroken, piercing sobs that brought Ana to the top of the stairs once again. "Aunt Gussie's trying to rest. Can't you stop that noise?"

"Oh, sure," said Joe, "if I smothered him. Why don't *you* come down and keep him quiet, if you think it's so easy?"

Emmy, rummaging in the closet, came up with a lady's leather glove. Joe yanked it on and began to horsey-ride the Rat once more.

Ana came down the stairs with a tray in her hands and glanced at Ratmom. "I've been thinking. The fern didn't become a *baby* fern—it went all the way back to being a spore, right?"

Ratmom wiped her nose with her paw and then nodded.

"But Ratty only went back to being a baby. And he didn't go all the way back to newborn, either, because newborn rats don't have any fur."

"Hey, that's right!" Joe looked at Ratmom. "Does a teardrop just take off a certain number of years, then?"

235

Della shrugged. "Maybe."

"How many?" Emmy asked at once. "In human years, I mean, not rat years."

Ratmom brightened. "Let's see . . ." She began to calculate on her paws. "Four point three times seven, to the nth power, divided by x squared, plus or minus the gradient of the coefficient in the vector analysis in base eight . . ." Her voice trailed away in confusion.

"I'd say ten years or so," said Ana firmly. "In human years, Ratty was about your age or a little older. Take ten years from your ages and you get a baby. It stands to reason."

"But how do you know he was our age?" Joe asked, still gently bouncing the Rat up and down.

"He couldn't have been *much* older. He wasn't interested in getting all mushy with girl rats yet."

Joe grinned. "Good point." He glanced down at the small rat on his finger. "Hey, I rocked him to sleep! About time!" He laid baby Raston carefully down, and Ana covered him with a doll's blanket.

"I hope he sleeps the night through," Ana whispered. "Don't you, Emmy?"

Emmy did not answer. She was staring at the

bottle between Ratmom's paws. *Ten years . . .* She looked up the stairway to the second-floor landing, where a thin sliver of Aunt Gussie's bedroom door could be seen. "I wonder if a teardrop would work on a human?"

Ana's hand flew to her mouth.

"There's only one way to find out," said Joe.

"*No,*" said Ana. "What if something goes wrong?" She poured Aunt Gussie's medicine into a small plastic cup and filled a glass of water at the kitchen faucet.

"Just *one* drop can't hurt," Emmy argued. "If she was ten years younger, she wouldn't be sick anymore."

"Make it two drops," Joe said. "One drop will only bring her down to seventy or so. That's still really old—how are we even going to tell the difference?"

"Hey, maybe we should do three!" Emmy followed Ana into the hall. "If we put it in her water, it's diluted!"

Ana set down the tray on the table beside the dollhouse with a thump. "Look. I'm the oldest, and I say we shouldn't."

Emmy stood a little taller. "She's *my* aunt. I say we should."

Joe looked from one to the other.

Della gasped, pressing a paw to her heart. "You're going to use *my* tears to help Gussie?"

"Yes," said Emmy.

"No," said Ana.

"What's the matter?" Della threw back her head to glare at Ana. "Aren't my bodily fluids good enough for you?"

"I didn't mean—"

"I suppose it's because I'm a sloppy torch singer who does cheap parlor tricks in a rowdy riverfront bar!" She twisted a corner of her shapeless cardigan sweater. "Not *everyone* can be flabulous, you know!"

"Use the tear bottle," Joe reminded her.

"Maybe I *am* a failure!" sobbed Della. "Everything I do is wrong!"

"Not *everything*," said Emmy.

"It's true! I left the nest, and my children were stolen. I tried to save Rasty, but I almost drowned him. Sissy is still lost, I'm not fit *or* flabulous, I can't work at The Surly anymore—"

"Not since you cracked the bouncers' heads together," Joe agreed.

"And now I've turned my son into a screaming baby!

I'm a *bad mother!*" She reared back, swaying on her haunches, and reached for her bottlecap. It was dry.

"And now I'm even out of—*hic!*—root beer. Pleeeease can I have some more?"

"It doesn't do you any good," said Ana severely.

"I could give it up," said Della, pressing a paw to her heart, "if I knew I wasn't a total failure. If I thought that . . . maybe . . . I could help old Gussie?" She sniffled, wiped a paw across her eyes, and looked up hopefully.

The children turned their backs to confer.

"Give me a break," said Ana. "I'm not going to agree just to get a rat to give up root beer."

"You should agree for Gussie's sake," said Emmy sternly.

"But you can't just decide to make someone younger without their permission!" Ana cried. "It's not medically ethical! It's against the Hippocratic oath!"

"I don't even know what that means," said Joe, "but I vote with Emmy."

"Something could go wrong," Ana insisted.

Emmy gripped Ana's wrists. "But if we don't do something, Gussie is going to *die.*"

Ana was silent a moment. "Let's ask Aunt Melly. If *she* says we can use the tears on Gussie, then all right." She glanced past Emmy. "Hey! Get off the tray!"

Della turned, the tear bottle clutched in her paws. "But I want to come, too! I want to watch my tears make Gussie well!"

"We don't even know if we're going to use them." Joe took the bottle and set Della back in the dollhouse. "You'd better stay with Ratty. He might start crying again."

The children knocked softly at the sickroom door and entered.

A single lamp lit the curve of Aunt Melly's neck as she knelt by the side of the bed, her face buried in the bedclothes. On the pillow, Aunt Gussie's white hair looked like a halo, and she breathed in long, raspy sighs.

Joe tried to back out. Emmy caught him by the sleeve.

"This is creepy," he whispered.

Ana set down the tray and knelt on the other side of the bed. "Aunt Melly," she began, and hesitated.

"Go on," Emmy said, very low. "You're the one who wanted to ask her."

Ana pushed her bangs out of her eyes and started to explain about the fern and Ratmom's special power. She didn't get very far before Aunt Melly lifted a tearstained face.

"I'm sorry," she faltered. "I can't really listen right now . . . oh, Gussie! Dear sister!" She pressed her face back into the blankets, and her shoulders shook with muffled sobs.

Emmy ducked down behind the bed. "This isn't going to work," she muttered.

Joe nodded. He picked up the tiny bottle of tears and uncapped it. "One drop or two?" he mouthed.

Emmy held up two fingers.

"Hey!" Ana whirled around, jostling Joe's elbow. "What do you think you're doing?"

"Yikes," said Joe, looking in dismay at the water glass.

"How many drops?" Ana hissed.

"I don't know! You bumped against me when I was pouring!"

"More than two, anyway," said Emmy. "Nice going, Ana."

"It wasn't my fault!" said Ana. "I wasn't the one putting in drops after we *agreed*—"

"Please!" Aunt Melly struggled to her feet. "I don't know what you're bickering about, but enough! Hand me the tray. It's time for Gussie's medicine."

Ana shot one more glare in Emmy and Joe's direction and handed over the tray. "Don't give her the water, Aunt Melly, it's not safe—"

"Yes, I know. There'll be less chance of her choking if we give her ice chips. But help me give her the medicine now. Joe, Emmy, get on either side and prop up her shoulders."

Emmy slipped an arm beneath Aunt Gussie's back, feeling her slight weight and the shoulder blades that stuck out like wings. Joe's hand crossed under hers and gripped her forearm.

"Now, lift." Aunt Melly put the cup of medicine to her sister's lips. "Swallow, Gussie, dear."

Aunt Gussie's cracked lips fumbled on the edge of the plastic cup, and Aunt Melly tipped it carefully, not losing a drop. The sick old woman swallowed convulsively and her eyelids fluttered.

"Is that better?" Aunt Melly caressed her sister's thin, pale hand. "I think it does you good . . ."

"Oh!" Gussie's eyes opened wide. "Oh, my!" She sat up in bed. "I feel so much better!"

"Really?" Aunt Melly's face was joyful. "Oh, darling Gussie, suddenly you look ten years younger!"

"I *feel* ten years younger!" cried Gussie. "No, twenty!"

Emmy looked at Joe across the bed. "Did you put teardrops in the *medicine*?" whispered Emmy.

"Not me," said Joe.

"Well, somebody did," Emmy said, unable to take her eyes off the middle-aged Aunt Gussie sitting bolt upright in the middle of her bed. No, not middle-aged—

"Gussie!" Aunt Melly's hands flew to her throat. "You don't—you don't look a day over *thirty*—"

Aunt Gussie's wrinkles smoothed out. Her hair went from white to a deep chestnut brown. Her eyes grew bright, and her skin youthful, and all at once she looked younger than thirty, she looked *twenty*.

The young Aunt Gussie gave them an enchanting smile.

"You're so pretty!" breathed Ana, and Joe nodded, mesmerized.

"I feel a little gawky," said Aunt Gussie, and it was

true—she was changing before their eyes again, looking awkward and coltish, her arms too long for her body, her face angular, her mouth too wide for her chin.

"She's a teenager," said Ana. "Maybe fourteen—no, thirteen—"

Emmy found she was gripping Ana's and Joe's hands tightly. Would it ever stop? Had they killed her in the end? The teenage Aunt Gussie shrank, dwindled, and turned into a slender child with brown curly hair and an impish grin, smaller than any of them.

The children held their breath, but Gussie seemed to have stopped the youthening process. Aunt Melly sat back on her heels, looking stunned.

There was a skittering of claws at the doorway and Ratmom slid into sight. "Hi, all!" She scampered across the wood floor, swarmed up the bedpost, and gave a wide, toothy smile. "Looks like someone took her medicine!"

"You?" Emmy stared at Ratmom. "You put tears in Aunt Gussie's medicine? How many?"

"Oh, seven or so. I had to calculate for the extra body mass of a human, you understand." Ratmom

shook her head, looking puzzled. "But I guess the size doesn't matter, because she looks about—"

"Six!" shouted Gussie, beaming. "I'm *six*! Let's go out and play!"

"I feel . . . a little faint," said Aunt Melly, fumbling with the tray. "Perhaps . . . a drink of water . . ."

"No!" CRIED EMMY, but it was too late. Aunt Melly took a final swallow and set down the empty glass with a bemused expression.

"Do you know, I feel remarkably well," she began, but stopped as she caught sight of her hands.

She held them out before her, openmouthed, watching as the ropy veins subsided, the age spots disappeared, and the knobby knuckles slimmed. The delicate, long-fingered hand grew smaller, plump and dimpled—and a very young Aunt Melly looked up at her sister on the bed.

"I want to play, too!" She leaped onto the pillows, screaming with laughter. "Look, Gussie, I'm littler than you! I always *wanted* to be the youngest!"

Emmy, Joe, and Ana conferred by the window while the little girls jumped merrily on the bed.

"It's weird how they don't seem to worry about any of this," Joe said. "Aunt Melly would have—when she was old, I mean."

Emmy nodded. "Maybe little kids don't worry that much."

"I'm worried enough for both of them," said Ana, gnawing on a fingernail.

"I'm not!" said Ratmom from her perch on the bedpost. She leaped to the nightstand, knocking over the bottle of tears in the process—"*Oops!*"—and from there to the windowsill, where she sat with her tail dangling, looking pleased with herself.

"You don't have to look so happy," said Joe. "You messed up *everything*."

"Gussie's alive, isn't she?" Ratmom put her paws on her hips. "So she's a little younger. She has longer to enjoy life, that's all! And besides, you were going to do the same thing. *You* put the drops in the *water*."

"We weren't going to use it," snapped Ana. "From now on, let people know when you're going to take seventy or eighty years off their lives, will you?"

Ratmom looked from one disapproving face to the next, and her whiskers drooped. "But don't you think it's kind of fun to have it be a surprise?"

"*No*," said all three at once.

"But you wanted to use the teardrops! I heard you!"

"Sure," said Emmy, "but only one or two. We wanted her to get *well*, not get youthenized!"

Thump! Thump! Melly and Gussie tumbled off the bed and began to chase each other around the room, shrieking.

Ana shook her head at Ratmom. "What were you thinking?" she demanded, jumping back as Melly ran past. "Two little girls can't live on their own. And two old ladies can't just disappear. The police will search for them, the judge will ask questions, and everybody's going to get in trouble."

"I was only trying to help." Della's furry shoulders slumped. "Humans make things too complicated. It's simpler to be a rat."

"I might have to turn rat myself," Ana said gloomily. "It *would* be simpler. I could use seeds for money—there are plenty in Aunt Melly's spice cabinet. I could hop on the train, jump off at Grayson Lake, live in Rodent City, and never worry again."

"You *can't* turn rat," said Emmy. "You promised Aunt Melly you wouldn't."

"Sure, because she promised to speak to the judge for me! But who's going to listen to a five-year-old Aunt Melly? Nobody, that's who."

"Do you need someone older to help?" Della looked up hopefully. "I could talk to the judge—"

"No," said Ana. "You've helped enough already."

"Oh." Della reached wearily for the window-blind cord and slid down to the floor. "I guess I'll just be going, then . . . since nobody needs me."

"Ratty needs you," said Joe. "He's a baby, remember? You'd better make sure he's still okay."

Ratmom shuffled off toward the door, her tail dragging.

Emmy sighed. Ratmom's feelings didn't seem important compared to the very real problem of what to do with Melly and Gussie. What on earth could she tell her parents? She gazed moodily at the little girls, who had dragged the blanket off the bed to make a tent. "They sure have a lot of energy, don't they?"

Joe grinned. "I bet they'll calm down after a while. They've been old and stiff for so long—no wonder they want to run around."

"They're awfully cute," said Ana, watching the two curly heads bob up and down as the little girls shut one end of the sheet in a dresser drawer and tried to find a way to hold down the other end. "I wonder if they remember being grown-up?"

The five-year-old Aunt Melly looked up and wrinkled her nose. "Course we remember—but it's no *fun!*"

Gussie nodded vigorously, her brown curls bouncing. "It's booooring! Taxes and dusting and everything stupid!"

"We want to play tent," said Melly, flapping a corner of the blanket at Gussie's head.

"And horse," said Gussie, dropping to all fours with a whinny and a toss of her mane. She pawed the floor and pranced up to Joe. "Do you give horsey rides?"

"No," said Joe.

"I will," said Ana. "I'm the biggest, anyway. Come on, Gussie, climb on my back."

Emmy leaned on the windowsill. The sun had set long ago, and the sky was dark, with a narrow band of deep blue lingering in the west. Out of habit, she scanned the sky for bats, but she hardly knew what she would do if she saw one. She felt as if her brain had been stunned.

The wooden floor creaked beside her as Joe shifted from one foot to the other. "Now what?" he said simply.

"I have no idea." Emmy stared out into the night

again, gazing at the dark expanse of the Mohawk River. "Maybe Ana has the right plan. We could all become rats and then we'd never have to explain anything."

"Giddyap! Go, go!"

Joe glanced at the far side of the room, where Ana had collapsed under the weight of the two giggling girls. "Don't you think we should tell them to go to sleep, or something? It's got to be past their bedtime."

Emmy leaned her forehead against the window sash. "But they've been grown-ups for sixty *years* or more. And this is their house. How can we start telling them what to do?" She shut her eyes. If only she could just shut her eyes and let someone else figure everything out. She could wake up in the morning, and it would all be fixed—Melly and Gussie would be old but healthy, Sissy would be found safe, Miss Barmy and Cheswick would be captured or gone away forever, and there would be no more misunderstandings with her parents. Oh, and Ana would have a home that she actually wanted to go to . . . Emmy rubbed her eyes tiredly. It was a long list already, but it seemed as though she was forgetting something.

"They act like little kids, though," Joe argued. "I

mean, you wouldn't want to let them run around on their own, would you? It wouldn't be safe." He looked over his shoulder at Melly and Gussie, who were now playing leapfrog over Ana's back. "They might remember grown-up stuff, but they don't seem interested in anything but playing."

Emmy stared at the little girls as a thought slowly emerged through the fog in her brain. "Maybe they *know* about the grown-up stuff, but they *feel* like kids. So they'll act the way they feel."

Joe looked interested. "Do you think it's that way for Ratty, too?"

Emmy clapped a hand to her forehead. "I knew I'd forgotten something! Ratty's still a baby!"

"That's the least of our worries," muttered Joe as the little girls pounded out into the hall and down the stairs, with Ana staggering behind.

Emmy and Joe caught up to Ana at the front door. "I can't go outside after them," she said worriedly. "The police are still looking for me."

"Gussie! Melly!" Emmy opened the front door and called out into the night. "Come back! It's too late for you to be out!"

Two little girls streaked past, laughing as they

tagged each other. "We're going to the river park!" called Melly.

"I haven't been on a teeter-totter for sixty-five years!" cried Gussie.

Emmy looked at Joe. "Come on," she said. "I'll take Melly. You get Gussie."

"Oh, my aching back," muttered Joe, but he jumped off the front steps and broke into a sprint.

Emmy and Joe were more than a match for five- and six-year-old runners, and they caught up to the little girls at a low fountain with a bronze Indian in the middle.

"Come home, Gussie," Joe coaxed. "We'll take you to the riverside park in the morning, okay? You'll have more fun when you can see where you're going."

Gussie sat on the edge of the fountain and swung her legs. "But I *want* to be out at night." She grinned up at Joe, and the light from a streetlamp edged the dimple in one cheek. "Mama and Papa *never* let me play outside after dark. But I'm old enough now! I'm seventy-six!"

"Still, it's important to be safe," Joe began, knowing his words were lame, but feeling he had to say them anyway.

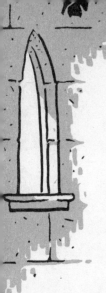

Gussie threw back her curls and laughed, showing a mouthful of baby teeth. "I've been safe my whole life. It's boring. I want to run fast and climb high and go out after dark—"

"And have all the fun we ever missed," finished Melly. She snuggled up to Emmy on the fountain's stone rim. "Come and play?"

"Joe and I shouldn't be out this late, either," said Emmy, feeling like a hypocrite.

Gussie jumped up on the fountain and edged along the rim, her arms outstretched for balance. "You were out late when you got Ratmom."

"Er—" said Joe. He looked at Emmy for help. "It wasn't *that* late."

"Later than it is right now," said Gussie. "*And* you went on the river."

"How did you know about that?" Emmy asked curiously.

Gussie shrugged. "You talked over my bed all the time. You thought I was asleep, but I heard you." She cocked her head. "Old people aren't dumb, you know. They're just old."

"I'm starting to figure that out," said Joe, catching her as she began to teeter. "Listen, why don't we go

back home and talk about it? I'll give you a piggy-back ride."

"Yay!" cried Gussie, leaping on his back and drumming his sides with her heels. "Hi-ho, Silver!"

"Me, too!" begged Melly, tugging at Emmy's hand.

Emmy and Joe staggered on toward the house under the weight of the little aunts. But as they paused to rest for the third time, something darted past in the soft night air.

"Hey!" Emmy whispered, letting Melly slide off her back. "It's a *bat!*"

Joe set Gussie down and got a firm grip on her hand. "Let's go!"

The children ran, Joe and Emmy half dragging the little girls, catching glimpses of the bat as it swooped in and out of the shadows. It headed toward Cucumber Alley, and as the children turned the corner, they saw it clearly for a half second, etched plain against the streetlamp's glow. It seemed to be carrying some kind of paper in its claws. As they watched, the bat fluttered down to the brick face of Melly and Gussie's home and pushed the envelope into the mail slot.

"Catch it!" Emmy whispered, and Joe started

forward, but stopped, confused, suddenly bathed in the circling blue and red lights from a patrol car.

"Now, kids," said Officer Crumlett, "you know it's too late for you to be out. Where are your parents?" He heaved his bulk out of the car and stood looking sternly down at Emmy. "Say, aren't you the Addison ladies' niece? Where are your aunts? Who are these kids?"

Emmy's heart was beating hard and fast. "Um— this is my friend Joe, who is visiting. And"—she hesitated. "These are Melly and Gussie, my . . . relatives." She watched, her fingers itching to grab, as the bat detached itself from the brick wall and fluttered up to the porch roof.

"Melly and Gussie, eh?" Officer Crumlett frowned. "Are you *all* staying with the old ladies?"

The children nodded. Emmy kept an eye on the bat.

"They're not *that* old," said Melly.

"You're only as old as you feel!" Gussie tipped her head back and shook her curls, smiling adorably.

Officer Crumlett's expression softened. Emmy took advantage of the moment to march the little girls up the steps to the front door. "We're really very sorry,

sir. Melly and Gussie wanted to play tag in the dark."
She ushered the little girls inside and wagged her
finger at them. "Go put on your pajamas right this
minute, and I'll be up to tuck you in. Try not to wake
the aunts!"

Officer Crumlett cleared his throat. "I really
should talk to your aunts, but if they're asleep—"

"They've gone to bed," said Emmy firmly, eyeing
the little girls as they skipped up the stairs. "I think
maybe we wore them out. But I'll be sure to tell
them tomorrow what you said about staying inside
after dark."

"Well . . . all right. But you kids turn on the porch
light now, and go in and lock the door. Come on, I
don't have all night."

Emmy cast an anguished glance at the bat hanging upside down from a corner of the porch roof, but
there was nothing she could do. She reached inside
and flicked the light switch. The bat, startled, re-
leased its perch, and flew off into the night sky as
she closed the front door behind her.

The letter was typewritten, addressed to both aunts,
with claw marks on the corner where the bat had

gripped it. When they were sure the policeman had gone away, Gussie and Melly came down again, and the five children crowded around the letter in the front room.

"Aren't you going to open it?" Joe asked Gussie.

She leaned against him on the couch and yawned into his sleeve. "You read it, Joe. I'm sleepy."

Ratmom scurried down from the dollhouse and up onto the back of the couch, where she leaned over Joe's shoulder as he read aloud.

```
My Dear Misses Addison,
    I feel it is my duty to inform
you that your niece Emmaline is
not all she pretends to be. She may
look like a nice girl, but she is
nas$ty and obnoxious, as I have
reason to know. She sneaks out of
your house at night and steals
your boat to go on the river at an
hour when good children are in
their beds. I wonder what she is
hiding from you?
    It is painful to write, but she
```

has been seen at low riverfront bars
with ~~disrip~~ disreputable characters.
Personally, I would not want <u>my</u>
niece hanging about with sleazy
drunks, but of course you may not
mind it. Everyone to her own taste.

> Very Truly Yours,
>
> A ~~Fiend~~ Friend

No one spoke as Joe folded up the paper and put it back in the envelope.

"What does *sleazy* mean?" asked Ratmom.

Emmy stroked Ratmom gently between the ears. "Somebody mean wrote that," she said. "It's not true."

"It's a poison-pen letter," said Gussie. "Don't read it again."

"Do you think it was one of our nosy neighbors?" Melly asked.

Ratmom climbed down from the couch and crept along the baseboards to the bookshelf, where she pulled out something that looked like a dictionary.

Emmy shook her head. "Your neighbors wouldn't know anything about a rodent bar on an island. This

has to be from Miss Barmy. She's hired postal bats before, too, remember?"

She wrinkled her forehead again, trying to think. What had she forgotten? Something about the letter was nagging at the corner of her mind—

"Seedy," said Ratmom in a hollow voice. "Sordid. Squalid."

Emmy looked up. Ratmom was hunched over a book, running a single claw along a line of type. "Grubby," Della went on, in tones of increasing disbelief. "Dodgy. Shady."

"I guess she found the thesaurus," Gussie murmured.

"Untrustworthy?" Della's voice rose. "*Slimy?* That's what they're calling me, now—a slimy drunk?"

"Don't take it personally," Ana said, but the thesaurus slammed shut, and soon after, the sound of sobs came from the interior of the dollhouse.

Emmy opened her mouth to remind Ratmom to cry into the bottle, but then she remembered that it was upstairs where it had been knocked over. Oh, well, Della's tears wouldn't hurt the dollhouse carpet, and Ratty was at a safe distance, sleeping under a blanket on the terrace.

Emmy looked at the letter again. There was a certain amount of truth to it—she *had* gone out at night in the canoe to visit The Surly Rat. And though Emmy wouldn't have called her a sleazy drunk, Ratmom *did* have a root beer problem.

Still, there was a tone of malice to the letter that made it awful to read. At least it had been sent only to the great-aunts, who knew all about Ratmom anyway and understood. It would have been much worse if a letter like that had been sent to her parents . . .

Emmy felt suddenly chilled. That was just the sort of thing Miss Barmy *would* do. What if her parents opened such a letter? Would they come to get her and find the escaped Ana living there? If they did, they would never trust their daughter again. And Emmy didn't even want to think about trying to explain the little aunts to them.

They just *had* to find Sissy and stop Miss Barmy. "If only we could have followed that bat," Emmy muttered.

Joe's eyes strayed to the front window and the streetlamp beyond. "I bet that was one of the bats who carried Sissy off. It might have told us where they took her."

"Do you want to talk to bats?" Gussie sat straight up, wide awake again. "I know where they live."

"Where?"

"In the belfry at St. George's!"

Emmy gasped. How could she have forgotten? Her father had told the story of ringing the bells at the church over and over, but she hadn't remembered the most important part. The bats would fly out of the belfry when the bells rang!

Gussie ran to the front door and turned the knob with both her hands. "Come on, Melly, let's go show them. I always wanted to climb up to the belfry, and they never would let us!"

"Hey, wait!" said Joe. "You heard what Officer Crumlett said—"

Melly giggled behind her hand. "He can't tell me what to do. I was his mother's third-grade teacher!"

"But you can't climb a belfry in the middle of the night!" Ana moved to block their way. "It's too dangerous!"

"That just makes it more *fun!*" cried Gussie, grabbing Melly's hand. Laughing, the two little girls dodged Ana's outstretched hands, dashed down the steps, and disappeared into the dark.

23

EMMY AND JOE caught up with the little aunts at the heavy wooden door of the church.

"We're faster!" crowed Melly.

"Yeah, well, we were watching out for Officer Crumlett," muttered Joe, trying the door. "Come on, it's locked. Let's go home."

Gussie shook her head. "I played the organ here for thirty years. I ought to know where the spare key is by now!" She ran past a corner of the building and out of sight.

Emmy, who was bent over with a stitch in her side, slowly straightened and looked around her. A restless breeze curled around the stone church, and all was dark, shifting shadow, but there was enough light from a thin moon to show the churchyard with its row upon row of gravestones.

She shivered. "Ana's right—it will be dangerous, climbing in the dark."

Melly looked up at her. "But if we try to climb in

263

the daytime, somebody might tell us not to. And then we'll never get to talk to the bats." She paused. "Why didn't Ana come, too?"

"Because the police are *really* looking for her. If Officer Crumlett sees us tonight, we'll just be in trouble. But if he sees Ana, he'll take her away to live with people who don't want her."

"Oh. I remember now." Melly twined her legs around each other and sucked on a strand of her hair. "I don't have a mama and papa anymore, either."

Emmy looked helplessly at the little girl, unsure of what to say. Aunt Melly's parents had been dead for a long time, and Emmy assumed she had gotten used to it—but the five-year-old Melly wanted her mom and dad just like any other kindergartner.

A creaking sound made Emmy startle. The great church door swung open a foot, and Gussie's small face appeared in the gap. "Come *on!*"

Their footsteps echoed loudly in the dark, still church. Faint light from moon and stars filtered in through tall, arched windows and fell in long stripes on the stairs to the choir loft. The organ pipes gleamed coldly as three shadows moved past, following the sound of Gussie's voice ahead.

"Ow!" Emmy banged her shin on something she couldn't see. "Gussie must really know her way around," she muttered.

"Joe!" called Gussie, from far above. "I can't push open the first trapdoor!"

"Coming," Joe called back. "Melly, let Emmy come behind you. That way she can grab you if you fall."

Emmy groped for the next rung of the ladder, hoping it was true. How could she catch someone she couldn't see? "Hang on *tight*, Melly."

"What?" Melly stopped and took a step down.

"And *don't* step on my *hand*," said Emmy through her teeth.

There was a sound of something heavy scraping above and grunting from Joe. A thin, pale light filtered through the trapdoor and was blocked by the children's bodies as they went through one by one.

Emmy moved upward. She hauled herself past the trapdoor and tumbled onto the floor of a square room with pale starlight coming through a narrow window, only to see Melly's shadowed legs already moving up the next ladder.

"How many ladders are there?" Emmy called, but the answer was indistinct. Hand over hand, rung

after rung, she crawled up another long ladder and then another, until at last Melly paused above her.

"Why is everybody stopping?" Melly's childish voice sounded high and excited.

"There's another trapdoor—and it's heavy." Joe's words drifted downward and echoed in the vast immensity of the attic spaces. Something flew past Emmy swiftly in the dark, and she gripped the ladder more tightly, strangling a cry. If the little aunts weren't scared—and they didn't seem to be, they seemed to think it was all a big adventure—then Emmy wasn't about to show any fear. All the same, it was good that it was too dark to see much. If she happened to look down, she wouldn't see how far she had to fall.

Emmy looked up at a scraping, sliding sound and a last grunt of effort from Joe. Moonlight streamed in from the open trapdoor, lighting the arms and faces of the four children on the ladder beneath. Joe stepped up and pushed his head and shoulders through. "Whoa," he said at once. "This is *serious*."

"What?" Emmy called. Her hands were cramping.

Joe stepped carefully down two rungs, standing side by side with Gussie on the ladder. "It opens onto the roof," he said, leaning over. "And it's a loooong way down."

"I want to look!" Gussie cried.

"It's dangerous," Joe said. "Just poke your head through. You'll see."

Joe bent down as Gussie climbed past him, and spoke to Emmy. "I don't think the little girls should go on the roof. There's nothing to stop them from rolling right off."

"If it opens onto the roof," said Emmy, puzzled, "where's the belfry part?"

"There's a side door into the bell tower," said Joe. "You have to crawl along the roof a little ways and then go through— Hey! Gussie! Come back!"

Too late, Joe reached for the little girl's feet, but they disappeared through the square hole as Emmy watched in growing dismay.

"Don't worry, I'm not afraid! It's fun!" Gussie's voice came faintly through the square hole, accompanied by a scrabbling sound on the roof above. There was a creaking sound and a sudden slam, and Emmy's heart jolted.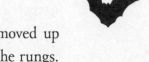

Joe must have jumped, too, or Melly moved up and bumped him, for his feet slipped off the rungs.

He dangled from the side of the ladder and for a moment the moonlight etched his frantically scrabbling legs. Emmy's throat was so thick with fear it felt like cement. And then Joe wedged a knee between the rungs at last, and Emmy was just about to breathe again when the light from the moon was suddenly blocked. Melly scrambled up the rungs past Joe and through the trapdoor. "I'm coming, Gussie!"

"Melly! No!" Emmy cried, but the little girl was already on the roof.

Joe got his feet back on the rungs and looked down at Emmy. "I'm going after them," he said, breathing hard. The moonlight was blocked yet a third time; then Joe's feet kicked briefly in the square space and he was gone.

Emmy had very little interest in climbing along a roof in the middle of the night, but she had even less interest in hanging on a ladder all alone in the dark attic of a church. Besides, Joe would probably need her. Melly and Gussie were as take-charge as any grown-ups, but as reckless as little kids, and it was a dangerous combination. And anyway, wasn't this what they had been trying to do for days now? Find the bats and find Sissy?

Emmy pulled herself gingerly out of the trapdoor, gripping the edges with both hands. She sat with care on the roof, one leg on either side of the peaked ridge, and looked down.

She felt a lightness in her stomach and a quiver at the base of her spine. It was a *very* long way down. The gravestones in the churchyard glimmered like teeth in the moon's light, and Emmy's mouth went dry. If she lost her balance she would land in the graveyard—which would be about right, because she would be dead.

All right, so it had been a mistake to look down. She looked up at the moon, saw a winged shadow dart across it, and followed with her eye as it swooped down and into the open slats of the belfry ahead. Just below the slatted windows of the lower belfry was a square wooden door, and it banged again as Joe went through.

If Joe could do it, so could she. Emmy scooted forward, inch by inch, her palms pressing hard on the split-wood shingles. She reached for the white wooden door, pulled it open, and went through headfirst.

Naturally there was another ladder. She knocked against it in the dark and got a splinter under her

thumbnail. She stumbled, reached blindly for a rung, and found instead a rope that sank with her as she grasped it. High above, a deep, sweet tone sounded.

Childish giggles came from overhead, and a shadowy head popped down from the trapdoor. "Stop ringing the bell, Emmy, and come up here!" said Joe. "The bats won't talk!"

A musty odor filled Emmy's nostrils as she poked her head up into a room already crowded with three children and a looming dark mass that she took to be the bell. She put a hand out to steady herself and felt its cold, pitted iron sway slightly beneath her hand.

A muted light from the high slatted windows lay in stripes across Joe's face. He was speaking to something small and furry, and as the creature spoke in return, Emmy could see a faint gleam of fangs.

"I don't know nothin'," said a squeaky voice that somehow still managed to sound tough. "We got clients, we got a business, and the business don't include talkin'."

Emmy sat on the edge of the trapdoor and braced herself with one foot. "But I thought you were postal bats."

The bat bristled. "Who wants ta know?"

"I'm Emmy Addison. I'm here visiting family—Gussie, here, and Melly, over there—"

"Family? I understand family. Look here." The bat fluttered behind Emmy, who turned and saw another ladder—of *course* there was another ladder, she should have known—and up through yet another trapdoor.

Emmy followed. The musty smell grew stronger and began to take on an odor of gerbils, or sweaty socks. She poked her head through the trapdoor and breathed shallowly through her mouth.

"See? The *famiglia*! Mamas, babies, all safe, and soon the babies will learn to fly! And me, Rocco, I guard them!"

Emmy felt a soft rustling in the air and all around her a sense of something breathing. The fine hairs lifted on her neck, and slowly she backed down the ladder.

Rocco followed, still talking. "Me and the boys—and the girls who ain't mamas—we're the postal bats. But we keep the business in the family, see? We don't blab about our clients, see? You want information, you gotta talk to the boss."

"Where's the boss, then?" Joe asked.

"And *who* is the boss?" Emmy added.

Rocco gave a whistle of surprise. "Everybody knows Manlio's the boss bat. You *must* be from out of town."

"But where *is* he?" Joe repeated.

Rocco shrugged. "He's out on business. I'm not sayin' where. I'll send one of the boys to find him."

Emmy leaned against the wooden slats and looked down at the narrow strip of churchyard that she could see. The view was cheerless, gray and black, with here and there a cold glint of moonlight on an iron railing.

The little aunts were getting tired, too. Emmy could see their lumpy shapes on either side of Joe, and one of them yawned audibly.

"I know how to wake us up," said the other, and a shadowy leg stretched out to nudge the bell wheel. The bell bonged once, loud in the small space, and again before Joe stilled the clapper. "Hush! You don't want to wake the neighbors, do you?"

"I don't want to stay here," said Gussie suddenly. "I want my own bed."

Joe shifted his position and gathered the girls in close. "Lean on me and go to sleep," he said. "It won't be long."

There was a soft smacking sound, as if one had given him a good-night kiss. "I always wanted a big brother," said Gussie sleepily, and nestled beneath his arm.

Emmy sighed. She wasn't excited about staying in the belfry, either, but they *had* to find out where Sissy was. Who knew what trouble she was in?

The sound of the bell had ceased, but another thin sound went on and on, almost like a voice—no, it *was* a voice, and it was coming from outside, far below.

"Listen!" Emmy said softly, and put an ear to the slats.

"It sounds like Ana," whispered Joe after a moment. "But I can't understand the words."

"She shouldn't be outside," said Emmy, alarmed. "Not with the police looking for her. And what's she making noise for?"

"You'd better find out," said Joe. "I'd go, but Gussie and Melly are asleep."

Emmy winced. All those ladders, alone and in the dark . . . "Okay," she said, sounding braver than she felt.

It was a relief to breathe fresh air after the stale, musty odor of bats. Emmy was determined not to look down this time, but once on the roof she

realized that she could call quietly to Ana if she crawled just a little way around the side of the belfry.

"Come . . . down!" Ana's voice was high and thin and urgent, with an edge of hysteria.

"What's wrong?" Emmy called back softly.

"All . . . come down . . . now!" Ana's shadowy form ducked as a car's headlights moved slowly down the street.

Emmy wriggled backward to the trapdoor on the ridgepole. They couldn't keep this up. Someone would call the police on them. She'd have to go all the way down and see what was the matter.

Hours later—well, it *seemed* like hours—Emmy stepped off the last rung, groped her way past the choir loft, and moved cautiously down the broad staircase to the entryway below. Ana was waiting for her just inside the heavy front door.

"This had better be good," said Emmy. "You wouldn't believe how many ladders I had to climb. And I think I swallowed about seven spiders, with all the cobwebs that hit my face."

"Where are the rest of them?" Ana's voice was urgent. "Where are Melly and Gussie?"

Emmy looked at her in surprise. "Up in the belfry with Joe. He just got them to sleep."

"They have to come down! Right now!"

"But we're waiting for Manlio to come back—"

"I don't care!" Ana's voice was panicked. "We have to go up! We have to get them!" She started for the staircase, stumbling in the dark. "I'll go up by myself if I have to!"

"You'll never find it without me along," said Emmy. "It's way too dark."

"I have a penlight," said Ana grimly, switching it on. "Come *on*."

"But I still don't understand why—"

Ana stopped suddenly and pointed the penlight at a bulge in her pocket. "Look. *Now* do you understand?"

"Hey! Get that light out of my eyes!" said Raston, poking his head out. "What is this? The Spanish Inquisition?"

Emmy gasped. "Ratty! You're not a baby anymore! Did Ratmom do something to reverse it?"

"Nope, it just wore off all by itself." Raston turned his head from side to side. "Now, where are those bats?"

Emmy clapped her hands in delight. "Now we don't have to worry about the aunts staying little forever! It will wear off for them, too—"

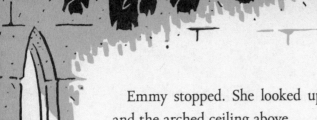
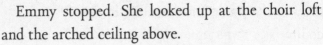

Emmy stopped. She looked up at the choir loft and the arched ceiling above.

"*Now* do you get it?" Ana demanded.

Emmy moved uneasily. "Well, if it wears off, we can just give them some more of Ratmom's tears, right?"

"Ratmom's gone." Ana started for the ladder.

Emmy followed. "You mean you can't find her? Maybe she's sleeping somewhere besides the doll-house—"

"I mean she's *gone*. She left a note and everything. She said she was heading to Rodent City on the train. She said that Ratty hadn't been able to find Sissy here, and so maybe the bats had taken Sissy back to Rodent City. And she said she was *not* too fat and slow to hunt for her daughter."

Raston popped his head out again as Ana climbed. "I didn't want her to go *away*. I just wanted her to get in shape!"

"Oh, no . . . oh, *no* . . ."

"*Hurry*," said Ana.

Up ladders, through trapdoors, up still more ladders, and out onto the roof—it was windier than before, and brisk gusts of air plucked at Emmy's clothes, but she hardly noticed the long drop, this time—then the squeeze through the square wooden door to fall at the foot of yet another ladder. Up and up, rung after rung . . .

There was a sound of rasping breathing and a muffled moan. Emmy took the penlight from Ana and shone it slowly around the lower belfry.

The beam of light was narrow. But it was enough to illuminate the sleeping forms of the aunts, now long and spindly.

Joe's arms were around their frail, elderly shoulders. Something wet glistened on his cheekbone and dropped into darkness. "Gussie's *dying*," he said, very low.

"How are we ever going to get them both down?" whispered Ana.

THE WIND PICKED UP, shearing through the slats of the belfry. Emmy's skin prickled beneath her thin cotton shirt with something more than cold as she looked at her great-aunts. What to do?

"We could ring the bell," said Joe. He wiped his eyes with the back of his hand. "Somebody would come, if we rang it loud and long enough. And then they'd get the fire truck and put a ladder up to the belfry and break a window and carry Gussie and Melly down. But we'd never be able to explain, not in a million years. And they'd find Ana."

Ana smoothed a hand over Gussie's ankle. "I don't have to be here when they come. I could hide."

"But then where would you go afterward?" Joe turned his head, and dim light outlined his cheek. "If Gussie and Melly have to be rescued from the belfry, they're going to be put in a nursing home—or *something*. People are going to think they're crazy or can't take care of themselves. So they sure won't be able to take care of you."

Ana put her chin on her knees. "I could become a rat. Rodent City isn't a bad place to live. I'd get used to it, after a while."

Emmy didn't say anything. An idea was nibbling at the edge of her mind . . .

Joe looked down. "No matter what we do, Gussie isn't going to make it," he said quietly. "But I don't want her to die up here. So whatever we do, we'd better do it fast."

In the darkness, something stirred and pulled away from Joe's side. "Oh, no," said Aunt Melly. "Oh, my dears—oh, *Gussie*." She bent over, as if under a heavy weight.

Emmy shut her eyes, the better to concentrate as her idea took shape. She ran through the possible steps in her mind, one after the other. Could it work? It was complicated. Maybe if everyone helped . . .

There came another gust of wind and with it, a small dark creature blew in, fluttered briefly, and settled on the great bell wheel. "And so we meet again! *Fortunato!* And you have business for to discuss with Manlio, no?" The boss bat looked around, his eyes glinting. "Or there is maybe some *other* reason you intrude my belfry?"

"We need to know where you took Sissy," said Joe.

"Cecilia," Ana added.

"Ah, the sweet fuzzy one!"

"My *sister*," said Raston, between his teeth. He leaped from Ana's pocket to Emmy's shoulder, where he could stare directly into Manlio's small, bright eyes. "And we want her back."

Manlio shrugged. "But this is impossible. I deliver the oh so beautiful Cecilia to the Mamma, I am paid, and this business, it is concluded. Now you want me to take her back? It is against all bat honor! It is against the postal code!"

Raston stiffened. "I don't know where you took my sister, but it wasn't to her mamma!"

Manlio's small eyes narrowed. "Are you to calling me a liar?"

"If the shoe fits, Bat Boy!" said Raston hotly.

Manlio smiled, showing his pointed fangs. "And as for you, if you are to calling me Bat Boy one time more, I tell the boys to sprain your toes, no?"

Emmy covered Ratty's mouth with a finger. "He's sorry, Mr. Manlio—he didn't mean it. But *somebody* lied. Because we *found* Sissy's real mother, and she hadn't seen her daughter for years."

Manlio stared at them, expressionless.

"Who paid you?" asked Joe. "Was it a patchy-looking rat? Or a black rat?"

"A black rat," said Manlio hoarsely. "Are you for to saying that the sweet fuzzy one, she is in *danger*?"

"Terrible danger," said Raston with a sob.

"We need you to help us rescue her," said Ana.

"We have to figure out how to get the aunts down from the belfry, too," said Joe.

"I'm afraid," came Aunt Melly's quavering voice, "that we are causing a great deal of trouble."

"Don't worry, Aunt Melly." Emmy leaned forward. "I have a plan. It might not work, but it's the best I can come up with. Listen."

Sometime later, Emmy leaned back. "What do you think?"

There was quiet in the belfry.

"I like it," Joe said at last. He smoothed Aunt Gussie's hair. "It can't mess things up any worse than they already are, that's for sure."

"Except for you, Emmy," said Ana. "I don't know how you're going to explain these things to your parents."

Emmy sighed. That was the weak point of her plan.

"Explain things later!" cried Raston. "Rescue Sissy now!"

Emmy stroked his back with a soothing hand. The Rat was right. Rescuing people—and rodents—came first.

"I'm sorry to make you so responsible for us," said Aunt Melly. "And we were the ones who got you into this belfry trouble, too. So it must be your choice as to what we do."

Emmy winced. She was starting to hate the word *responsible*. But it sounded different, the way Aunt Melly used it. She didn't mean just checking off a list of chores.

"Okay," said Emmy with sudden decision. "Let's try it. Ana, you'll need your penlight. Ratty, start biting."

"Oh, dear," said Aunt Melly again, looking shocked as she shrank to a tiny version of a little old lady. "Must I really go all the way to a rat?"

"It's better that way," Emmy said. "Nobody thinks twice about a pet rat. But if anyone saw a tiny lady . . ."

282

"I understand," said Aunt Melly, holding out an arm. "Just a little nip, though, Raston, if you please. And be very gentle with dear Gussie."

"I'll do my best," promised the Rat. In moments there were two white rats on Joe's knee—bony, desiccated, with patchy fur and loose folds of skin. One looked to be in a very deep sleep.

Joe bent over the sleeping rat, put an ear to her chest, and listened to the quick rasp of breath. "Hang in there, Gussie," he whispered. "We'll get you to Rodent City as fast as we can."

"And when we find Della, we'll use just *one* of her tears at a time," said Aunt Melly. She looked up, smiling faintly. "I'm afraid we really were quite a handful as youngsters."

"You think?" said Joe, forcing a smile. He tucked Gussie gently into his pocket and stepped over Emmy to get to the trapdoor. "Come on, Ana. Bring Melly and let's get a move on. We've got a train to catch."

"Look for a freight train!" called Manlio. "Tell the yard bats where you want for to go! Giovanni—hey, Giovanni!"

A sleepy-looking bat poked his head downward from the upper belfry. "Yes, boss?"

"You must for to bring them on the night freight—the one that will to pass through Grayson Lake, no? Stefano, at the station, he has the schedule. And then you must to wait for me and the boys. We've got a little, how you say, *business* first."

Emmy watched Joe and Ana start down the ladder, carrying the shrunken aunts. She waited until the top of Ana's head disappeared into darkness and she heard the door to the rooftop slide open.

"Okay, Ratty, my turn." Emmy held out her finger. "Don't chomp. Two bites, please. I'll do my part better if I can scamper."

She shrank like a collapsing balloon, her insides pulling together and the rest of her following. She had barely a moment to feel her legs as small as chalk sticks, and sense the sudden great loom of the bell overhead, when another small nip from Ratty transformed her into something furry with a sniffing nose, alert ears, a long tail, and eyes that were perfect for night vision. All at once she could hear much more bat noise, too. Clicks and peeping calls filled the air around her, higher pitched than she had been able to hear as a human, and louder, too.

Meanwhile, Manlio had been giving orders.

"Ready?" he asked from the windowsill as he hooked two harnesses together. All around them, bats descended, wings fluttering like falling leaves. One by one, they hooked their claws around the long, looped filaments attached to the harnesses and squeezed through the window slats to wait on the sill outside.

Manlio strapped the dual harness on Emmy and Raston, gave a final yank to the buckles, and shoved the two rats out onto the narrow wooden sill.

The wind blew back their fur and pushed at their bodies like an unseen hand. Emmy teetered on the ledge, dug in her hind feet, and gripped Ratty's paw, her small rodent heart pounding many times faster than a human one.

Raston swayed unsteadily.

"Don't look down!" Emmy pitched her voice to be heard above the wind and the peeping bats.

Raston turned and said something that she couldn't hear.

"What?" Emmy shouted.

"What if the harness breaks?" Raston clutched at Emmy's arm, his mouth to her ear. "The buckles looked a little rusty! Maybe I'll just go down the ladders after all—"

285

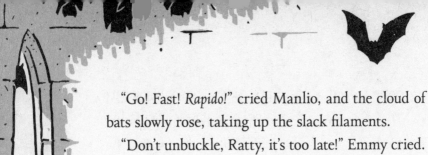

"Go! Fast! *Rapido!*" cried Manlio, and the cloud of bats slowly rose, taking up the slack filaments.

"Don't unbuckle, Ratty, it's too late!" Emmy cried. "Hang on!"

The slender filaments of fishing line tightened and pulled them off the ledge, their toes dragging. Emmy's stomach flipped to her throat as they dropped like two stones, and her mouth opened to scream. But then the cloud of bats adjusted to the weight and they stopped falling, flying instead in fitful jerks as the bats fluttered and dipped, darting forward in a confused pandemonium of wings.

Emmy found herself grinning and unable to stop. She had always wanted to fly! And not in an airplane, either, but like this, blown about by the wind and soaring over rooftops on a starlit summer night.

"Whaf—ats—oop?" Raston's question was half blown away by the wind.

Emmy leaned in close to the Rat's ear. "What fat soup? What kind of a question is that?"

Raston shook his head and put his muzzle next to her face. *"What if the bats poop?"*

Emmy looked up involuntarily.

"Don't look up! You might get it in your eye!"

Emmy looked down, grinning again. Between worrying about a breaking harness and what might land on their heads, the Rat was nervous enough for both of them. "Try not to think about it," she said in his ear as they dipped lower, passing the train station and a pair of traffic lights blinking yellow. "We'll be landing soon, anyway."

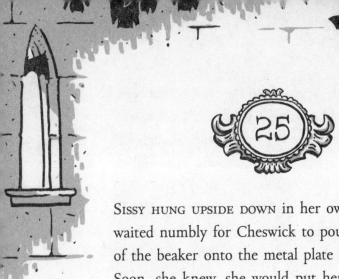

25

SISSY HUNG UPSIDE DOWN in her own harness and waited numbly for Cheswick to pour the contents of the beaker onto the metal plate and roll it out. Soon, she knew, she would put her ulcerated lips on the amber goo and begin yet another round of kissing.

She was weary beyond exhaustion. The pain from her lips had spread past her muzzle, up into her head, and down her neck; the spots where the harness chafed had become oozing sores; and her tail was singed where Cheswick had been careless with the Bunsen burner. Worst was the knowledge there was no one here who cared about her at all, except for how they could use her. And it would never, never end.

There was no chance of rescue. No one knew where she was—except for Manlio and his bats, and they were paid by Miss Barmy. And before long, even the bats wouldn't know, because Miss Barmy was planning a move.

"Hurry up with that, can't you, Cheswick?" The piebald rat, lounging on the windowsill, swung one clawed foot over the edge and bobbed it impatiently. "Don't we have a thousand patches *yet?*"

"Patience, my little lilac blossom," said Cheswick, breathing hard as he pushed the beaker across the counter. "It's difficult to do all this while I'm a rat. Everything takes much longer."

"Well, turn human then," said Miss Barmy, waving a careless paw. "Have the rat kiss you, I don't care."

"You won't mind if I'm a grown human while you're still a rat? Really?" The black rat blinked. "You won't feel as if we're somehow . . . unequal?"

"I've known we're unequal for a long time, Cheswick. But you're improving in many ways. I've quite liked you as a rat, you know."

"That isn't exactly what I—" Cheswick stopped, his pink nose quivering. "You've *liked* me as a rat, Jane?"

"Yes, yes, but go on, get kissed. I want you to pack up everything as soon as we have a thousand patches. Father has the money ready, and he'll pick us up and take us to the airport in the morning. You can take me out of the country as a rat, and we'll start over somewhere—"

"In the south of France!" gasped Cheswick.

"Paris is better," said Miss Barmy. "I hear they have more mirrors. Go on, hurry *up*!"

Cheswick squared his fuzzy shoulders and reached to release the crank arm that held Sissy in place. He lowered her to the counter, where she lay on her side in the harness, unable to move but grateful that she was no longer upside down.

Cheswick pushed her into a sitting position and held on, his paws on her arms. "Kiss me, then," he said. "Kiss me tw— Good heavens!" He peered into her face, looking shocked. "What happened to your lips?"

Cecilia stared at him. What did he *think* had happened? She looked pointedly at the amber goo in the beaker and blinked back the sudden tears that rose against her will.

Cheswick flinched, looking ashamed. "I couldn't help it, you know. I had to get the patches made. You understand, don't you?"

A wave of sudden anger washed over Sissy, leaving her trembling. It wasn't enough that he tied her up and took her away from family and friends and used her cruelly. *Now* he wanted her to say that it was perfectly reasonable. If it wasn't for the fact that she was tied up so tightly that only her paws were free, she would have scratched him.

Cheswick flushed pink from his nose to his tail at her scathing glare. "I'm sorry," he whispered. "But I simply *must*—" He stopped. "Oh, what's the use." He loosened her harness and bent forward. "Just hurry up and kiss me."

Sissy shuddered. She didn't want to kiss this evil man—or if he wasn't evil, he was weak, and that was almost as bad—but she knew she would be made to kiss him in the end. So she got it over with, half wondering whether he would grow or stay a rat like Miss Barmy.

But apparently Cheswick Vole did not have the blocking hatred and resentment of his lady love. He turned first from rat to tiny human, then went from tiny to large as Sissy had seen so many times before. He slid off the countertop, a wizened, skinny man with trousers belted high and greasy hair combed over a bald spot on top.

"You were better-looking as a rat," observed Miss Barmy from her windowsill.

"I know, dear," said Cheswick humbly. He fumbled

with Sissy's buckles, turning his eyes away from her damaged lips. She whimpered a protest, for he had tightened the harness one notch past the usual, but he did not seem to hear.

"*La la la la*," Cheswick sang under his breath. He cranked Sissy up, poured the goop, rolled it flat, and lifted off the top sheet. "Go ahead and kiss. It's the last batch for a while," he added in a low voice, reaching for the X-Acto knife to cut the squares.

Sissy was buckled so tightly that she could not bring her paws up to hold back her whiskers. And if her dragging whiskers ruined this set of patches, Miss Barmy would punish her.

Cheswick lowered and raised the rat and moved her steadily along with the crank arm, looking away all the while. Sissy, trussed so tightly that her arms were going numb, had never felt so helpless. Each kiss burned like fire. She could not use her paws to wipe the caustic goop away between kisses, and when a scab broke open on her lips, it took all her strength not to cry out in pain.

But though Sissy held in her cries, she could not stop her broken lips from bleeding, nor her tears from falling. And with her tears, the blood fell in droplets, splashing onto the goo and sinking into the patches without a trace.

It was dark in the boarded-up laboratory. The Bunsen burner, connected by a rubber tube to a gas tank beneath the counter, burned steadily, turned down low for the night. On the window ledge, Miss Barmy snored faintly.

Cheswick was still awake. He sat at the desk across the room, making tally marks on a sheet of paper as he counted the thousand patches he had stockpiled, and packed them in a carryall bag.

Cecilia had been taken out of her harness and put in a cage on the counter for the night. She peered through the bars at the final batch of Sissy-patches, cut and ready on the metal plate. Would Cheswick forget to pack them with the others? Maybe she could avoid punishment for ruining them after all.

She shut her eyes wearily, too tired and heartsick to care. If only she had not trusted Manlio—if only she hadn't been so stupid about the letter! But she had so wanted to believe it came from her mother.

And now she was going away forever. Not only would she never see her mother—she would never

see her friends or her beloved brother again. And what must Rasty think of her? Would he think that she was happily living with their ratmom and had forgotten her promise to send the bats for him?

Sissy felt a pain in her heart that was worse than anything she had suffered so far. She could not bear to think that her brother would believe she had abandoned him. If only she could give him a message!

She *could*. She knew how to write, now. But she had no pencil, no paper . . .

Sissy blinked. Had something moved, in the corner? She stared at the flap of tar paper that covered the opening to the street. No, it was perfectly still. It must have been Cheswick's moving shadow.

She shook her head impatiently. She had something more important to think about than shadows. She had her claws, and she had the bottom of the cage, and she had the whole night ahead to scratch out a message for Rasty. Someday, Professor Capybara would come back to his old lab, and sooner or later he would clean the cages. And when he did, he would find her message and tell Raston. Someday, her brother would know the truth.

Sissy had painfully scratched the first

word—"Dear"—when she saw another moving shadow out of the corner of her eye, then another. She lifted her head, ears pricked and nose at the alert. There was a musty smell, somehow familiar.

Bats. Bats crawling in, moving crabwise along the baseboards, one after the other in single file. Bats that had carried her away, bats that could not be trusted—

Sissy nearly squeaked out loud as a fluttering shadow fastened itself to the side of her cage. There was a tiny *click*, and the door swung open.

"The lock, she does not exist that can stop Manlio!" whispered the bat, and his fangs gleamed as he grinned.

Sissy stepped back. "You *lied* to me!" she whispered.

Manlio put a wing to Sissy's lips. "Hush, my sweet fuzzy one. The bad rats lied to *me*, and now I come to set you free."

Sissy winced as his wing touched her fresh scabs.

Manlio turned her shoulders so that she faced the glowing Bunsen burner. "*Mamma mia!*" he gasped. "The poor sweet lips! I did not know the Barmy rats could to be so cruel! I was to believing what they tell

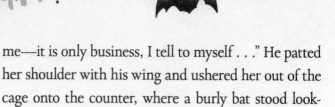

me—it is only business, I tell to myself . . ." He patted her shoulder with his wing and ushered her out of the cage onto the counter, where a burly bat stood lookout, eyeing the Bunsen burner with interest.

"Keep the eyes open, Rocco," murmured Manlio. "Is possible we can to do this quietly."

A slender shadow scrambled up the counter leg, crouched with ears alert, and resolved itself into a soft gray rat with a white collar of fur around its neck. "Good to see you, Sissy," whispered Emmy Rat. "Okay, let's go."

A second rodent shape scrabbled over the edge of the counter, panting. "Sissy!" cried Raston hoarsely, staring at her lips in shock.

"There goes the quiet," muttered Manlio. "I thought the Ratty brother was to wait outside with the harness?"

"But how could I, when my sister was in here? Anyway, you need someone fit, someone flabulous—Sissy, I'm going to *rescue* you!"

Sissy embraced her brother, weeping for joy.

"Cry later," said Emmy, glancing at Cheswick across the room. "Go *now*."

"But look what they've done to her!" Raston reared

back, his tail stiff with fury, and caught sight of the patches on the metal plate that Cheswick had forgotten in his haste. He took two hops toward it, cocked his hind foot, and kicked.

"Don't bother, Rasty!" Sissy put a paw on his arm as the first patch went flying. "These are ruined—they've got whiskers and blood and tears in them, so they'll never work for Miss Barmy."

"I'd like to kick *her*," said Raston.

On the windowsill, the piebald rat's snores stopped abruptly. She flicked an ear, rolled over, and was still.

"Hush, Ratty!" Emmy was tense beneath her fur. "Take Sissy and get out of here!"

Raston hopped off the metal plate—and landed on the X-Acto knife handle. It rolled under his hind foot with a metallic sound, his feet flipped up, and he landed on his backside, yelping. Cheswick Vole jumped up from the desk, startled, and came at them with urgent strides.

Manlio gave a piercing whistle. From all over the room, small black shadows uttered shrill battle cries and darted straight for Cheswick's head in a wildly fluttering cloud of leathery wings and sharp fangs.

"Get away!" he bawled, flapping his hands like frantic windmills. "Jane!"

The piebald rat on the windowsill awakened with a snort.

"Go *on!*" cried Emmy, shoving Cecilia and Raston.

"Move, sweet fuzzy!" screamed Manlio, fanning his wings at Sissy, who seemed to be paralyzed with fear. "Go!"

"Cheswick! *Stop that rat!*" Miss Barmy leaped off the windowsill, teeth bared in a snarl.

The darkened laboratory was filled with swooping dark shapes and the *flit flit* of bat wings. Cheswick groped blindly, grabbed the first thing his hands touched—the video projector—and swung it by the cord with a muffled grunt. The bats, with their built-in sonar, easily eluded this, but as Emmy watched, the cord detached and the projector went sailing. It crashed into the window in a shattering sound of breaking glass, hit the boards behind it, and fell to the counter with a heavy *thunk*, just missing Miss Barmy.

The sound jolted Sissy and Ratty out of their paralysis. The two rats skidded down the counter, across the floor, and under the tar-paper flap.

"Noooooo!" cried the piebald rat, high and despairing.

"Jane—I'll get her back, I *will*." Cheswick fumbled with the front door deadbolt.

"Go, go, go, GO!" shouted Manlio, and the bats streamed past him and out beneath the loose tar paper.

Miss Barmy started toward Emmy, her claws outstretched. "I recognize you, Emmaline Addison! It's all *your* fault!"

"Stay back!" shouted Rocco, picking up the X-Acto knife and holding it like a bayonet. Out of the corner of her eye, Emmy saw the last column of bats filing out the hole.

Manlio fluttered back up to the counter. "Emmy, *now!*"

But Emmy was fascinated by the drama unfolding before her. Miss Barmy, her whiskered face distorted with rage, was backing away on the counter in defeat. And over at the front door Cheswick, full size as he was, desperately rattled the knob but couldn't seem to get it to turn.

"You want me to trim her claws, boss?" Rocco grinned, showing Miss Barmy his fangs. "Maybe clip her ears a little?"

Manlio shook his head. "We must to catch the

train," he called over his wing. "Hurry, we meet you outside!"

The piebald rat suddenly jumped off the counter and scampered behind the sheet that had served as a screen.

Emmy grinned at the rodent shadow moving behind the screen. Good riddance! She turned to follow Rocco but paused at the metal plate with its sheet of patches.

"Wait a second." She grabbed one of the small bags nearby.

"Hurry, there is no time!" Rocco fluttered back to the counter. "Anyway, those are the bad patches, no?"

"I don't care." Emmy stuffed the patches rapidly into the bag. "I don't want Miss Barmy to get her paws on *any* of these, bad or not—"

She stopped with her paw in the sack, frozen, as behind the screen a shadow grew suddenly large.

Emmy's mouth went dry. Miss Barmy must have had more patches lying around . . . *lots* more.

Emmy took a step back, stumbling, and hid the bag behind her. "Rocco," she cried, sick with dread as Miss Barmy, human and tall, headed straight toward them.

Rocco grabbed the Bunsen burner and held it like a flamethrower, sweeping it from side to side to make an arc of protection for Emmy and himself. Miss Barmy stopped and smiled nastily.

The front door burst open with a splinter of wood, a screech of hinges, and a manly grunt from Cheswick. He dashed out into the windy night, but after a few moments, he came back in, slowly.

"Well?" said Miss Barmy, never taking her eyes off Emmy and Rocco.

"No luck," Cheswick said. "The bats had the kissing rat in some sort of sling, and they flew up as soon as they saw me."

"Never mind," said Miss Barmy. "I heard the bat say they were going to the train station. We'll follow them. And, Chessie?"

"Yes, my little turtledove?"

"Is there any way to shut off that annoying Bunsen burner?"

"Why, of course!" Cheswick Vole reached under the counter and turned a knob on the propane tank.

"Excellent," said Miss Barmy, and her smile widened as the flame sputtered and died.

Rocco dropped the useless Bunsen burner and

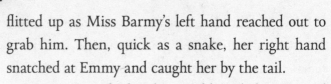

flitted up as Miss Barmy's left hand reached out to grab him. Then, quick as a snake, her right hand snatched at Emmy and caught her by the tail.

Emmy squeaked—she couldn't help it—and clutched the bag of patches to her chest as Miss Barmy lifted her by the tail and dangled her in the air. Rocco fluttered fiercely about Miss Barmy's head, but he was just one bat, and the woman simply ignored him.

Emmy twisted in a frantic effort to free herself, as Miss Barmy's fingers pinched tighter.

"Go, Rocco!" Emmy cried. "Keep Sissy safe, and make sure they bring Gussie to Ratmom for the tears!"

Rocco swooped off toward the open door. Emmy squealed helplessly as she was swung around and dropped.

There was a metallic scrape; there was a click.

She was locked in a cage. And Miss Barmy had the key.

26

EMMY STARED at Ana's face, which looked out plaintively from the poster on the train station wall. MISSING, it said above the picture, and below was a lot of small print Emmy couldn't read from her cage.

She wished she had Manlio's skill at lock picking. But even if she did, it would be hard to pick the lock while Cheswick was holding her cage to his chest—and harder still to get out of the train station with its heavy doors and bright lights.

"What do you mean, there are no trains to Grayson Lake this time of night?" Miss Barmy demanded. "I *know* there are night trains. I've *heard* them. They have a very *distinctive* whistle."

"They sound like this," said Cheswick helpfully. "Whoooo . . . whoo whoo whooooo . . ."

The stationmaster looked at him over his half glasses.

"Well?" Miss Barmy tapped her fingernails against the ticketing booth.

"You must have heard a freight train," said the stationmaster, shuffling through a stack of papers. "They only stop here to pick up crew; they don't carry passengers. Is there anything else I can help you with?" He looked up, and his bored expression changed. "Are you allergic? Your nose seems to be . . . twitching."

"Another patch, Cheswick!" Miss Barmy cried.

Emmy slid into the wire wall of her cage as Cheswick set it on the ticket booth ledge. He dug in the carryall bag slung over his shoulder, pulled the backing off a patch, and pressed it against Miss Barmy's neck. Her nose, which had turned pink, moist, and twitchy, subsided into a more human aspect, and the light coating of fur that had begun to sprout behind her ears disappeared.

The stationmaster blinked.

"I have a medical condition." Miss Barmy pulled a hand mirror from the carryall and glanced at it with satisfaction. "It comes and goes."

"I see," said the stationmaster faintly. He stared at Miss Barmy and adjusted his glasses.

"When does the train to Grayson Lake pick up crew tonight?" Miss Barmy's voice was smooth as syrup as she tucked the mirror in the bag once more.

The stationmaster stared at her, seemingly fascinated. "I don't know that I should tell you. There are rules about giving out information to the general public, and regulations . . ." He extracted a paper from the pile before him and held it up. "See?"

Jane Barmy leaned forward, ignoring the list of rules. "But I just love trains, and I so *admire* anyone who *knows* about them . . ."

"Hey! *I* know about trains—*eep!*" Cheswick's voice cut off abruptly as Miss Barmy kicked him beneath the counter.

"Could you possibly tell me?" Miss Barmy ran a finger along the edge of the ticket booth and lowered her eyes, smiling. "I can see you're the kind of man who decides things for himself. You look so terribly *strong*. Do you work out?"

"Er . . ." The stationmaster flushed pink and loosened his necktie.

"Perhaps we can watch the train together!" Miss Barmy fluttered her eyelashes. "Nighttime arrivals are so exciting, don't you think? And then after it

goes away, you can explain the policies, and show me *all* your regulations."

Emmy gripped the metal bars of her cage, hanging on by her claws. Cheswick Vole was not a smooth jogger. With every lurching stride, the cage banged against his leg, giving Emmy a jolt that she felt in her stomach. She tried very hard not to throw up.

The small drawstring bag was loose in the cage. It sailed past her head and she ducked, glaring at it. If only she hadn't wasted time collecting that last batch of bad Sissy-patches! They weren't worth getting caught by Miss Barmy, that was for sure.

And now what? She could hardly think. Almost every idea she'd tried so far had gone wrong, starting with not telling her parents about Ana and Aunt Gussie. She should have just let her mother and father take care of everything.

But no. If she had done that, then right this minute Ana would be living with people who didn't want her and Aunt Gussie would be dying in a nursing home.

The cool night air blew through the bars and ruffled Emmy's fur. Was it any better, she wondered miserably, for Ana to be without a home at all? Or for Gussie to be four inches tall and dying in Joe's pocket? Or for herself to be locked in a cage, with no way out?

Cheswick slowed to a walk, and then stopped, breathing hard. He set the cage down and conferred with Miss Barmy in a low voice.

Emmy rocked on her hind legs as Cheswick picked up the cage once more. They were in a dark section of town, between streetlights. There was a sound of sliding gravel, and the metal floor tilted—they were going uphill—and then branches scraped her cage as they pushed through a belt of undergrowth.

She knew she should have tried to explain to her parents about the rodents. She could have shown them, the way she did with Aunt Melly, and they would have had to believe her. They would have understood about her messy room then, too.

But Aunt Melly had been willing to keep the rodents' powers a secret because she, herself, had a secret she needed kept in return. Emmy's parents had no such reason to keep quiet. And what would happen to Sissy and Ratty and Ratmom if the world found out there were rats who could shrink people

and make them grow—not to mention a rat whose tears could make someone young again?

Emmy knew exactly what would happen. Raston's teeth would be worn to nubs, Sissy's lips would never heal, and Ratmom would be forced to cry for the rest of her life.

The cage leveled. Miss Barmy whispered something to Cheswick that Emmy didn't quite catch. Hands fiddled with the lock on Emmy's cage.

All at once Cheswick reached in and grabbed her around the middle. Swiftly he forced her mouth open while Miss Barmy wedged a shoelace behind her gnawing teeth and between her jaws, tying it tightly behind her head, and then around her front paws. Before Emmy had time to realize what was happening she was back in the cage. The lock clicked shut.

Miss Barmy looked in through the top of the cage, sneering. "Just to make sure you can't warn your friends . . . if they *are* your friends. They abandoned you, didn't they?"

Emmy, tied, gagged, and caged, with the taste of shoelace in her mouth, felt a rising fury and despair that almost choked her. The floor of the cage tilted beneath her like a ship at sea as Cheswick moved forward and Miss Barmy whispered at his side. Emmy swayed back and forth with each stride, hardly caring that she couldn't understand what they were saying. Even if she did hear their plans, what could she do to help herself or her friends? Just exactly *nothing*.

It seemed a long time before Cheswick set the cage silently on the ground and squatted beside Miss Barmy. Emmy rubbed her muzzle with her tied paws and looked out from behind the crisscrossed bars. Just ahead, untrimmed trees swept their branches low to the ground. Beyond the open lacework of leaves were twin rails, gleaming coldly in the moonlight.

The station lights were not too far away. For just a moment Emmy was confused—surely they had walked farther than that?—until she realized what must have happened. Cheswick and Miss Barmy had gone a long way down the line and then had come back secretly, downwind from the station.

There was no train that she could see.

There were bats, though. She could see them huddled near the steel rails, and she could hear them somewhere in the shadows on the other side of the

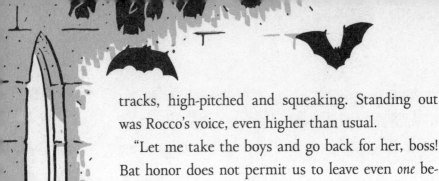

tracks, high-pitched and squeaking. Standing out was Rocco's voice, even higher than usual.

"Let me take the boys and go back for her, boss! Bat honor does not permit us to leave even *one* behind!"

Emmy glanced quickly up at Miss Barmy. Had she heard?

But Miss Barmy, peering through low-hanging branches, was turned away, her whole body tense as she looked down the long tracks. And Cheswick, the carryall slung on his shoulder, was watching Miss Barmy for the first clear signs of approaching rodenthood.

Emmy let out her breath softly. Perhaps the bat voices only seemed loud to her sensitive rodent ears. She wished she could tell Rocco to be quiet. It was nice that he wanted to rescue her, but if he kept talking, Miss Barmy would find Sissy for sure.

"No." Manlio's voice was piercingly high, too. "We must to send away the sweet fuzzy one safe, no? And the old sickly one, she must to go also, with the harness—"

"But, boss! We can do that *and* pick up Emmy, too!"

Emmy looked up at Miss Barmy and Cheswick in alarm. They *must* have heard that . . .

But no.

"Later, Rocco," said Manlio. "No time now—the train, she comes soon."

Emmy pricked up her ears. It had been so gradual that she had hardly noticed, but now she realized she had been hearing it for a while—a low hum, a distant rumble, growing in volume as she listened. And then came the sound of another voice from the shadows—Joe's voice.

"Hey, you guys!" Joe's whisper carried clearly. "I can hear the train!"

Miss Barmy turned her head at once, clenching Cheswick's arm. The two of them stared in the direction of Joe's voice, their eyes searching the shadows.

Emmy's whiskers stiffened. There was something here she didn't understand. Why could Miss Barmy hear Joe's voice—but no one else's?

There was a high snickering from the bats near the tracks. "*We've* been hearing the train, like, for-*ever!*" piped a young voice. "Doesn't he ever listen to the rails?"

"Hush! For shame!" An older bat voice overrode the thin, peeping laughter. "Never make fun of those who are less fortunate! Not *everyone* can have bat ears!"

"*Scusi*," piped the young bat. "Sorry. But at least I didn't say it so the humans heard me."

"Very noble," said the old bat dryly. "Now, lower your pitch. It's not polite to talk about people at a frequency they can't hear."

Emmy nearly choked on the shoelace. That was why Miss Barmy and Cheswick hadn't heard the bats! Bats could speak at a higher pitch than humans could hear! And now that she was a rat, she could hear that frequency, too. Could she speak at that high pitch, too? Not with a stupid shoelace in her mouth, she couldn't . . .

"Here is what we must to do." Manlio's voice from the shadows was low enough for humans to hear. "Dry your tears, my sweet fuzzy Cecilia. We *will* to rescue Emmy Rat—but *first* we see you off safe on the train, we send a message to Guido to expect a so large package, we take care for the old sick one, no? And then—"

"And then," finished Rocco, "we will mount a bat attack! For honor! For *famiglia*!"

"Emmy's like family to *me*," came Raston's voice. He sneezed twice.

"I don't want to leave without her," said Sissy.

The train's rumble grew louder. But Miss Barmy paid no attention. She gripped Cheswick's sleeve, her body rigid, as she listened to the conversation she could now hear.

"But you must, sweet fuzzy," said Manlio. "Leave all to the bats. We will to outwit the Barmy person!"

Unnoticed in her cage, Emmy worked her paws together, trying desperately to hook one of her claws in the shoelace knot. If she could get her paws free, she could untie the gag. Then she could warn her friends that Miss Barmy was there and listening to every word.

"We promised we'd get the aunts to Rodent City and find Ratmom," came Ana's voice from the shadows, "but if Emmy's a *prisoner*—"

Joe's voice tumbled over hers, rough with worry. "Are you *sure* you and the bats can deal with Miss Barmy?"

Manlio chuckled. "We make her the offer she can't refuse, see?"

"I can't leave Gussie . . . but how can I leave dear Emmy?" Aunt Melly gave a terrible sob. "After all, I'm her great-aunt, even if I am a rat now. And I still don't see," she added, her thin tones quavering up the

scale, "why you had to turn me into a rat. I simply can't get used to these *whiskers.*"

"I have explained this already, no?" Manlio sounded impatient.

"She didn't hear," said Ana quickly. "Aunt Melly, it's *safer* if we're rodents."

"It's dangerous for *people* to hop a freight train," Joe put in. "But rodents are quicker and way more agile—"

"They can leap, and climb straight up, and fall fifty feet without getting hurt," Ana said.

"And flabulous rodents (I name no names)," said Raston, "can leap even farther, and climb higher, and—wait a minute. We're talking fifty *rat* feet, right?"

"Er . . ." said Ana.

"Plus it's illegal for humans to hop a freight," Joe went on, "but there's no law against a *rodent* doing it. Not so far, anyway," he added.

"I'm afraid," came Gussie's voice, weak and low, "I'm causing you all . . . far too much trouble."

"Don't worry about that," said Joe swiftly. "Manlio, are you sure the train is going to stop here?"

Manlio grunted. "If Stefano says it stops—then it stops."

The earth trembled and a whistle sounded piercingly, two long tones, one short, one long again. A bell clanged—ting *ting*, ting *ting*—and around the curve a dark looming shadow appeared, with a bright headlight high and centered, lighting up the track before it. The engine passed them with a roar and a clatter, the great steel wheels singing, and then car after car went by in a screech of metal and a clanking, hissing sound of brakes. At last, with a sliding sound as of something heavy dragging, the train stopped. But still the engine hummed and whined, breathing as if it were a live thing.

A bat swooped in fast from the eaves of the station, calling, "Hurry! *Presto!* Get on one of the hopper cars—the train's going as soon as the new crew gets on!"

Emmy peered into the night. Her friends were hidden on the other side of the train, but she could see two hopper cars shaped like two thick, flat Vs. At the front and back ends of each was a little platform or ledge with space to sit, and at the side was a ladder to the top of the car. Between the cars, and joining them, was a knuckle of steel. But the ledges were high off the ground—could rats really jump

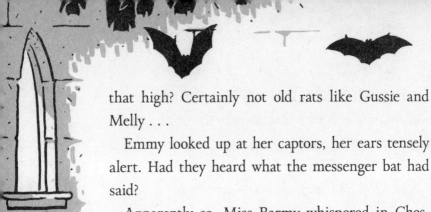

that high? Certainly not old rats like Gussie and Melly . . .

Emmy looked up at her captors, her ears tensely alert. Had they heard what the messenger bat had said?

Apparently so. Miss Barmy whispered in Cheswick's ear; Cheswick nodded and moved stealthily to the train, taking up a position out of sight. Emmy, left behind with Miss Barmy, tried vainly to spit out the shoelace gag.

The shadow of a girl appeared in the gap between the cars. Ana hoisted herself up onto the front hopper's platform, and reached down to take a much smaller shadow, one with a dangling tail, from Joe's hands. She tucked the rodent carefully in a corner, and reached for the next, and then a third.

"You don't need to hand *me* in!" cried Raston, and a fourth small shadow showed briefly above the ledge, leaping. There was a thud, another leap, and then a scrabbling sound of claws on metal. Joe gave the Rat a boost and climbed up on the platform himself.

"You didn't have to help me," said Raston, breathing hard. "A flabulous rat likes to challenge himself with ever-increasing levels of fitness difficulty—"

"Shut up, Ratty, and just bite us, okay?" said Joe. He sat down on the platform next to Ana, his legs dangling. "Bite us twice!"

"You *could* say *please*," said the Rat. He sniffled and sneezed again. "Is there some ragweed around here? I have allergies."

"Hurry, Ratty!" Ana said through her teeth.

The two child-sized silhouettes dwindled, shrank, and grew fuzzy around the edges. At the distant station, a door banged and human figures stepped onto the train. "Good-bye! Good-bye!" called the bats, fluttering up and away from the tracks. And then, from the shadows, a tall, bony shadow moved in—and grabbed.

There was a squeal of terror. But Cheswick Vole, his hands gripped around a small gray rodent, was already trotting back to the cage where Miss Barmy waited with her fingers on the latch.

"Quick! Give the rat to me!" Miss Barmy reached out eagerly.

"Watch out! It's trying to bite!" said Cheswick, gripping tighter.

"And when I do, you're going to shrink!" howled Raston, as Cheswick shoved him in the cage head-first.

Miss Barmy gasped. "You got the wrong rat, Cheswick! You got the shrinking one!" She staggered to the hopper and leaped onto the platform. "I'll get you!"

The train emitted a sudden series of clanks. The engine noise increased. Miss Barmy was kneeling on the platform, her hands snatching and grabbing.

"I've got them cornered, Cheswick!" Miss Barmy cried. "Bring the cage! Hurry!"

Cheswick snatched the cage and ran, joggling Emmy and the Rat from side to side. "Here, Jane! Which one is she?"

"They're going to tell me right now," said Miss Barmy, smiling with bared teeth. "Is it *this* one?" Her fingers tightened on something furry.

"No!" cried Joe, his voice both fierce and frightened. "She's old! She's sick! Put her down!"

"Then give me the kissy rat!" snarled Miss Barmy. She opened her clenched hand to show a frail, elderly rat, its sides heaving with the effort to breathe.

Emmy felt a cold shiver run beneath her fur as she stared out between the crisscrossed metal bars at her helpless great-aunt.

There was the sound of a bell, a clank. The train lurched forward.

Cheswick trotted alongside the slowly moving train. "Hurry, Jane! Get off *now!*"

"I'm not getting off until I get the right rat, Cheswick! I'll squish them one by one if I have to!"

Sissy stepped forward, her paws in the air. "Put her down," she said, her voice trembling but stern. "And let Rasty and Emmy go free. I'll come."

"Jane!" yelped Cheswick, jogging faster and gripping the ladder with his free hand.

Miss Barmy smiled cruelly. She reached out and gripped Sissy's unresisting body, discarding Aunt Gussie on the platform floor.

Cheswick threw the cage onto the empty platform of the car behind, took three running steps, and heaved himself on board. Emmy and Raston bumped heads as the cage landed with a bang.

They were passing the station. The yard lights flashed briefly on Cheswick, Miss Barmy, the huddled rats, the cage, and then all was dark again. The bats, realizing too late that something had gone wrong, surged up to them in a flapping cloud, only to fall back as the train gathered speed.

"Shove the kissy rat in the cage," said Miss Barmy. Cheswick lifted the unresisting Sissy from Miss

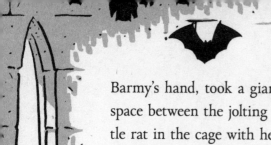

Barmy's hand, took a giant step across the rackety space between the jolting cars, and tumbled the little rat in the cage with her brother and Emmy. He snapped the lock shut.

"Hey! Let the others go!" cried Sissy in a passion, rattling the bars with her paws. "That was the deal!"

"Oh, I'll let them go," said Miss Barmy. "Just not right *now*."

27

EMMY SAT HUDDLED in the cage and watched the countryside flash past, gray and formless in the hour before dawn. Now and then she could pick out a stray pinprick of light from a house or farmyard, gone so fast she wasn't sure she had seen it at all.

Leaning against her in a warm and fuzzy bunch were Ratty and Sissy, fast asleep, lulled by the steady *clack clack* of rolling wheels and the rocking sway of the hopper. And across the rattling space between the cars, on the rear platform of the hopper ahead, was everyone else.

Miss Barmy sat curled up in one corner, a dark, malevolent shadow, with Cheswick next to her, keeping watch. Every time she got a little furry around the edges, he would dig in his carryall bag for yet another patch to keep his lady love human.

Cheswick watched the four rodents in the other corner, too. And he had told them strictly not to move from their corner or talk. But what he didn't

realize was that Joe had been steadily insulting him for hours, in the high-pitched squeaks no human could hear.

Emmy had been too worried to laugh. Once Sissy had untied the shoelace gag with her clever paws, Emmy had spent most of her time trying quietly to pick the lock on the cage. But she was no Manlio; she had not learned to pick locks from babyhood; and when her claw broke off in the lock, jamming it completely, she gave up in despair.

She and the others had discussed plans, of course. They had discussed them all night long, in the ultrasonic frequency that Miss Barmy could not hear. But every idea seemed stupid, or hopeless, or both. And when Joe tested Cheswick's watchfulness—when he moved just slightly away from the corner of the platform—Cheswick's big hand had come down around the unconscious Gussie, and his thumb and forefinger had encircled her small neck, and Joe had not tried to move again.

Emmy's eyes fell on the small drawstring bag with its damaged Sissy-patches, crumpled in a corner of the cage. She had managed to keep those few patches from Miss Barmy, but it was probably a useless gesture. Cheswick had a huge bag full, and they seemed to be working just fine.

Sissy shifted in her sleep, and a moan of pain escaped her damaged mouth. Emmy put out a paw and stroked her gently, but Sissy's moan turned into a short, distressed sob.

Emmy's whiskers stiffened. Sissy was having another nightmare. And if Miss Barmy succeeded in taking her to France, Sissy would probably have many more.

Emmy's small rodent heart beat high in her throat. She had heard all of Miss Barmy's plans now: details about how they would elude the police, get money from the bank, fly out of the country. Cheswick and Miss Barmy had discussed everything, raising their voices to be heard over the clank and rumble of the moving train. Emmy only wished the train noise had been louder so she didn't have to listen—it made her ill.

The miles rolled on, and the sky grew lighter. The dark, windy night had given way to a clear, windy morning, and on the eastern horizon the deep blue sky curved down to a pink edge, just showing above the distant trees. Chuk *chuk*, chuk *chuk*, chuk *chuk*

went the train, like the tick of a clock, and Emmy knew that time was running out.

There was one idea—a hopeless, stupid idea—that had been dismissed as too dangerous by the others. But it lingered on the outskirts of Emmy's mind, refusing to go away. It was a simple plan. And it *might* work.

Or course if it failed, she would be squished, suffocated, and cut in little pieces.

Ding ding ding ding came the train's bell, then the whistle: *DOOoot! Doot DOOOOoooot!*

A crossing flashed past. Was it the town before Grayson Lake? Emmy wasn't sure, but she knew they must be getting close.

Miss Barmy leaned forward to look at the passing countryside. The houses were more frequent now, and the roads had an occasional car or truck.

"The moment it stops, Cheswick, we jump off," Miss Barmy said. "Get everything ready—we can't waste any time. Father was going to take us to the airport, and he still can."

"Yes, my little chrysanthemum." Cheswick settled the carryall more firmly on his shoulder, stepped across the gap between cars, and bent down to grip the handle of the cage. "Aren't you excited?" he said to Emmy. "You're going to travel overseas! You'll learn to speak French like a native!"

Emmy stared at him through the bars of the cage. It was true. If they didn't get away—today, this minute—she and Ratty and Sissy would all end up in France. And they *would* be there long enough to learn to speak the language. They would be there for the rest of their lives.

Emmy felt a gathering sensation inside her, as if all her whirling fears had compacted into one still point of furious rebellion. "I'm going to do it." She said the words before she could change her mind.

"Do what?" Joe spoke as she had, in a frequency higher than any human could hear.

Emmy told him.

"But you might die!" cried Joe. "All of you might die."

Ratty clutched Sissy with both his paws.

"Do you think I don't know that?" Emmy reared back, her muzzle high. "But if we go to France—if we stay their prisoners for the rest of our lives—we're going to *wish* we were dead, every single day."

There was a silence.

"She's right," said Ana at last. "I ought to know."

The train's sound changed and grew suddenly louder—*WHAPPETA WHAPPETA*—and Emmy looked up to see that they were passing through a cut in a hill, with stone layered high on either side. And then they were through, and the sunrise flamed into the gap in colors of peach and gold. A water tower stood guard as the train passed, and the morning light glinted on the rooftops of a town and danced in sparkles across a familiar lake, beautifully blue and clear.

"Listen." Emmy stared hard at Ana and Joe. "Miss Barmy and Cheswick will follow us because it's Sissy they want. But no matter what happens, you have to take care of the aunts. Promise?"

Joe pulled at his whiskers and looked at Cheswick and Miss Barmy, who were leaning out in their eagerness to see their destination.

"Promise!" demanded Emmy. "You won't be able to help us if things go wrong, but you *can* help Gussie and Melly. Do you have the harness ready? Do you remember all of Stefano's instructions?"

Ana nodded. "The harness, the signal, the postal bats, then on to Rodent City to find Ratmom."

"The bats won't be able to fly all the way to Rodent

City. It's almost too bright for them already. So one of you will have to go, and one of you stay with the aunts at the station."

"Why don't you just send an Emergency Rodent Alert?" Raston asked.

"Oh, Rasty!" cried Cecilia. "What a wonderful idea!"

"But what's a—"

"*Aiiiieeeee! Aiiiieeeee! Aiiiieeeeeeeeeee!*" shrieked Raston.

Emmy glanced quickly at Miss Barmy. It seemed almost impossible that she hadn't heard. But, no, as long as it was a high enough frequency, a sound could be as loud as a jet engine and no human would ever hear it.

"Let me get this straight," said Joe. "We do this sort of screechy thing—"

"*AIIIIEEEEE! AIIIIEEEEE! AIIIIEEEEEEEEEEE!*" screamed Raston.

Joe removed his paws from his sensitive ears. "Right. Like that. And then we add our message?"

Ratty and Sissy nodded together. "Keep it short," said Ratty.

"Say where you are and that you're in danger," added Sissy, twisting her paws.

"And don't forget to ask for . . . for Ratmom."

Raston buried his face in his paws and broke down completely. "Oh, Mommy, my ratmommy, I'm sorry, I didn't mean to criticize—I don't care if you *never* get flabulous!"

The rooftops were getting closer. Emmy knew they would be passing her house soon—would her parents be out this early? She had an overwhelming longing to run to them and tell them everything, let them fix it all . . .

But she had to get out of the cage first. She looked at the faces of her friends.

"Emmy," said Joe, his voice cracking, "maybe you shouldn't. Even if you'd be in a cage the rest of your life, at least you'd be *alive*."

"What?" said Aunt Melly, sitting up and rubbing the sleep from her eyes. "What do you mean, she'd still be alive?"

Emmy clenched her paws to keep them from shaking. There was no time, not for explanations, not for anything. "Do it, Sissy," she whispered. "Kiss me twice."

Emmy's body went through the familiar change from rodent to girl, and then from tiny to large. But this time there was a cage around her. She could feel herself filling all available space, her back up against the crisscrossed bars, her elbows in the corners, her skin trying to push out through the holes—

It wasn't working. She couldn't breathe. There was no room for her chest to expand and her knees were pressing against her throat and then somewhere beneath her, right before everything went black, she heard a small whimper.

28

AND ALL AT ONCE it *did* work. The metal cage creaked and suddenly popped under the pressure of a girl growing large and strong inside it. Pieces of metal sproinged out as if shot from a catapult, tinging against the hopper car and flying out the side of the train and hitting Cheswick in the back of the neck.

The man whirled.

"Ratty!" cried the full-sized Emmy. "Bite me twice!"

Cheswick Vole's hands clenched on air as Emmy shrank down and became a rat once more. Three rodents skittered out of the way of his feet, faster and more agile than the big, clumsy human.

"Go, go, go!" Emmy cried, snatching up the draw-string bag with her paw, and the rodents swarmed up the ladder to the top of the hopper car, with a sure-footed scamper in spite of the train's rocking sway.

"NOOOOOOO!" wailed Miss Barmy, scrabbling for the ladder with her manicured hands.

"Jane, don't climb up! It's too dangerous!" shouted Cheswick.

"I'm not staying a rat, Cheswick! I'd rather die!" cried Miss Barmy, twisting on the ladder.

"But, my little sugarplum—you were darling as a rat! So sweet and fuzzy!"

Emmy pelted along the top of the moving train, following Ratty's and Sissy's bounding gray forms. As they leaped to the next car, the early morning light caught their ruffled fur, edging them in pink. And then Emmy, too, came to the end of the hopper and the yawning space between cars.

It would have terrified her if she had been human. But she was a rodent now, and so she bunched her hind legs and sprang across the gap as lightly as she would jump a curb. She landed on the boxcar with a scrape of claws, flicked her tail for balance, and looked back, settling the drawstring bag more securely around her shoulder.

Miss Barmy was struggling to hang on to the ladder, her hair and clothes whipping wildly. Cheswick was pulling at her urgently from below.

Emmy grinned. Miss Barmy would never catch Sissy now. What the nanny didn't know was that the

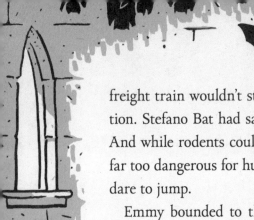

freight train wouldn't stop at the Grayson Lake station. Stefano Bat had said it would only slow down. And while rodents could leap off safely, it would be far too dangerous for humans. Miss Barmy wouldn't dare to jump.

Emmy bounded to the last boxcar, skidded to a halt next to Ratty and Sissy, and looked around. On her left was the town of Grayson Lake, spreading up a wide hill, and down the embankment on the other side was the lake. Out in Loon's Bay was a white blotch that must be a sail. Someone had gone out early and was rounding the point—was it her father? Emmy squinted, but her rodent eyes couldn't focus that far.

The train was slowing. The trees were going by less quickly, and the warning bell had begun to ring. Emmy shouted in Ratty's and Sissy's ears, "Go down the ladder and get ready to jump!"

Raston clambered over the edge first, followed by Cecilia. Emmy, waiting her turn, watched intently as the long, gabled train station grew steadily larger. She could see a cloud of bats swooping out from beneath the station eaves. They darted toward one of the hopper cars in a fluttering mass, and flew off again somewhat more slowly, dangling two elderly rats in the harness beneath them.

Emmy's heart gave a sudden leaping beat. It had worked! The great-aunts were safely off the train and away from Miss Barmy and Cheswick!

Emmy narrowed her eyes, still watching. A moment later, two young brown rats leaped from the hopper and landed, somersaulting, on the ground. Joe and Ana took off for the station at a scamper, crying an ultrahigh *Aiiiieeeee! Aiiiieeeee!* as the bats lowered Gussie and Melly onto one of the benches. Behind the station, on the sloping ground, hundreds of small rodent heads suddenly popped out of their burrows at once. Then, all together, the shrill cry of the Emergency Rodent Alert went up, winging its way back toward Rodent City and Ratmom.

Emmy slid joyfully down the ladder after Sissy and Ratty. "Jump!" she cried, and leaped clear of the tracks. She landed, tumbling like an acrobat, the drawstring bag whipping around and around.

It was true! Rodents could fall hard, even from a moving train, and not get hurt! And the train was pulling away, with Cheswick and Miss Barmy still

hanging on to the hopper car ladder, leaning out on the lake side of the train, afraid to jump.

Cheswick leaped—or was shoved—and Miss Barmy, hanging on to him, leaped, too. Emmy watched with horrified fascination as Cheswick hit the ground and Miss Barmy hit Cheswick.

There was a sound like a dry branch snapping, then a piercing scream. The carryall, torn off Cheswick's shoulder, split open, and the Sissy-patches flew up and scattered in swirling, windy gusts as Cheswick and Miss Barmy rolled heavily down the lake side of the embankment and out of sight.

The train rumbled distantly and disappeared around a curve. The bats, done with their task, streamed back under the station eaves to roost.

Sissy whimpered.

Emmy turned immediately. Sissy had not quite jumped clear of the tracks, and her front paw had jammed in the narrow gap between rail and crosstie. Raston, bent over the paw, was yanking at it vigorously.

"Stop that, Ratty, and let me see." Emmy crouched over Sissy's paw, swollen now and even more tightly wedged. She glanced up the tracks and blinked as a sudden gust blew grit in her small rodent eyes. It would probably be a while before another train came, but they had to get the paw out somehow. Maybe someone from Rodent City would come with Rat-mom and could help? Emmy found herself wishing it would be Mrs. Bunjee, who always seemed to know what to do in an emergency.

Raston gave a low rodent growl, his fur bristling. Emmy looked back to see Miss Barmy struggling up the embankment, using a stick to help her climb. Her hair was wild, and her eyes stared piteously at the carryall bag, lying split and empty on the rail-road tracks.

"My patches!" she cried. "They can't all have blown away." She struggled to the damaged bag and picked it up. "Cheswick!" she bawled down the embank-ment. "Help me!"

A low moan floated up. "My leg . . . I think it's broken . . ."

"You think that's bad? I broke two nails!" Miss Barmy held a manicured hand out in front of her, and shrieked, "No! *Three!*"

Raston sniffled.

"*Shhh!*" Emmy said. She flattened her small rodent

body between the railroad ties. With her hind foot, she carefully slid the drawstring bag behind her, out of sight.

Raston sniffled again. Emmy glared at him.

"I'm very allergic!" he whispered desperately. "There's—ah—ragweed! Ah—ah—"

Emmy shut her eyes and prayed.

"—CHOO!"

Raston had not managed to make his sneeze ultrasonic.

Gravel scraped. Miss Barmy bent over them with a hideous smile.

"Bite her, Ratty!" cried Emmy.

But before he could move, Miss Barmy shifted her weight. Her heel dug into the ground next to Sissy's tail. The rest of her foot rested, ever so lightly, atop the rat's small, defenseless body.

Emmy stared hopelessly up at Miss Barmy's powerful leg, at her ankle, scraped and bruised from the fall—and then she forced her gaze down to the lizard-skin shoes with the metal tips and Sissy's terrified face.

"Run!" whispered Sissy. "Leave me! Find a hole and hide!"

Raston reared back. "I'll bite you if you don't let her go! I'll shrink you!"

Miss Barmy pressed down lightly with her foot. Sissy screamed.

"Are you *sure* you want to do that?" Miss Barmy swung her stick idly beside her ankles. "Because if you and your little rat friends get any closer, I might do something you won't like at all."

Emmy turned at the sound of pattering feet. Joe, scampering to the rescue, had left Ana on the station bench to watch the aunts—but he skidded to a stop at the sight of Sissy beneath Miss Barmy's shoe.

Raston looked frantically at his friends. Then, with a sudden spurt of gravel beneath his paws, he whirled and took off running toward the station.

Emmy stared. Ratty had abandoned his sister! It hardly seemed possible!

Miss Barmy snapped her fingers at Emmy and Joe. "You two, pick up my patches!" She reached into the carryall and pulled out a shard of broken mirror, patting her hair back into place. "And you'd better hurry, if you want to keep your precious kissy rat safe. I'm going to need more patches soon." Her

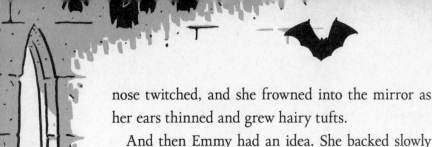

nose twitched, and she frowned into the mirror as her ears thinned and grew hairy tufts.

And then Emmy had an idea. She backed slowly away.

"If you don't go find my patches this instant," said Miss Barmy coldly, "I won't let the kissy rat turn you human again. How would you like to stay a rat forever, Emmaline?"

Emmy stopped just out of Miss Barmy's reach. She pulled the drawstring bag from her neck. "I have patches," she said.

Miss Barmy stared at her intently. "You do not."

Emmy pulled out a Sissy-patch and held it up. She backed up a few more steps.

"Bring that bag here!" Miss Barmy commanded. "Bring it here, or I'll squish the kissy rat!"

Emmy felt her whiskers trembling, but she forced her voice to remain calm. "No, you won't. You need her too much."

"So do you," snarled Miss Barmy, but she lifted her foot.

"Come and get them," said Emmy, backing away still farther. She glanced over her furry shoulder at the rising ground beyond the station and the line of woods beyond. Were there wild rodents who might help?

"You nasty little *rat!*" cried Miss Barmy, lunging forward. Emmy whirled and ran, but Miss Barmy caught up all too quickly, and her metal-tipped shoes stamped far too close to Emmy's tail.

Emmy threw the small drawstring bag with all her ratty strength. It sailed a foot and a half into a patch of weeds, and Miss Barmy laughed aloud, pushing aside the prickly stems with both hands. She pounced on the small bag where it lay and pulled open the drawstring.

"I've outsmarted you again," she crowed, throwing aside the shoelace and slapping the Sissy-patches on her neck. "I'll take these, and then I'll just go back and get the kissy rat in the end. She's still stuck, or hadn't you noticed?"

Emmy's tiny heart was beating like a humming-bird's. She looked sideways toward the tracks where Joe and now Ana, too, were struggling to free Sissy. If only she could keep Miss Barmy distracted for just a little longer!

Emmy looked up at Miss Barmy's sneering face— and gasped.

"What?" Miss Barmy looked down at her in scornful triumph.

Emmy blinked, staring. "It's just that I've never seen such a . . ."

"Such an incredibly beautiful woman?" Miss Barmy smiled.

Emmy shook her head, unable to take her eyes from Miss Barmy's changed face. "Such a monster," she finished unsteadily.

"Ha! Everyone *else* thinks I'm beautiful. Everyone *else* thinks I'm stunning. Everyone *else* thinks I'm the most attractive, lovely, gorgeous—"

Emmy reached in the carryall bag and threw a piece of the broken mirror at Miss Barmy's feet. "See for yourself."

It wasn't just the whiskers sprouting everywhere that made Miss Barmy look so loathsome, Emmy thought as she listened to the woman's shattered cries, nor the repulsive half rat, half human features, nor the spasmodic twitches that shivered over the furry skin.

No. What gave Miss Barmy an air of pure evil was the hideous red splash that stained her from head to foot. Dark like old blood, glistening as if with tears, it had a look of raw liver.

"*Aaaiiieegh!*" Miss Barmy's wail had the crimson edge of despair. "I'm ugly! *Ugly!*"

Emmy glanced over at the tracks again. Aunt Melly was there now, too, struggling with Joe and Ana to free Sissy's paw. Emmy was surprised—had Melly left Gussie alone on the bench? And then suddenly Aunt Melly grew less furry and larger, going up and up until she was full sized once more. Looking slightly disheveled but very much the schoolteacher, she straightened her skirt and marched firmly across the gravel toward the monstrous Miss Barmy.

Miss Barmy turned, snarling, but a sudden shadow overhead made her look up. From the air came a fluttering, and a high peeping, and a shrill whistle.

Raston, dangling from the harness beneath a canopy of bats, lifted his paw to his mouth and whistled again, a short, sharp signal. "Operation Guano Drop! Bombs away!"

Guano? Emmy had heard that word before somewhere. But what did it mean?

Splat. The first guano bomb hit Miss Barmy on her forehead and dripped down. It was white, and sloppy, and smelled of—

"*Bat poop!*" screamed Miss Barmy. "In my eye! Cheswick, help!"

But Cheswick didn't come. Miss Barmy, half blind, tried to dodge the bat guano plopping down, blob after soft, wet blob, but it landed on her head, her shoulders, her red ears, until she was sobbing with rage and humiliation. Joe and Ana, now full sized, came running, and Emmy darted on rapid rodent feet back to Sissy to get kissed and grow and join in the circle of humans that surrounded the monster that was Miss Barmy.

The bats dropped Raston gently lower, lower, until he tumbled, sneezing, into the ragweed. Joe and Emmy lunged for Miss Barmy's feet—Ana and Aunt Melly grabbed a wrist each—and between them they held Miss Barmy down while Raston spit on her grazed ankle with scorn.

Miss Barmy shrank. Emmy and Joe tied her up with the shoelace. And through the thin line of woods and down the hill came an army of rodents, led by a familiar-looking chipmunk.

"Where's the emergency?" said Mrs. Bunjee. She looked at the trussed-up Miss Barmy, put her paws on her hips, and chuckled richly, her chipmunk cheeks bunching. "It looks as if you have the situation under control."

"Well," said Emmy, glancing over her shoulder, "not exactly. We found Sissy, but she got her paw stuck between the rails—"

A massive gray rat burst forward from the ranks of rodents. "*My baby!*" screamed Ratmom. "On the train tracks!"

29

EMMY KNELT DOWN on the gravel railbed, joining the huddle around Sissy. Ratmom, who had left a trail of bare earth behind her as her tears landed on the vegetation, wept from a safe distance as she gazed at her long-lost daughter.

"Pardon me," said Aunt Melly, bending over with a limp and furry Gussie in her hands. "I just need one tear. Maybe two . . ."

She caught one of Della's tears on her finger and dropped it in the corner of Gussie's half-open mouth. The elderly rat shivered slightly, opened her eyes, and sat up, smiling. "Oh, my! How wonderful I feel!"

"And now two kisses, Cecilia?" asked Melly. "I'm sorry to bother you, dear. I know your paw must be hurting you terribly."

Sissy's smile was strained, but she leaned in to kiss Gussie once, then twice. Everyone backed away to avoid the suddenly growing arms and legs of the not-quite-so-elderly Aunt Gussie.

Aunt Gussie combed the twigs out of her hair with her fingers, beamed down at the rats, and pressed her sister's hand. "My, what an adventure we seem to be having!"

"Er—" said Emmy, looking down the tracks. There was a vibration in the rails that she didn't like. "It might be *more* of an adventure if we don't get Sissy's paw out soon."

Whooo . . . whooooo . . .

Aunt Gussie exchanged a startled glance with Emmy and bent over Sissy's paw. "I can try to pull it free, dear," she said to the little rat, "but it's going to hurt. Are you ready?"

A gust of wind blew grit across the tracks, and Gussie's grip tightened. Sissy cried out in a high squeal of pain, but the paw remained stuck, now more swollen than ever.

"I'm afraid to pull harder!" Gussie's face crinkled with concern. "I don't want to pull her in two!"

Emmy stroked Sissy's back gently. The little rat trembled beneath her hand, whimpering.

"I've heard of animals chewing their paw off, if they were caught in a trap," said Joe in a low voice. "It's better than dying."

Whooo . . . whooooo . . . the whistle sounded again, louder this time. There was a humming vibration in the rails.

A shudder rippled over Sissy's body from ears to tail. She looked at her weeping mother and brother; she looked at her paw. She stiffened her whiskers and lowered her head, placing her mouth with its sharp teeth around the tender wrist bones.

"Oh, my brave little ratling!" sobbed Della.

"Sissy, no!" Raston buried his face on Ratmom's damp shoulder.

"Hey!" Joe said sharply. "Stay away from those tears—the last thing we need right now is a screaming baby Ratty!"

"Everyone off the tracks," ordered Aunt Gussie. "You too, Melly. Joe and Emmy, keep the rodents back." She gazed at Cecilia with compassion. "Do you want me to pull until you come free—even if I pull your paw right off?"

Sissy looked up with wide eyes and nodded. Aunt Gussie took hold of the small, furry body and braced herself.

"No!" cried Emmy. "Wait!"

Aunt Melly lunged ahead to clutch Emmy's

shoulder with fingers of iron. "Get back this instant, Emmaline Addison! The train is coming!"

Somewhere ahead, there was a series of clanging noises and the *ting ting ting* of a bell. *AWHOOOO! AWHOOOO!* A whistle echoed in the rocky cut and back from the rooftops of Grayson Lake. Emmy, unable to make herself heard, twisted hard and ducked out from under Aunt Melly's grasp. She scooped up Della Rat and ran to Sissy, pushing Aunt Gussie's hand aside.

"One tear!" Emmy shouted. "Just one!" She wiped a forefinger under Ratmom's brimming eye and dropped a shining crystal tear into Sissy's startled mouth. "Swallow!" she yelled in Sissy's ear.

Cecilia gulped—and dwindled under Emmy's hand. The rodent's fur became finer and silkier, the tail short and curly, the little paws smaller than ever . . .

Baby Sissy's tiny paw slid easily out from the narrow gap where it had been wedged. Emmy felt hands seize her collar and she was violently yanked backward as the train went ringing and thundering past, car after car.

Stunned, flat on her back, with a scrape on one

elbow and a bump on her head, Emmy gazed up at the distressed faces of her great-aunts.

"What were you thinking?" demanded Aunt Melly, still gasping for breath. "You could have been killed!"

Della Rat climbed slowly out of Emmy's hand.

"Ratmommy!" shrieked Raston, breaking free from Joe's restraining hand. "Where's Sissy? She's not—" He choked and didn't finish.

Della lifted her muzzle, her pink nose quivering, her eyes wet. She looked at Emmy, waiting.

Emmy opened her other hand. Squirming on the palm was a tiny rat, waving her paws and gurgling.

"*Sissy?*" Raston's mouth hung open.

"Watty!" cried the baby, with a charming squeak of laughter. She held out her forepaws in a clear demand to be picked up.

Raston stared at his tiny sister. "I don't know anything about babies. Let Ratmommy take her."

"Oh, no you don't." Joe's hand came down, blocking Ratmom's path. "Sorry, Della," he added, looking down. "If even one more tear got into her mouth—"

"I know, I know," said Della, still crying but this time for happiness, her eyes bright and shiny with joy. "Go on, Rasty. Pick up your sister!"

Raston edged forward. He flexed his paws, gripped Sissy gingerly under her forearms, and lifted. She hung in the air, kicking her hind feet.

"Don't hold her out like that, son! She's not a wet rag; she's a baby. Cuddle her. Pat her on the back."

Raston pulled his sister awkwardly to his chest and gave her back several experimental thumps.

"No, Rasty, not so hard! She might spit—"

Urp!

"—up," finished Della, a moment too late.

Raston stared in horror at the glob of regurgitated food dribbling down his front, and then at baby Sissy, still blurping out messy little bubbles.

Joe made a sudden choking noise and turned away.

"If anyone," said the Rat bitterly, "thinks this is *funny*—"

"Not me," Joe gasped, hiding his face in the crook of his elbow.

Raston muttered something under his breath and shifted baby Sissy to his other arm. "I can still *shrink* people, you know," he said pointedly. "I do have my dignity."

Emmy grinned as she fished in her pocket and

handed the Rat a crumpled tissue. He took it and dabbed moodily at his chest fur.

The final car of the freight train went rattling past, and in the sudden quiet, Aunt Melly's voice could be heard. "Yes, but what now? And what should be done with Ana?"

Emmy's grin faded. She lowered her voice. "Joe, where *is* Ana? I don't see her anywhere."

"She was on the other side of the tracks when the train came." Joe abruptly sobered, looking at the embankment where it dropped off suddenly. "I don't see her now, though."

A squeaking cheer came from a little distance away, and a sound of many small paws clapping. The crowd of rodents from Rodent City had been busily tying Miss Barmy to a long, sturdy stick and now they hoisted her above their shoulders, hung from the middle like a roasting chicken on a spit.

"And off she goes to jail!" shrieked a gopher.

"Good riddance!" said Joe, grinning.

"Mmpph! Rmmph!" Miss Barmy, though tied and gagged with a shoelace, wasn't going down without a fight. She glared with helpless fury.

Emmy didn't feel sorry for her at all.

"But where is Cheswick?" asked Aunt Melly. "He shouldn't go free."

Joe turned. "Didn't he jump off with Miss Barmy?"

Emmy nodded. "Last I saw, he rolled down toward the lake. But I think he broke his leg or something."

"Cheswick? Cheswick VOLE?" Della's voice, husky and powerful from years of singing in noisy bars, soared over everyone else's and the crowd of rodents hushed. "Do you mean the Big Hand—the *nest robber*—the *criminal who stole my children?*" She shook her paws in the air. "Oooh, let me get my paws on him just *once*—"

"We have to find him first," said Joe.

Emmy frowned slightly. The sound of clapping went on and on. Why?

She turned her head. It wasn't the rodents clapping. It was the sound of a sail a little way off, flapping in the breeze as it was furled. And now that she was looking in the direction of the lake, she could see the bare top of a mast showing behind the embankment.

Emmy whipped around and put a finger to her lips. "Everyone, *shhh!*"

A deep, familiar voice drifted up from behind the

351

high embankment. "Ana! We've been looking for you!" Then the voice changed and hardened. "Cheswick Vole. So *you* took her. Get behind me, Ana."

"But he's hurt, sir," came Ana's voice.

"It doesn't matter. I'm going to tie him up and call the police."

Joe looked at Emmy. "Your father," he whispered. "He thinks Cheswick kidnapped her or something!"

"I need to sit down," said Emmy faintly.

Emmy sat in a state of dazed calm. The aunts, on the next bench over, were in a flutter, trying to figure out what they should say to Jim Addison. But somehow, after all Emmy had been through, she couldn't work up the energy to worry about a few explanations.

And she was looking forward to seeing her father. He might be upset—she had certainly done some things he wouldn't have approved of—but she had just escaped the clutches of someone who *hated* her. Having a parent upset at her for a while didn't seem like that big a deal, anymore. Her dad might not understand her but Emmy knew he loved her, and that was enough.

Joe flung himself on the bench next to her and

nodded toward the belt of trees behind the station. "The rodents are all going to wait there," he said. "To see what happens to Cheswick, I guess." He grinned. "And baby Sissy burped all over Ratty again."

There was a sound of sliding gravel. Emmy saw her father's head appear over the embankment, then his upper body, and his hand on Ana's shoulder.

"Gussie! Melly!" Jim Addison stood before them, his hair rumpled. "What a surprise! Did you take an early train?" He scooped up Emmy and gave her a hard hug, lifting her off her feet and kissing her cheek.

"Yes," said Aunt Melly after a pause. "We took an early train."

"You should have called! I would have been glad to pick you up. I know it's a short distance to the house, but you two aren't as young as you used to be—" He stopped a moment, grinning. "Actually, you look livelier than ever. Over your cold, Gussie?"

"I feel better than I have in years," said Aunt Gussie, giving Emmy a wink. "And we wanted to surprise you."

"Oh, you have." Emmy's father set down his daughter, shook Joe's hand, and gave the aunts a hug

apiece. "But look—here's Ana! I've found the little girl they've been combing the county for. Will you take care of her while I go in the station and call the police?" His mouth set in a grim line. "I've tied up Cheswick Vole, the man who kidnapped her. I had plenty of rope in the sailboat, and he's not going anywhere—I think he's broken his leg, too."

"Of course we'll take care of Ana," said Aunt Gussie. "Come sit by us, dear."

"I think you'll find the station is closed, though," said Aunt Melly.

"Really? Wasn't it open when your train stopped?"

"The ways of train companies are really beyond me to explain," said Aunt Melly briskly. "The important thing, Jimmy, is for you to go and make your call. We'll wait."

The scrape of Jim Addison's feet on gravel had hardly faded into the distance when Professor Capybara trotted up from the road carrying a small black satchel. "I came as soon as I heard about the rodent alert. Am I too late to help?"

A scuffling sound came from the underbrush behind the station, and a rippling mass of rodents moved out together like a restless, furry carpet. In

the middle, carried high, was a struggling red-splotched rat on a stick.

At the head of the procession marched Della Rat with her children. Her heavy hips bunched as she moved; her cardigan sweater was soiled and missing a button. But her whiskers were stiff and her ears alert, and all her claws were ready. She looked up at the professor. "You're not too late. You're just in time to help us bring that *snake*, Cheswick Vole, to JUSTICE!"

CHESWICK VOLE, scraped and bruised, smudged with dust and tied with every sailor's knot Emmy's father knew, looked up helplessly at the top of the embankment where three grown-ups, three children, and an army of rodents watched him with eyes of judgment.

"Please," he begged them, "let me go. I didn't take Ana. You know I didn't."

Baby Sissy shivered at the sound of the man's voice and pressed her tiny face into Raston's shoulder.

"You've done other things just as bad," said Aunt Melly coldly.

"You took my children!" Della snarled.

"You kidnapped Sissy!" cried Ratty.

"And put Emmy in a cage," Joe added.

"You threatened to squish me." Aunt Gussie shuddered. "I still remember your fingers around my neck on the train."

"In addition, you stole patches and you forged letters," said Professor Capybara. "And you broke into

my old laboratory in Schenectady. So far that's breaking and entering, robbery, forgery, kidnapping, and reckless endangerment. So why on earth do you think we should let you go?"

Cheswick blinked up at them with damp eyes. "Because I'm sorry?"

The professor gazed at him sternly. "And you seriously think that makes it all better?"

Cheswick sniffled. "What if I said I was really, really, *really* sorry?"

Joe snorted. "You're just sorry you got caught."

Ratmom stood high on her hind legs and pointed a claw in accusation. "Now you say you're sorry! I've cried a river over you!" Tears spilled down her furry cheeks and splashed on the gravel embankment.

"Oh, how I wish we had an empty bottle!" Aunt Melly cried. "We should be saving these tears for Gussie!"

"Now, now." Aunt Gussie patted her sister's hand. "I'm not afraid to die, Melly. I wouldn't have played the organ in church for so many years if I didn't believe what I was playing, you know."

"Well, I don't want you to die yet!" said Melly. She sank down on the embankment, sniffling.

"Never fear, dear ladies. I brought some things along just in case they were needed—and I'm sure I have a bottle you can use." The professor rummaged in his satchel amid the sound of glass clinking. "Not the vials—they're full of potions—but I did throw in a bottle of something just in case I got thirsty. Ah, here it is!" He pulled out a bottle of root beer and twisted off the cap. "Anyone want a drink before I pour it out?"

Ratmom turned. There was a dreadful pause.

"Not for me," said Joe swiftly.

"There's a drinking fountain at the station," said Emmy. "I think I'd rather have water."

"Me too," Ana added.

"There's really too much sugar in root beer for us," said Aunt Melly, with a meaningful look at Gussie.

Ratmom threw back her head. Raston and baby Sissy watched her with wide eyes.

"Dump it," said Ratmom. "I don't need it."

Ana took the bottle gently from the professor's hands. "I'll let Cheswick have a drink," she said. "And then I'll rinse the bottle in the lake and bring it back for Della's tears."

A pitiful moan rose from Cheswick below, and

Aunt Gussie looked down the gravel embankment. "Ana," she said, "why *did* you go down there by Cheswick? Why didn't you just wait until the train was past and then come to the station? Didn't you know he might still be dangerous?"

Ana curled her fingers around the root beer bottle. "I thought he might have hurt himself," she said. "Doctors help people even if they've done something bad, you know."

The elderly sisters looked at one another as Ana slid down the embankment and gave the wounded man a drink. "She sounds just like Papa," said Gussie.

Melly nodded. Then she whispered something in Gussie's ear.

"Ana, dear," said Aunt Gussie—and stopped. "Do you hear that?"

Everyone listened to the sound of a police siren some distance away.

Cheswick groaned aloud. "*Please!*" he begged, his voice cracking. "Don't let them take me! They'll give me life in prison for kidnapping Ana—but I didn't do it!"

Emmy had never seen such frightened eyes on a

grown man. She looked at the others. "They will," she said. "They'll lock him up and never let him out."

"Wasn't that what he was going to do to us?" demanded Raston.

Emmy had to admit this was true.

"Well, then." Raston tightened his hold on baby Sissy, who was wriggling to get down.

"But you're not supposed to put someone in jail for something he didn't do, even if he's done other bad things," said Emmy. "Right?"

"Quite right, dear," said Aunt Melly.

"And we could never explain what really happened," Ana said. "Not so that anyone would believe it."

"Better decide," said Joe. "They're coming."

Emmy chewed on a fingernail. "We can't untie the knots in time, anyway. But—"

"But *what?*" cried Cheswick.

"Ratty could bite him twice. Cheswick would become a rat and shrink right out of the ropes."

"What? You'd let him go?" demanded Raston. "Over my dead body!"

"And mine!" cried Ratmom, shaking her paw.

"You don't understand," said Emmy. "I mean, once

he's a rat, he can be taken to Rodent City like Miss Barmy and put in jail."

Cheswick looked up. "In jail? With *Jane*?"

"Well, probably not in the same cell," said the professor.

"But I could speak to her through the bars? I could . . . touch her paw?"

Emmy glanced behind her. She could see what Cheswick could not: Miss Barmy, splotched with the dark red of blood, her fur damp and stringy as if with tears, and as tightly bound as a fly in a spiderweb. Her rodent eyes showed above the shoelace gag, crazed with hatred. Emmy could not imagine anyone less likely to inspire love, but Cheswick was beyond all reason.

"All right, then," said Professor Capybara. "Bite him, Raston—but hang on to him. The rest of you rodents, are you ready?"

Four strong-looking squirrels scampered down the embankment, carrying a piece of twine. Raston started to follow and stopped.

"Here, somebody take her!" He pressed his baby sister into the arms of a convenient gopher and dashed down to do his duty. There was a shocked

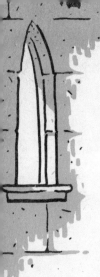

pause—long enough for one deep breath—and then the thin, high screech of an enraged baby rat filled the air.

"Good heavens," said the professor, plugging his ears. "I had no idea something so small could make such a noise."

"She's got my lungs," said Ratmom proudly. "We'll make a singer of her yet."

Emmy and Joe watched with deep satisfaction as Cheswick Vole shrank, turned furry, and was promptly tied up with twine. Ana made a tiny splint for his broken leg, and the squirrels carried him up the embankment. The army of rodents, cheering in their high, squeaky voices, set off for Rodent City, carrying Miss Barmy and Cheswick in their midst like trophies of war. The professor went with them, his satchel clinking slightly as he brought up the rear.

"She's all yours!" squeaked the gopher, and the screaming baby Sissy was thrust back into Raston's arms. "Good luck getting her to shut up, and next time put her in diapers, why don't you?"

Raston looked aghast at the baby rat, who was not only still howling furiously but leaking as well. He held her at arm's length and turned, searching for Ratmom.

But Ratmom, emotional at the sight of her ancient enemy being carted off to jail, was crying *again*. Ana picked her up, held the root beer bottle to catch the tears, and walked toward the station benches where Gussie and Melly already had gone to sit.

"Come on, Rasty!" cried Ratmom. "Bring little Cecilia, the darling!"

The police siren blared again, closer than ever, and Emmy hurried to the train station parking lot where her father and mother were just pulling in.

Joe, lagging behind, turned to give Raston a wicked grin. "Why don't you try giving the little darling a horsey ride?"

"Oh, shut *up*," said Raston.

"So this is the little girl who gave us such a lot of worry," said a tall officer, smiling down at Ana. "We've been looking everywhere for you." He glanced at the station, where a poster that said MISSING was tacked to the door.

Ana gazed at her own face on the poster and then at Aunt Melly, who had turned pale. "I didn't mean to cause everybody so much trouble."

"We're just glad to have you safe," said the officer,

hitching up his belt. "Now then, Mr. Addison, where is the suspect?"

"I'll show you," said Emmy's father. "He's tied up tight, don't worry."

Emmy's mother didn't waste words. She knelt and folded both Emmy and Ana into her arms, and when she let them go, her cheeks were wet.

A second policeman got out of the car and opened the back door. "Ana!" cried a frantic voice, and a woman leaped out, losing a shoe in the process.

"It's Squippy!" whispered Joe, smothering a laugh.

"No kidding!" Emmy watched as Ana was grabbed yet again and cried over noisily. The second policeman followed his partner and Jim Addison across the tracks to the embankment.

"I was so worried!" Gwenda Squipp dabbed at her eyes. "Did that man take you? How did you get off the train? I looked for you everywhere!"

"I don't remember him taking me off the train," said Ana truthfully. "But I do remember a lot of strange stuff. Like becoming very small. And then turning into a rat."

"My poor dear!" said Squippy. "You must have

been drugged. Well, we'll talk more later, dear, when you've recovered. And, my goodness, that family of yours has been worried, too!"

"You mean the relatives I was going to live with?"

"Yes, indeed. They were calling every day."

"I didn't know they wanted me that much," said Ana slowly. "I kind of thought they didn't."

"They wanted you, all right. They kept asking if they'd get their check for the whole month, even if you weren't there for part of it. Oh, they were *very* anxious to have you." Squippy's mouth turned down. "A little *too* anxious, I'd say."

Ana's face fell into lines so sad that Emmy had to look away.

Aunt Melly put a comforting hand on Ana's shoulder, and drew her close. "My dear Miss—er?"

"Squipp. Gwenda Squipp."

"I wonder what is the trouble with the officers over there. Would you perhaps go and find out? We'll stay with Ana. We don't want her to have to get any closer to that man than absolutely necessary, wouldn't you agree?"

"Of course," said Squippy, shading her eyes as she looked to the embankment. One officer was

standing at the top, looking around, and the other two men were climbing up, arguing loudly.

"I'm telling you, I tied him up perfectly well! I'm a sailor, and I ought to know how to tie a knot!"

"*Ought* to know is right, sir," said the officer heavily.

Emmy's mother glanced hurriedly around and headed off in their direction, followed by Squippy. Aunt Melly waited until they were several yards away, and then drew everyone together.

"We don't have much time, Ana, so listen carefully," Aunt Melly said. "Gussie and I have discussed this already, and we would like you to come and live with us."

Ana lifted her head quickly.

"It will take some time to arrange, and we will have to persuade the judge, but if you *would* like to live with us, dear girl, then you have a home."

"But—" said Ana.

"Now, I know we're far too old," Gussie broke in, "and maybe you would find our life too dull."

Ana shook her head, her eyes brightening.

"But if Della is willing to supply us with tears," Melly interrupted, with a fond glance at the big gray rat, "we should both be able to stay alive until you graduate from medical school."

Ana did not gasp or cry out. She merely sat very, very still, as if someone had handed her something incredibly precious and fragile. "Medical school?" she said at last. "You're sending me to medical school?"

"If you still wish to go," said Aunt Melly, smiling.

"You see," Gussie explained, "our dear papa studied to be a doctor, but *his* father died and Papa had to run the family business."

"Bootmaking," said Aunt Melly. "Hurry, sister— they're coming back."

"So that's how he made his fortune. And here we have all this money just sitting in the bank, and we are quite sure that he would have wanted us to use it to help another young aspiring doctor reach her dream."

"Really?" Ana breathed. "Truly?"

"Truly," said the aunts together.

"And you can visit them in Schenectady," Emmy said to the rats.

"I wouldn't mind," said Ratmom. "I could swim across to The Surly now and then, for old times'

sake. And I have a feeling that Rasty wants to finish *Get Flabulous.*"

"I'm getting plenty of exercise right now," muttered Raston, who had taken Joe's advice and was letting baby Sissy ride on his back. "Hey! Stop pulling my whiskers!"

"Go, orsie!" shouted Sissy. "Orsie, go! Go! GO!"

"I'm going, already," muttered Raston, bucking his hindquarters up and down, up and down. "Sheeesh. Isn't it your naptime or something?"

Joe grinned at Emmy. "And they all lived happily ever after."

"Well, almost," said Emmy, glancing over her shoulder.

"But I tied him up like a Christmas present!" said Jim Addison, following the police officers as they headed to their cars. "It just doesn't make sense!"

"Maybe you tie your Christmas packages a bit loose, sir." The tall policeman was elaborately polite. "Now, Miss Squipp, if you're ready, we'll accompany you and the young miss to the Children's Home. And we'll be wanting to talk with her there."

"Can they come with me?" Ana asked, holding out her hands to the aunts.

"Er . . ." said the officer.

"I really, *really* want them to come," said Ana. "Please, Squippy?"

Squippy leaned over to the officer and whispered behind her hand. "The poor child was so traumatized, she bonded with the first mother figures she met after her ordeal."

"But there's not enough room in the squad car," said the policeman.

"My nephew will drive us to the Children's Home; won't you, Jimmy?" Aunt Melly looked over at Emmy's father.

"You'll want to drive carefully, sir," said the tall officer.

"A little more carefully than you tie knots," said the second.

"And we'd better take the little girl in our car," said the first. "Just to make sure she actually gets there."

Emmy's father, very red in the face, walked toward his car. "I *know* I tied him!" he insisted to his wife. "I trussed that man like a Thanksgiving turkey!"

Emmy watched as her father's shoulders slumped.

She knew how terrible he felt. It was awful to have people think you had done something wrong when you hadn't.

Joe shifted uncomfortably. "I wish we could tell them what really happened."

"I know. But the police would never believe it, anyway." Emmy peered under the station bench. "Are you rodents coming with us, or what?"

Ratmom climbed into Emmy's waiting hands. She had stopped crying at long last, but she was still a little damp. "Come on, Rasty!"

Raston, sweaty and harassed, looked up wearily. "I can't," he said. "As soon as I stop bouncing, she—"

"*EEEEEEEEEEEEEEEEEE!*" screamed baby Sissy. "Orsie orsie orsie orsie—"

"I don't know what to do!" cried Raston. "I haven't even passed the Rodent City Babysitting Course yet! I'm too *young* to be this dependable!"

"Poor Ratty," said Joe. "I know how you feel." He reached down and scooped up the baby rat. Sissy, startled into silence, gazed up at his face.

"This is the way the horsey goes, walk, walk, walk," Joe began, bouncing his finger up and down.

Baby Sissy hiccuped, gripped his finger with her forepaws, and looked up adoringly. "Mo!"

"Come on, everyone," called Kathy Addison from the lot. "There's plenty of room in the van. We'll drop you off, Joe."

"Did you get some new pets, Emmy?" Jim Addison frowned as he held the door open. "Don't you have a cage for them?"

"Um . . . the cage broke," said Emmy. She thought with satisfaction of *how* it had broken. Her shoulder was still sore where it had pressed up and into the wire mesh of the cage, but she didn't mind at all. She had saved her aunts, and she had saved her friends. And Cheswick Vole and Jane Barmy were locked up for good.

Mr. Addison got behind the wheel and started the engine. "Emmy, if you're going to have pets, you've got to be more responsible for them."

Meaningful looks were exchanged behind his back.

"James Addison," said Aunt Melly in her clear, firm teacher's voice, "your daughter is the most responsible child I have ever known. Far more than you were at her age, if I remember correctly."

"Yes," said Aunt Gussie, laughing, "you were a rascal, Jimmy."

Emmy's father chuckled, and the back of his neck turned pink. "I don't remember it that way. But I guess there's no way to prove what I was *really* like when I was ten."

Emmy and Joe glanced at each other and tried not to laugh.

"You'd be surprised," said Emmy.

GOFISH

LYNNE JONELL

What did you want to be when you grew up?
A writer, an artist, a singer, an actor, a brain surgeon, a pilot, and a superhero. Oh, and a missionary, during my holy periods (admittedly somewhat short).

When did you realize you wanted to be a writer?
I got the first real inklings in third grade. But I was sure one day in sixth grade, when I read the last page of *A Wrinkle in Time.* That's when I knew that what I wanted most of all was to write books like that, for kids just like me.

What's your first childhood memory?
Being tossed in a blanket by my big brother and sister. The heart-stopping swoop and drop—and laughing out loud in the middle of it, delight and terror mixed!

What's your most embarrassing childhood memory?
The day Rick Johnson caught me crawling on my stomach at the local park with a stick. Rick started to

laugh and accused me of playing army. I was too embarrassed to tell him I was a Dakota scout, about to save my tribe from the warring Apaches.

As a young person, who did you look up to most?
My dad. He was my first hero and still is.

What was your worst subject in school?
Math. It took me a long time to get over my habit of counting on my fingers. (Actually, I may not quite be over it yet.)

What was your first job?
Taking out the wastepaper baskets (when I was a kid). First job when I was a teen was working the Christmas rush at a store called LaBelle's. Two weeks of horror, as I recall, trying to look busy dusting useless objects on glass shelves, and a break room full of cigarette smoke.

How did you celebrate publishing your first book?
I can't even remember, can you believe it? I'm brain-dead, I tell you! Brain-dead! But it probably involved wine and song. And a fabulous meal with someone I loved.

But I can tell you how I celebrated when I got an offer for a second and third book together: I bought a little sailboat and hit the water!

Where do you write your books?
Wherever I can. I start in my office at home, and when that fails, I go to the kitchen or dining room. Pretty soon, I'm out on the patio (if it's warm enough) or at a coffee

shop (if it's cold). I've written in airport terminals and at resorts and on planes and in hotels, on notebooks and computers and paper napkins. Basically, if one place doesn't work, I try another until something clicks.

Where do you find inspiration for your writing?
Also wherever I can!

Which of your characters is most like you?
I am a nice combination of both Emmy and the Rat. Part of me is Emmy, the good girl who tries very hard to do the right thing—and the other half is the Rat, who is the type to slouch in the back row and make sarcastic comments. Oh, and the Rat is also impossibly sensitive, egotistical, and dramatic. It gets a little uncomfortable in my head, sometimes, with the two of them battling it out.

What sparked your inspiration for *Emmy and the Rats in the Belfry*?
In *Emmy and the Incredible Shrinking Rat*, I had given Ratty a birthplace of Schenectady for no good reason except that it came into my head and I loved the sound of the word. I told in that book how he had been taken from the nest when he was just a little ratling, and never saw his Ratmom again. One day Ratty and I were blogging with a group of schoolchildren about this tragedy, and one boy wrote, "Ratty, why don't you ask Lynne Jonell to write another book and have you go find your mom?" I thought that was a marvelous idea, and I went right to work.

Another thing that sparked this story was the fact that

I had been watching elderly relatives growing more and more frail. Their bodies were failing but their spirits were as strong as ever. I wanted to explore that in a book, and so ended up writing about Emmy's great-aunts, who had a brief spell of being children again before they returned to their proper age. That adventure helped Emmy see them more fully than she ever had before.

If you could transform into an animal, which one would you choose and why?
I love the idea of being a bird. I would like to soar very high, and ride the thermals in steep canyons, and watch the light grow and change on the canyon walls.

What is the biggest challenge of writing the conclusion to a series?
Well, I haven't written the conclusion yet! There is one story yet to tell. I know how it will end, and I know what will finally happen to Miss Barmy and Cheswick, and Ratty of course. . . . I can see it all in my mind, quite clearly. Someday I will put it down on paper, and then perhaps I will be able to answer this question.

When you finish a book, who reads it first?
My husband, Bill, is my first reader. He's a good one, too!

Are you a morning person or a night owl?
I am a night owl, nighthawk, nightjar, night crawler . . . my eyes don't really focus until about three in the afternoon. And then I sometimes work all night, to the dismay of my dear first reader.

What's your idea of the best meal ever?
Oh, wow. So many delicious thoughts suddenly flooded my brain that it's paralyzed. Let's see. It would have to involve a green salad that absolutely sings in the mouth—let's say it has red onions, a little prosciutto, maybe gorgonzola cheese, a light fruity vinaigrette . . . then a soup, something with clams and lobster maybe? And—oh, a lovely little pasta dish with an absolutely decadent sauce, butter and cream and wine to start, with some tantalizing spice that I can't quite name. And a very good wine, and maybe some thinly sliced marinated beef that is paired with some lovely, big, fat mushrooms and a few roasted potatoes, crispy on the outside and steaming and tender inside . . . mmmm. And then some cheese and fruit. . . . And, of course, something fabulously chocolate, with raspberries and cream and coffee. And—why not? I think a little champagne!

Which do you like better: cats or dogs?
Oh, cats, no question. They're independent, mysterious, and they have dignity. They don't drool, sniff in embarrassing places, or smell like wet dog.

What do you value most in your friends?
Loyalty, kindness, humor, and a noble heart.

Where do you go for peace and quiet?
My house is actually pretty quiet most of the time. But my favorite spot would be up high, among rocks and a few trees, with the scent of pine and a long view.

What makes you laugh out loud?
Almost everything. I am easily amused. I often laugh at what I write, especially when it's about rabbits.

What's your favorite song?
That changes constantly. But I have to say I love old jazz standards, like "God Bless the Child" and "The Nearness of You."

Who is your favorite fictional character?
David, from *North to Freedom* by Anne Holm.

What are you most afraid of?
Failing to do what I was meant to do with my life.

What time of the year do you like best?
Fall, no question. September is the loveliest month of the year, for me. Warm, glowing, golden, and fleeting.

What is your favorite TV show?
I actually don't have a regular show that I watch. But I used to love *Batman* when I was a kid. *Biff! Bam!! Pow!!!*

If you could travel in time, where would you go?
To the future. I'd like to see how my kids turn out in the end.

What's the best advice you have ever received about writing?
That revision is what separates the women from the girls, the men from the boys, the sheep from the goats.

And to not write at all if you don't *have* to . . . but if you do have to, then don't give up until you get it right.

What do you want readers to remember about your books?
The sheer joy and delight of being swept away into another reality and out of their own. . . .

What would you do if you ever stopped writing?
I imagine at that point I really would be brain-dead. I can't really imagine it.

What do you like best about yourself?
That I'm honest.

What is your worst habit?
Checking e-mail a gazillion times a day.

What do you consider to be your greatest accomplishment?
Not quitting when things got tough—whether in writing, marriage, parenting, or any other sphere.

What do you wish you could do better?
I would really love to have a photographic memory. I hate to forget names, and I do it all the time! Plus, it would make memorizing music so much easier.

What would your readers be most surprised to learn about you?
I'm not all that funny in real life. I just think I am.

Adventure on the high seas, a missing princess, swordfights, and secret identities combine in this tale of a boy who can speak to cats, from the author of the Emmy and the Rat series.

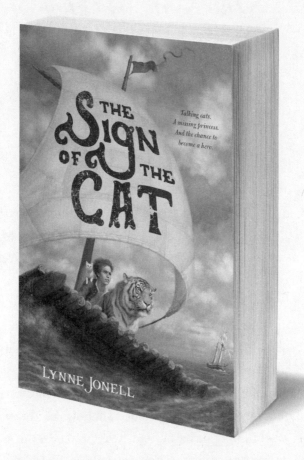

Keep reading for an excerpt.

CHAPTER 1
The Cat Speaker

DUNCAN WAS A BOY WHO COULD SPEAK CAT.

He had known cat language since he was small, because the cat who lived at his house took the trouble to teach him. It wasn't until he was a little older that he realized this was highly unusual.

Of course, all humans would be able to speak Cat if they were taught at the right age. But as most cats can't be bothered, the right age goes by for nine hundred and ninety-nine out of one thousand, and the chance is lost forever.

Duncan McKay was one in a thousand. Maybe even one in a million. Not that it was helpful to him now. He fingered the report card in his pocket nervously as he sat on the second-floor landing, watching through the window for his mother to appear on the crooked street below their house. He had gotten too many As this term, and she would be upset.

"Why me?" he asked Grizel, who was a very old cat by this time. "Why did you teach me to speak Cat?"

Grizel did not answer. She was crouched halfway down the stairs, watching a mouse hole. There had never been a mouse there, not once, but she was not a cat to neglect her duty.

Duncan kicked a heel against the old black sea chest that served as a window seat, and gazed out over the island cliffs to the sea. He hated not getting answers to perfectly reasonable questions. He was eleven and big for his age, and he was tired of being treated like a little boy. "Why me?" he asked again, a little louder.

"Why not?" Grizel snapped. She was testy about the subject; the other cats made fun of her because of it, and she had regretted teaching him more than once. Still, she was not a bad-tempered cat. She wouldn't have snapped at him if she hadn't been cranky from hunger and disappointed about the mouse.

She turned away from the mouse hole and looked up at the boy who sat on the second-floor landing. His face was shaded, but the afternoon sun streamed through the stairwell window and brightened his rough gray pants with their twice-patched knees.

A cat will hardly ever apologize for being rude. It usually doesn't see the point. But Duncan's lap looked warm and full of sun, and Grizel's spot on the stairs had fallen into shadow. She butted her head against Duncan's leg, blinked, and opened her eyes wide, with a tiny upward twist between her brows. This was Cat Trick #9: Melting Kitty Eyes. She had not been a kitten for a long time, but she could still act adorable when necessary.

Duncan took her on his lap and began to stroke her behind the ears.

Grizel kneaded his stomach with her paws. "I taught you to speak Cat because I felt sorry for you when your father died," she said. "All in all, I think I did a good thing. I've been able to explain why fresh tuna is better than the stuff in a can, for instance. And you have quite a knack for purring."

"That's nice if you're a cat," Duncan said, watching out the stairwell window for his mother. "Only, I'm a boy."

"You can't help that," said Grizel. "I've never held it against you."

Duncan didn't answer; he was trying to remember when his father had died. Had there been a funeral? He had been very small. There had been a forest of black-trousered legs around him, and someone smelling of pipe tobacco had picked him up and whispered gruffly in his ear. "You'll be the man of the house now," the voice had said. "You'll have to take good care of your mother."

Duncan had tried. While he was still too young for school, he tied an old shirt around his neck for a cape and practiced fighting evil villains. When he was a little older, he gave his mother all the copper pennies he found in the street. And when he was older still, he began to do small jobs at the houses where his mother taught music lessons. He gave her the coins he earned—at first the common five- and tenpenny pieces, later the larger brass barons and, on occasion, a silver-edged earl—and he tried hard to obey her rules, even the strange ones.

But some of her rules were very strange indeed.

Duncan unfolded his report card and looked at his grades with a sigh. He had made sure to get five questions wrong on his last history test, but it hadn't been enough.

Grizel tapped at the report card with her paw. "You could tell her that A means 'Average.' Or 'Actually Not That Good.' "

Duncan snorted.

"It could also mean 'Annoying,' or 'Atrocious,' or 'Abominable'—"

"What are you, a dictionary?"

"Or you could change the As to Bs," Grizel suggested. "Just draw a line along the bottom. And smudge over the pointy top."

"That never works." Duncan knew this because he had tried it before. "I could make it an A minus, maybe, but that's about all."

Grizel yawned, showing delicately pointed teeth and a small pink tongue. "Why don't you just get a few more wrong? There's nothing so hard in that."

"I hate getting things wrong," Duncan muttered.

"Other boys," Grizel observed, "would be pleased to have a mother who didn't push them to get good grades. Other boys would be *grateful*."

Duncan did not particularly care how grateful other boys might be and made this point under his breath.

Grizel flicked her tail and went on as if she hadn't heard. "A good son might have a little faith in his own mother. A clever boy might understand that she had a *reason*—"

"For what?" The report card crinkled in Duncan's hand. "For telling me never to get a gold star, or earn a medal, or win a prize? For telling me I should never stand out?"

"For keeping you hidden," Grizel said sharply. "And safe."

Something cold patted quietly inside Duncan's chest. "Am I in danger?"

"Did I say that?" Grizel closed her eyes until they were slits in her furry golden face. "I don't recall using that word."

"You said 'safe.' And 'hidden.' So there's got to be something she's keeping me hidden from, right?"

Grizel sank her shoulders more deeply into the round curve of her body. She seemed to grow more solid. A faint snore escaped her.

Exasperated, Duncan bounced his knees up and down. The cat held on with her claws, her eyes tightly shut.

"There's no danger," said Duncan. "You made that up. This is the safest, most boring island in all Arvidia. It's even named Dulle, which should tell you something."

The snoring grew louder.

"Fine. Be that way." Duncan detached Grizel's claws from his leg one by one, set her on the floor, and looked through the window again. His mother wasn't on the street that led to their house, and he couldn't see her walking up the steep cliffside road.

Instead, he saw a striped tabby cat rounding the corner. Its head was up, its tail well back, and altogether it had the purposeful look of a cat with business to accomplish.

It stopped beneath their window and looked up, meowing.

Grizel put her forepaws on the windowsill. Duncan opened the window and leaned out. "What?" he meowed back.

Grizel nudged Duncan aside with her head. "It's for me," she hissed. And to the cat in the street below she meowed, "What news?"

"Cat Council tonight," called the tabby. "At moonrise. In the graveyard."

"What for?" Grizel asked. "What's on the agenda?"

"Kitten examinations," said the tabby. "Territory disputes. Dog-taunting assignments. Old Tom warning about impending disaster. The usual."

Duncan grinned. He loved kitten examinations.

"Can't stay to talk—lots more cats to notify," said the tabby, turning away.

"I'll be there," called Grizel to the cat's retreating back, and its tail swished once in acknowledgment.

"I'm going, too," said Duncan.

Grizel leaped onto his lap. "If you do, the other cats will make fun of me again. They'll say, 'Can't she go anywhere without that red-haired *master*?'"

Duncan rubbed the top of her head gently with his knuckles. "I'm not your master, and they know it. And my hair isn't red anymore. It got darker this year—it's practically brown. Especially on a cloudy day."

Grizel settled herself more comfortably, curling her tail around her flanks. "You shouldn't go. Your mother wouldn't like it if she knew you were sneaking out at night."

Duncan was silent. Of course his mother wouldn't like it. But it wasn't as if he was doing anything *bad*.

"If I don't tell her," he pointed out, "she won't need to worry."

Grizel looked at him through half-shut eyes. "A mother's rules are for her kitten's own good."

"I'm not breaking any rules," Duncan said firmly. "My mother never said, 'No going to cat councils in graveyards.' Not once."

Grizel made a small huffing noise. "She may not have said that *exactly*—"

"See? You even agree with me." Duncan curled his fingers around the cat's bony jaw and began to scratch her under the chin. "Good kitty, *nice* kitty." He let his fingers pause. "Promise you'll wake me up in time to go?"

Grizel tipped her head and squeezed her eyes almost shut. "Scratch a little more to the side, and I will . . . yes, right *there*." A rumbling vibration began in her chest as she subsided into a contented purring.

Duncan did not want to be a bad son. But there was no way his mother would understand about the cat council, and he would rather not mention the graveyard. She always got a worried look on her face when he visited the grave she had told him was his father's.

He scanned the cliffside road again. Maybe his mother was teaching an extra piano lesson today. He should probably set the table for supper. And maybe tonight he could offer to play their old game of Noble Manners. It was getting boring for him (what use was it to learn all the customs and dances and courtesies of nobles—barons and earls and dukes—when he would never be one?), but it seemed to please his mother. With any luck, she would forget to ask for his report card.

Grizel gave a little mew of protest. Duncan, who had forgotten to keep his fingers moving, began to scratch again, this time behind the cat's ears.

Petting a cat was not the most exciting thing in the world. Still, it was pleasant, sitting in his favorite spot on the stairs. The small window overlooked the bay far below, curved and shining in the late-afternoon light, and he could see the fishing boats coming in from the sea, floating like curled-up leaves on the water. Halfway up the hill, the rooftops of his monastery school flashed orange and gold in the sun.

Duncan and his mother lived in the cliffside part of the island of Dulle, where the sun scorched them in summer and the sea wind scoured them in winter. It was a long walk down to the bay, and they did not often have the money to pay for the freshest fish. But Duncan loved the little house that was tucked under the overhanging cliffs. He loved being up high where he could see everything spread out beneath him, as if he were a king looking out over his realm. And sometimes at night, if there was no mist, he could even make out the glittering lights of Capital City on the far curving edge of the sea.

Someday he would sail there to make his fortune. And then he would be able to take care of his mother so she wouldn't be afraid anymore. He didn't know what Sylvia McKay was afraid of, exactly, but he was sure that when he was a man, he would be able to protect her from whatever it was.

Something moved at the edge of Duncan's vision. He snapped his gaze to the street below and saw a tiny white kitten.

It looked like Fia, a kitten he had seen roaming the monastery school. He had given her treats once or twice. But what was she doing out alone?

The kitten blinked up at his window. Even from this height, Duncan could see the startling difference in her eyes—one blue and one green. It was Fia, all right.

He slid Grizel gently off his lap and thumped down the stairs in his socks. He undid the double lock that his mother had installed—*snick, snick*—and he was out on the cobbled street, paved with stones as smooth as the Arvidian Sea could make them.

"What is it, Fia?" He sat down on the doorstep, its rough edges warm beneath his hands. "Are you lost?"

"Not me!" Fia swiped a tiny paw at Duncan's knee. "Only *baby* cats get lost!"

"Ah," said Duncan.

Grizel slipped through the open door and gave the kitten a disapproving look. "Where's your mother? You shouldn't be out on the street by yourself."

Fia switched her tail. "I'm just as big as my littermates— well, almost—and *they* can go out by themselves. Anyway, I have a message."

Grizel shook her head. "You can't be a messenger cat. You haven't even passed your kitten examinations yet."

"I'm *going* to pass them," said Fia with dignity. "And I'm *practicing* to be a messenger cat. And I have news for Dunc—"

Fia stopped midword and swallowed hard. She tensed as if to dart away, but she was too slow for the cream-colored cat who streaked from behind a flowerpot and bowled her over with the force of a small, four-legged truck.

The white kitten squirmed under the pressure of two firm paws.

"*I* have news for *you*," said Fia's mother. "You do *not* leave the monastery grounds unless I am with you. Do I make myself clear?"

"But I want to tell Duncan something!"

The cream-colored cat stiffened her whiskers. "Are you a cat or a postmaster?" she demanded. "We cats do not concern ourselves with human affairs. We have enough to do with our own. And I certainly have enough to do with looking after one harum-scarum little kitten who can't seem to obey the rules."

Grizel coughed behind one paw. "Human affairs aren't *completely* without interest, Mabel. You have to admit that you usually wander down to the bay when the boats come in. And you're not too proud to beg for a fish head or two."

Mabel drew herself up with dignity. "Of course I don't expect you to understand," she said frostily. "You've never been a mother—you haven't a mother's feelings. But I, who must provide for my litters—"

"One every year," Grizel murmured to Duncan.

"—must get proper nourishment. Come along, Fia. We needn't waste any more time." She picked Fia up by the scruff of the neck and stalked away.

"But what about my message?" Duncan meowed after them. "What's your news, Fia?"

Fia's small voice came floating back. "Your mother is—"

Fia's words were cut short by a fierce shake, and Mabel, with the kitten dangling from her mouth, disappeared around the corner.